THE COSTUMED AFFAIR

A PAMELA WAINWRIGHT MYSTERY

Carsten Ford

DEDICATION

We dedicate this work to all those who enjoy reading, solving, investigating, or writing mystery and detective fiction.

CONTENTS

ACKNOWLEDGMENTS

We would like to thank all those who made this possible – G.Locke, my family, the publishers, and of course the readers who went over the manuscript to ensure it told a good story. Thank you all for the incredible work done and provided, it is that creativity and dedication to the written word which means so much.

1

MISS ELLERY VENTURES

Lord Carrington heaved a sigh of boredom and, adjusting his monocle, stared languidly about the scantily filled lecture-hall. Lectures always proved tedious to the young man and he had come to this particular one simply because he felt it his duty to the lecturer, who was one of his lordship's numerous protégés.

As Carrington's monocled eye swept over the audience, some members of which appeared mildly interested, and others as hopelessly bored as he, his notice was attracted to an extremely aristocratic, rather formidable-looking woman of middle age seated just across the aisle. She held herself stiffly erect, all attention to the lecturer, her sharp gray eyes never shifting from his face as he described, in what seemed to Carrington wearisome detail, the history and architecture of an old Castle in Yorkshire, whose two ancient towers framing a gatehouse whose passage to the manor was completely rose lined, from where its name "Rose Gardens" originated, were said to date back to the Wars of the Roses.

Carrington smiled to himself at Miss Ellery Flynn's absorption. He remembered that the study of the antiquities of England amounted with her almost to a passion, if so intense a term could be applied to the pursuits of a well-ordered British spinster and high-churchwoman. Miss Ellery possessed but this one little weakness, unless perhaps, an almost doting affection for her handsome nephew, Max, could be placed in the same category. But then what woman was there who did not look with indulgent eyes on Maxwell Flynn?

A stir at the back of the hall made Miss Ellery glance sharply over her shoulder in impatience of the disturbance. Then an expression of astonishment, if not of actual consternation, spread over her countenance. She half started up from her chair, then as suddenly sat down again.

Carrington looked curiously toward the back of the hall, but he could see nothing terrifying, though there was indeed something a little unusual, in the appearance of the two late comers. To begin with, both were obviously East Indians. The younger, a man in the early thirties, was dressed in correct European attire, silk hat, frock coat, and properly subdued tie, yet the very contrast of his Western garb with the black hair and eyes and brown face of the East Indian made him a striking figure. His companion, a majestic old man, with white flowing beard, wore full native costume, turban and loose robe.

The two East Indians walked to seats in the center of the hall, carrying themselves with the dignified and assured bearing of princes. At once they became thoroughly, almost breathlessly, engrossed in the lecture.

Miss Flynn's attention began to wander from the old Yorkshire Castle to the two East Indians, whose presence appeared to cause her great disquiet Carrington, on the contrary, commenced at last to feel a mild interest in the description of "Rose Gardens," mainly because of the extraordinary absorption evinced in it by the two stately East Indians.

While the lecturer was waiting for some stereoscopic views to be projected on the screen, the tension of the two foreigners relaxed. The younger glanced about the hall in a calmly curious and even detached fashion, as though considering himself immeasurably superior to the handful of Britishers comprising the audience. Suddenly his arrogant gaze rested on Miss Flynn, who was in the act of bowing to Carrington whom she had just recognized. Instantly a change came over the East Indian's face, his eye kindled and he addressed his companion in a fierce, eager whisper. The old man followed his glance and Carrington did not like the expression of grim resolve that settled over his harsh features as he surveyed Miss Flynn who, becoming conscious that she was the object of the East Indians' scrutiny, straightened in her chair with an air that plainly spoke defiance and an equally firm resolve.

Carrington was wondering how on earth this staid British spinster of excellent family could have incurred the enmity, for such it undoubtedly was, of these two men from the occult East, when the lights were switched off for the first picture. There was some trouble with the projecting lantern, and for two or three minutes the hall was in darkness. Carrington was startled by feeling a hand laid on his shoulder and hearing Miss Ellery Flynn bid him, in an authoritative whisper, get up and accompany her outside as noiselessly as possible. They had just reached the main exit when the lights went on again. The two East Indians had risen from their seats and were making their way down the aisle with undignified haste.

Miss Flynn clutched Carrington's arm. "Get me a taxicab as quick as you can!"

Carrington, in a state of bewilderment, hailed a waiting taxicab before the doorman could blow his whistle. Miss Flynn literally leaped into the cab, with a fine disregard of the usual composure with which she moved.

"Get in too, Carrington! Tell him to drive at the top of his speed to Cockerill and Waddington's in Oxford Street!"

Carrington obeyed, being accustomed, as all who knew Miss Flynn were, to her high-handed fashion of disposing of other people's time to suit her own pleasure. As the taxi shot forward, the two East Indians exited from the lecture-hall in an agitated state. Carrington, as the cab with a bold contempt for the rights and safety of others, plunged into that ceaseless stream of traffic which at certain hours makes the London streets fairly impassable, had a final glimpse of a distracted doorman trying vainly to secure a taxi in obedience to the impatient commands of the two East Indians.

Miss Ellery's expression was positively triumphant. "We've beaten them! Drive faster, my fellow!" speaking through the tube which she found by her side.

Carrington ventured a faint remonstrance. "My dear Miss Flynn, if he drives any faster, we will all be hauled into Bow Street Police Court for endangering the lives of the public."

"Don't try to be humorous, Carrington." Miss Ellery sat on the extreme edge of the seat, leaning forward as though hoping to increase the speed of the taxi by the very intensity of her impatience, "I tell you we haven't a moment to lose."

"Perhaps," suggested Carrington,"you will explain what sort of an enterprise this is we are embarking upon?"

"Carrington," in a severely rebuking tone, "you have an inordinate curiosity, I haven't the time now to gratify it. You must wait until we reach Cockerill and Waddington's. I trust this little trip is not inconveniencing you?"

"Oh, not at all." Carrington resignedly clasped his hands over his Malacca walking-stick. At least, this little excursion was a break in the boredom of social life, therefore I am entirely at your disposal, Miss Flynn."

She leaned suddenly from the window. "There is a taxicab following us! Offer that fellow any inducement — I don't care what — so that we outdistance it."

Carrington obediently called to the driver with such eloquence that presently the taxi, after having narrowly escaped running down several indignant "bobbies" who had endeavored to check its speed in the interests of humanity, stopped with a jerk before the impressive building in Oxford Street which contained the offices of Messrs. Cockerill and Waddington, the London estate agents who make a specialty of letting and selling old houses of historic interest. Miss Flynn sprang from the cab unaided before Carrington could collect himself sufficiently to assist her. She precipitated herself into the waiting lift while he was making a leisurely descent from the taxi.

But this unconventional haste on the part of one who had always hitherto shown a rigid regard for the proprieties of etiquette was beginning to enthuse Carrington, most unemotional of men, and he gained her side in the lift with something approaching celerity. He was even conscious of a little thrill of expectation as the elevator shot upward.

The offices of Messrs. Cockerill and Waddington were on the third floor. Miss Flynn swept through the swinging doors into the inner office with a vehemence that brought Mr. Waddington, a benevolent featured elderly gentleman, in amazement to his feet.

"Ill take it, Mr. Waddington," she cried.

He blinked at her dazedly over his gold-rimmed spectacles. "I beg your pardon, madam?"

"Rose Gardens! Mr. Waddington. I have come to sign the lease. That is plain enough, isn't it?"

Mr. Waddington gave a little cough of embarrassment. "The — ah — fact is, Miss Flynn, since our little talk yesterday morning when I gave you the refusal of Rose Gardens for twenty-four hours, that — that other client whom you met here — "

"You mean that brown-faced, insolent East Indian who thinks he has only to express a desire and the keys of every Castle in England will be given up to him?"

Mr. Waddington's embarrassment grew. "I was referring to — ah — to Prince Rajan Mohan of India, Miss Flynn. He made a — a really magnificent offer this noon. We should have closed with his highness at once had you not requested us over the telephone to extend the refusal until you had opportunity to hear the lecture and judge for yourself of the historic merits of Rose Gardens as compared with other old Castles on our list. Of course, Miss Flynn, you have the refusal until this evening, but — as I said — the prince's offer is magnificent — really extraordinary."

"How much?" demanded Miss Flynn sharply.

"Four thousand guineas per annum for a lease of five years."

"A rather extraordinary offer indeed!" interposed Carrington who, with his gloved hand resting on the back of a chair, stood listening in an attitude of courteous, if slightly bored, ease. "I shouldn't say the old place was worth it, Miss Flynn. Probably the drainage is bad."

"On the contrary, the drainage is excellent," defended Mr. Waddington." "It is the one modern thing in this wonderful old castle."

Miss Ellery stiffened with decision. "Get out the papers, Mr. Waddington, and I will sign at once. I duplicate the offer of that East Indian, whatever he styles himself, though I tell you frankly I consider four thousand guineas an outrageous sum. I only pay it on principle to keep our old castles in the hands of the English — where they should be. It is bad enough to see the Americans taking possession of them — but an East Indian adventurer, never! Where are the papers, Mr. Waddington?"

"Here on the desk, Miss Flynn. If you will take this chair, please." From the agent's tone, one might infer that he was a little disappointed at losing an East Indian potentate as a client."

"I think, Miss Flynn," he ventured, "it is hardly fair to term Prince Rajan Mohan an adventurer. He is a member of one of the reigning families of India."

Miss Flynn gave a grunt of disbelief. "They all are. It makes them popular in society. Haven't you a respectable pen in your offices, Mr. Waddington?"

The agent hastily procured another. "Perhaps this will suit you better, madam."

She accepted it with a curt nod. "It couldn't suit me less."

As she elegantly looped the "y" in her surname with a bold, masculine dash, the swinging-doors flew open violently and the younger of the two East Indians sprang into the office. The old East Indian stalked after him.

Both stopped short, there was desperation, rage, menace on the countenance of the younger man and a sort of restrained ferocity on that of his companion as they stared at Miss Flynn, who, after giving them one glance of unalloyed triumph, blotted her signature and wiped the pen with a maddening precision.

The younger East Indian seemed unable to control himself and made a threatening movement toward her. Mr. Waddington turned white with alarm and stood inert. Carrington, his air of languid ease gone, stepped quickly before Miss Flynn and confronted the East Indian.

"Can I accommodate you in any way? — Prince Rajan Mohan, I believe?" a sternness in his voice in place of its usual fashionable drawl.

The East Indian glared in speechless wrath at the Englishman, tall, broad-shouldered, one who might have been athletic if he had not chosen to be elegant. There was a light in Carrington's gray eyes that must have reminded Rajan Mohan of the calm masterful manner of those British rulers of India. His features worked convulsively, but the hand which had sought the ever-ready dagger fell at his side. His companion addressed to him words of advice and rebuke in Hindustani, and Rajan Mohan listened with respect and even awe to the solemn speech of the old man. The rage died from his face and his manner became more in accord with his quiet Western dress than had been his violence of a moment before. He removed his silk hat and bowed politely, if a little constrained, to Miss Flynn, who was still seated uncompromisingly erect at the desk, her hand upon the document she had signed.

"Madam, it is Gupta Singh's opinion that I owe you an apology." Rajan Mohan spoke perfect English with just a hint of the liquid quality of the Burmese tongue. "We men of the East are of ardent temperament, and we find it difficult to bear disappointment with equanimity. It has long been my wish to become the possessor of an old English castle and to make my residence there during several months of each year. Rose Gardens appeared to me highly desirable, but doubtless Messrs. Cockerill and Waddington have other old houses of equal desirability on their list I regret, madam, that my disappointment should have caused me to forget the respect due an English lady and I bet that you will permit me to wish you full enjoyment of Rose Gardens."

Rajan Moran bowed gracefully. One felt under the courtesy of his words a striving for effect rather than sincerity. He had not needed to say that he spoke at the instigation of Gupta Singh.

Miss Flynn rose with deliberation. She looked squarely into the handsome, swarthy face of Rajan Mohan.

"Thank you. I expect to enjoy Rose Gardens."

"I repeat, madam, I hope you may." Rajan Mohan's teeth gleamed.

2

THE VENTURE ASSUMES PROPORTIONS

Miss Flynn surveyed Carrington across the table in the restaurant at the Carlton. "I suppose, Carrington, you think I have committed a great folly."

Carrington eyed the hot buttered crumpet on his plate. "Well rather! Miss Flynn. I don't believe any old broken-down castle is worth such a rent as four thousand guineas per annum. There are other old castles in England that you could lease for much less. Why were you so determined to have this one?"

"Apart from its historic interest, there are two reasons. One is that I will permit no East Indian adventurer to get the better of me, and the other is that Rose Gardens is situated near Dormont Court."

Carrington smiled comprehendingly. "And Helena Dormont, the girl whom you would like to have Max marry, lives at Dormont Court."

"Precisely. It is time that Max married and settled down. He is thirty-three years old and yet he has no more serious object in life than horses and flirtations. But" — Miss Flynn's voice softened as it always did when she spoke of her nephew — "Max is good-hearted and a true Flynn in spite of his irresponsibility which, after all, is only the boyishness of one who will never grow old. Max needs nothing more than the steadying influence of a sensible, clear-sighted wife — not a society doll. Helena Dormont is just the girl to supply that influence."

Carrington ventured a question. "Does Miss Dormont happen to love

Max?"

Miss Flynn looked slightly nettled. "They have only met twice — but I intend to remedy that. Did you ever know a woman with whom Max did not find favor?"

Carrington winced a little. "No, I don't believe I ever did." His tone was somewhat regretful. He was thinking of a certain woman. — "Do you know, if Max feels any — ah — interest in Miss Dormont?" he asked abruptly.

Miss Flynn frowned. "You know perfectly well, Carrington, that at the present moment Max considers himself in love with Lady Susanna Helton. But it is nothing more than infatuation — senseless infatuation — a few weeks absence and he will forget her completely."

Carrington did not share Miss Flynn's hopefulness. He appreciated better than she did the charms of Lady Susanna.

"It is my intention to have Max spend the summer with me at Rose Gardens," resumed Miss Flynn. "I tell you frankly, Carrington, I will throw him and Helena Dormont together as much as possible. But I suppose, to begin with, I must have some less obvious purpose in bringing Max to Rose Gardens, or I will rouse that masculine obstinacy which all you men possess. A small house party would probably please him. You know his friends better than I, and I am going to do a rather unconventional thing and leave the selection of the guests to you. You may invite anyone you please — except Lady Susanna Helton."

"But Miss Flynn, I think Susanna is the very one Max would want the most."

Miss Flynn's mouth tightened. "You call her Susanna?"

Carrington flushed. "Why yes, we're old pals — Susanna and I — have been for years."

Miss Flynn settled back severely in her chair. "Well, you need not invite her to Rose Gardens. As I said, I wish Max to forget her. She is distinctly not the woman whom I could accept as his wife."

"Oh, come now, Miss Flynn, what have you against Susanna? She's a jolly good sort — a fine woman."

"That is just it, Carrington. I do not approve of women who are 'a jolly good sort', and, in the first place she is a divorcée."

"Her husband was a beastly cad!"

"But her husband," Miss Flynn said in an uncompromising tone, "nobody forced her to marry him. It was her own choice and her plain duty was to abide by it. 'Whom God has — '"

Carrington raised his hand in deprecation. "For Heaven's sake don't quote scripture in defense of a little beast like Bartholomew Helton. Susanna ought to have divorced him years before she did. Miss Flynn." Suddenly lowering his voice, "is not that his East Indian Highness just entering?"

Miss Flynn eagerly followed Carrington's glance. It was indeed Prince Rajan Mohan who was entering. He was accompanied this time not by the old man, Gupta Singh, but by a young girl. The latter, herself an East Indian, was slim and childlike in appearance, apparently not more than sixteen years of age. She had a delicate oval face, clear olive skin, and velvety dark eyes in which loomed the mystery of the East. A gown of white, simple but costly, set off her Oriental beauty and added to her air of extreme youth.

The lights, the music, the many people in the café seemed to frighten her and she shrank behind Rajan Mohan's imposing figure as a deferential maître d'hôtel conducted them to a table not far from that at which Miss Flynn and Carrington were sitting. The girl kept her eyes timidly lowered, but Rajan Mohan's calmly arrogant gaze, sweeping about the restaurant, soon settled on Miss Flynn. If he felt surprise, none at least was visible on his impassive countenance as, taking the privilege of a prince, he bowed to her with a grave, though somewhat elaborate courtesy, which savored slightly of the East. Gupta Singh's rebuke had taken root, and whatever passion of resentment Rajan Mohan might still cherish against the successful lessee of Rose Gardens was concealed under a bearing of conventional composure, no less correct than that of any well-bred Englishman.

Miss Flynn inclined her head stiffly in response. Rajan Mohan, for the first time since entering the café, addressed his companion. He spoke to her earnestly, in an undertone, and evidently in Hindustani. There was little doubt that Miss Flynn was the subject of the conversation and still less that the girl stood in abject fear of her escort and was both distressed and horrified by his words. She glanced across at Miss Flynn, her eyes filled now with pathetic appeal, touchingly childish. She appeared to be struggling with a desire to escape from Rajan Mohan and yet to lack the courage even to raise her voice in protest.

Miss Flynn was moved by the girl's obvious distress. "Carrington, I should like to go over and rescue that poor child from that East Indian adventurer, but I suppose it wouldn't do."

Carrington shook his head regretfully. "No! I don't believe it would. He evidently has some authority over her. Miss Flynn," leaning toward her over the table, "I have been thinking of Rose Gardens — Where have I heard of it before? I remember now that it figured in the newspapers as the scene of a mysterious murder which has never been cleared up. The murdered man was the late owner — a collector of East Indian curios and the possessor of large shares in the ruby mines of Burma. If I were you, Miss Flynn, I should give up the lease of Rose Gardens. I don't like Rajan Mohan, and I like that old graybeard even less."

"No!" Miss Flynn spoke with decision. "I will not allow myself to be driven away from Rose Gardens either by a couple of East Indian mountebanks or by the ghost of a curio collector who ought to have known better than to dabble in anything Oriental. I am going back to Cavendish Square. I can't stand the misery in that poor child's eyes. Have you finished, Carrington?"

Carrington politely assured her that he had, but, as they rose, he could not resist a rueful glance at his scarcely touched cup of tea. Their sudden departure evoked the interest of Rajan Mohan and Carrington, as he escorted Miss Flynn through the restaurant, was acutely conscious of the East Indian's intent gaze.

As Carrington helped her into a cab, she reminded him that she was leaving him the selection of the guests for her house party.

"Not more than four including yourself," she cautioned him, "and you know whom you are not to invite. By the way, I wish you could find it convenient to call on me tomorrow. Why not come to lunch? I expect Max then."

Carrington accepted her invitation and then reentered the hotel intending to ask the reception clerk if Prince Rajan Mohan was registered there. As he was crossing the office, he heard his name called.

Turning, he saw a petite, very pretty young lady, dressed in the extreme of fashion, hastening toward him, one small gloved hand extended.

He stared a moment in amazement. "Why Mimi!" shaking hands with her somewhat confusedly, "what are you doing in London? I thought you Were in

Paris with the Nortons and their party."

The young lady made an affected little murmur. "So I was, but I found Paris shockingly dull these last few days — Max was called back to London," she explained in a tone of confidence, the ingenuousness of which seemed slightly rehearsed.

In fact, as one looked closely at Miss Miriam Cramer, her prettiness and even her youthfulness seemed slightly studied. The golden fluff of hair, straying from under the brim of her smart Paris hat, was of a little too bright, almost hard shade, the delicate pink and white of her complexion appeared to owe something to art, the arch of her brows was almost too perfect, her baby-like mouth a bit over red.

Carrington surveyed her thoughtfully for a moment. "Ah! Yes. I knew that Max had returned."

"I hear that he and Susanna coached to the races," observed Miriam, striving to speak indifferently, but not altogether succeeding.

Carrington looked uncomfortable. He was sorry for Miriam, little Becky Sharp though he knew her to be. Max was treating her rather shabbily. True, they had never been formally engaged but, for a brief spell some three or four years previous, before Miriam's beauty had needed to borrow from art, Max had been no less devoted to her than he now was to Susanna. As a matter of fact, there had even been gossip, and then, Max's fickle fancy turning, he became no less assiduous in fleeing from Miriam than formerly he had been in running after her.

Carrington was aware that he must say something. "I believe Max did take several friends down to the races."

Miriam moistened her lips. "Do you know where I could reach Max with a telephone or letter? His rooms are closed, and the porter does not know when he will be back. He left Paris in such a hurry that he forgot to give me his address." Her tone was successfully light, but her expression a little tremulous.

Carrington did not know what to say, so he blundered into the truth, telling of Miss Flynn's renting of Rose Gardens and her intention to have Max pass the summer with her there.

"What a very peculiar woman Miss Flynn must be," remarked Miriam reflectively, "to leave the selection of her guests to you. Have you invited anyone as yet?"

"Not as yet." His manner was guarded. He instinctively knew what was coming next.

Miriam laid her little gloved hand appealingly on his arm. "Tom, couldn't you? — couldn't you invite me for one of the guests? I'd so love to pass a few weeks in Yorkshire. I dote on old castles."

Carrington felt utterly helpless. He knew what Miriam's persistence was and that she was almost always successful in securing desired invitations. In fact, extended visits at the houses of acquaintances, casual or otherwise, was Miss Cramer's favorite method of eking out the very slender annuity which was all that her father had managed to save for her out of an extensive patrimony which he had dissipated in the three popular pursuits of pleasure-living gentlemen.

"I don't know what to say Mimi," Carrington stammered in desperation, "you don't even know Miss Flynn."

"But I should like to! Tom," Miriam's voice became very plaintive, "I'm fairly down to my last penny. If you don't take pity on me, I will be forced to spend the summer here in London and I am sure the heat will kill me. Really, Tom, I'm half sick now."

Carrington's unhappiness grew. Max would never forgive him if he invited Miriam, and as for Miss Flynn, Miriam was another of her pet aversions. He stole a glance at Mimi. She didn't look strong, there were circles under her eyes not due to art and a drawn expression about her mouth. London would be a beastly hole in the heat of summer.

Miss Cramer, seeing his hesitancy, pressed her plea. "I should be so grateful to you, Tom."

He could hold out no longer. After all, Miss Flynn had named only one whom he was not to invite.

"Very well, Mimi," with what heartiness he could summon up, "you are to consider yourself invited to Rose Gardens. You'll enjoy it, I think. Ill let you know when Miss Flynn expects her house party."

He made his escape as quickly as possible from Miss Cramer and her rather gushing thanks, in case he was tempted to withdraw the invitation which he already regretted. As he stepped toward the mahogany counter in the office to make inquiries regarding Rajan Mohan, that gentleman himself entered from the direction of the restaurant and approached Carrington. The young East Indian girl was still with the prince, but she kept at a little distance, her eyes fixed anxiously on Carrington as Rajan Mohan addressed him.

"You will pardon me," the East Indian said, speaking in his correct, somewhat stilted English, "but I believe you are the gentleman who accompanied Miss Flynn this afternoon to the offices of Messrs. Cockerill and Waddington in Oxford Street?"

Carrington screwed the monocle into his eye and stared curiously at the East Indian. "I did accompany Miss Flynn."

Rajan Mohan plainly resented the Englishman's stare. A dark flush mounted to his face, but he contrived to hold his voice even. "Perhaps then you can inform me if you think it likely that Miss Flynn could be prevailed upon to reconsider — that is, to surrender the lease of Rose Gardens. There are several reasons why I wish to rent this estate. I am prepared to make Messrs. Cockerill and Waddington an even larger offer."

Carrington continued to find his eye-glass useful "You are jolly eager to get the keys of that battered old castle, Prince Rajan Mohan. Its fame must have penetrated to India. Might I ask," with an exasperating drawl, "which part of its history interests your highness most, the fifteenth century period when barons wore roses and battled for rival kings or," and Carrington's voice became suddenly crisp and stern, "a more recent period, say a year or so ago when the late owner of Rose Gardens, a gentleman who had many affiliations with your country was found mysteriously murdered? An East Indian dagger, I believe, was the death-dealing instrument" His voice had dropped again into a drawl and he readjusted the monocle for another scrutiny of Rajan Mohan's face.

There was a tiger-like glint in the East Indian eyes and his upper lip curled, showing the gleam of his teeth. But, in an instant, as though in obedience to some will mightier than his own, he crushed all outer semblance of passion. Once more he presented the composed and assured bearing of a man of caste. For the first time Carrington, observing the marvelous self-control which he exercised, believed in the reality of his being, a prince of India.

"I will answer your question" Rajan Mohan remarked, his tone perfectly modulated and even a little tolerant. "I am interested in the history of no period in the existence of Rose Gardens. As a matter of fact, I am interested only in the history of my own country of India, seat of the worship of supreme Brahma." The light of religious fervor, of exaltation illumined the features of Rajan Mohan as he spoke the name of the first of the East Indian triad.

Carrington felt almost a sense of awe. He glanced at the girl, standing a few paces distant. The mention of Brahma had set her to trembling and her olive cheeks were almost white. She was regarding the impassioned countenance of Rajan Mohan with an intensity of fear that was fairly heart-rending. Carrington's inherent hate of the East Indian revived.

Rajan Mohan again put restraint upon himself, seeming to resent the fact that even for a moment he had permitted an unbeliever to look into the soul of a worshiper of Brahma.

"No," he went on, clearly forcing himself to use a more conversational tone, "my interest in Rose Gardens is in no way connected with its historic merits — or demerits — either in the past or in the near present. As I told Miss Flynn in your presence, I find it desirable to spend a few months of each year in England and Rose Gardens exactly suits my purpose. In addition, I consider its location near the North Sea an extremely healthful one. The air there, they tell me, is very — what you English call bracing — and precisely what my sister, Princess Nora Mohan" — he indicated the young girl who was still regarding him with frightened, fascinated eyes — "is in need of. Her highness has a delicate constitution."

"It is a pity to deprive Princess Nora Mohan of the bracing North Sea air," observed Carrington dryly, "but Miss Flynn has signed the lease for Rose Gardens, and I assure you I am perfectly certain that nothing will induce her to give it up."

He had purposely spoken loudly, and he heard the girl utter a little moan of despair. She was a pathetic figure — this little East Indian princess, but Carrington judged her ailments to be mental rather than bodily and wholly due to the thralldom of terror in which her self-styled brother held her.

Rajan Mohan preserved an emotionless countenance. "If Miss Flynn is determined to occupy Rose Gardens, that of course ends the matter. I have the honor to wish you a good evening."

3

MAX

Lord Carrington stopped in at his club before going on to his rooms. He had learned from the reception clerk at the Carlton that Rajan Mohan was not registered at that hotel. It had occurred to him that some of the members of the club might be able to give information concerning the East Indian, for if he really was, as he claimed to be, a prince of India, he could not be entirely unknown in London.

However, there was only one man at the club who had ever heard of Rajan Mohan. This man was Dickerson, traveler and journalist of international reputation. He assured Carrington that Rajan Mohan actually was a member of a royal house of India, but for some mysterious reason had been an exile from his native land for several years. Dickerson believed that his exile was due to the fact that the family of the Mohan had in some way brought upon themselves the wrath of Brahma and that the priests of the triple god had forbidden Prince Rajan to return to India until he had performed some act of revenge which should appease Brahma.

"But," objected Carrington, "the old chap who travels around with Prince Rajan looks as I should imagine, as an East Indian priest would look and why should a priest travel about with a man who has offended Brahma?"

Dickerson shrugged. "I don't know, unless to see that he doesn't get lukewarm in the vendetta act. I know very little of the priests of that land of mystery and poisoned daggers — in fact, for prudence's sake, I have made it a point to remain ignorant — but this I do know, if I had incurred the enmity of anyone even remotely connected with that three-headed idol I should put the ocean between that person and myself and in addition build me an impregnable fortress. The wrath of Brahma reaches far. I trust that you are not in the black books of Prince Rajan or his priestly 'compagnon du voyage.'"

Carrington leisurely helped himself to a glass of Vermouth. "If I am, I fancy an able-bodied Englishman should be a match for even a worshiper of Brahma."

Dickerson laughed. "You are insular in your confidence. Don't you know that with the East Indians ablebodiedness and courage counts for nothing? With them it's a thrust in the dark and the coroner's verdict — 'persons unknown.'"

Carrington lit a cigarette and leaned back comfortably in his chair. "Confoundedly interesting, Dickerson. You should lecture on East Indian vendettas."

"But I'm serious, old fellow. If you have offended Prince Rajan or that other chap, take the advice of a friend — and hide!"

"I fancy hiding would bore me," Carrington blew out a little cloud of cigarette smoke. "Do you happen to know if the wrath of Brahma rests also on the sister of Prince Rajan?"

Dickerson looked interested. "I didn't know he had a sister. Did he?"

"So he says." Carrington threw away his cigarette and stood up, preparatory to leaving.

"If you should hear anything further in regard to vendettas and the wrath of Brahma, I should be grateful if you would pass on the information to me."

Dickerson stared at him curiously. "Why do you take such an interest in Rajan Mohan?"

Carrington decided not to gratify his curiosity. Undoubtedly Miss Flynn would not wish her affairs discussed at a club.

"One must have some interest in life," he answered guardedly. "Why not Rajan Mohan as well as another?"

Dickerson smiled without rancor. "Keep your own counsel by all means if you prefer, only" — and he lowered his voice to a dramatic tone — "be careful you don't bring on yourself the curse of the Surya's Eye ruby!"

"Is that intended for a joke, Dickerson?"

"I don't know whether it is or not. I don't fancy Sir Robert Williamson thought so. You remember a year or more ago he was found dead in the library of his castle with an East Indian dagger in his breast. There was a strip of parchment pasted on the wall above him and on it in red ink was printed the words, 'Per order the Surya's Eye ruby' — or some such rot. I don't remember the exact wording, but Williamson was dead right enough and there was poison on the blade of the dagger to make the thrust sure."

Carrington felt a slight shiver down his phlegmatic spine. "Where had this happened, Dickerson?"

"In Yorkshire at a place called Rose Gardens."

Carrington took up his hat and stick. "Sounds too melodramatic to have happened in England." His tone was perfectly colorless. "Goodnight, Dickerson."

Carrington's state of mind, however, was not as unemotional as his voice. He was determined to use every effort to induce Miss Flynn to give up the lease of Rose Gardens. The scene of a spectacular murder such as this was decidedly not the place for a respectable English lady to pass the summer. He felt indignant toward Messrs. Cockerill and Waddington for their silence in regard to the crime which had occurred in this Yorkshire Castle.

When Carrington entered his rooms, he discovered that he had a visitor. His favorite easy chair was drawn up before the electric-log fire — for the May night was cool — a chestnut head reclined against the cushions and a pair of graceful limbs clad in black evening suit were stretched in indolent comfort upon a leather ottoman. The visitor did not trouble to alter his position in the slightest as Carrington crossed the room.

"Making myself at home you see, Tom," he remarked in a lazy, rather musical voice.

Carrington caught in a cordial grip the slim, elegant hand held out to him. "Max, dear old boy, why haven't you been in to see me before this?"

Max laughed softly, "This is the first evening I've had to myself, Tom. I don't dare to cross through London in broad daylight — too many duns at my heels — rotten nuisance those chaps."

Carrington stood looking down at his visitor with an indulgent smile. Maxwell Flynn, for all his thirty-three years, looked entirely boyish, cheerful, and irresponsible as he reclined there in careless grace. In his very attitude was conspicuous his distinguishing characteristic — a calm confidence, an almost insolent assurance in his own powers of attraction — a characteristic which antagonized most men but won most women against their better judgment. Then, too, Max was undeniably handsome with his wavy chestnut hair, blue eyes, and his clear-cut features. Yet there was something not entirely lovable about his face — the reckless, half-mocking light in his eyes perhaps, combined with the cynical, almost sneering curl of his lips. But Carrington, who regarded Max, his boyhood's playmate, with the lenient affection which a man of his steadfast, slow-going nature would feel for a wayward younger brother, saw none of these defects in the smiling face, indolently upturned to his.

Though Carrington was only five years older than Max, he felt at least twenty years his senior, and his tone was almost paternal as he asked, "You backed the winner at the races, I hope?"

Max raised his hand in entreaty. "Don't speak of races, Tom! I lost heavily on Gypsy Queen. Susanna lost, too. She's no end worried. She's up to her ears in debts and had staked everything on the mare. Now she's no means to meet her creditors. I'm in the same predicament myself, but fortunately I am able to take it philosophically. 'Pon my word, Tom, after all it's jolly exciting dodging duns. You should try it to relieve that infernal boredom you suffer from."

Carrington drew up a chair near his guest and settled himself therein with a sigh of content. "It must be jolly wearisome for the creditors, though. I think I had rather bore myself. Have a Corona, Max?" as he pushed a box of cigars toward him.

Max selected one. "Thanks. Don't mind if I do. By the way, Tom, what is this wild-goose scheme my revered Aunt has in her bonnet about leasing a crazy old castle in Yorkshire and dragging me up there to lay the ghost? I couldn't make much out of what she said over the telephone except that it was bound to be a beastly place to pass the summer in. What about it, old man? She seems to have constituted you master of ceremonies."

Carrington lit his cigar with some eagerness. "It strikes me, Max, that it's bound to be a rather exciting place to pass the summer in." And he told of the East Indians' attempts to gain possession of Rose Gardens, the crime which had been enacted there, and Dickerson's revelations in regard to the younger East Indian.

When Carrington had finished, Max was no longer reclining in indolent ease. He was sitting up with animation, and his interest was so great that he even declined a glass of the Château d'Yquem which Carrington's manservant had brought in on a tray.

"What did you say that East Indian chap's name was?" Max demanded eagerly.

"Rajan Mohan."

"By George! I know him then. I've met him at 'The Foreign Club' and other places. He's a genuine prince all right, and I believe there was some talk about his being exiled from India because of some curse having fallen on the family. But that's not to the point, the main fact is that he's distinctly worth cultivating. Why, he's a modern Croesus, a walking treasury of bank-notes and jewels. You should see the huge ruby he flaunts at evening functions — a ball of red fire — biggest stone I ever saw. They say it once formed one of the eyes of an East Indian god and that Rajan can't go back to India until the ruby has done something or rather — I don't know what. Tom, do you happen to know where his highness is putting up?"

"Max," said Carrington gravely, "don't get mixed up with this East Indian. If you must have money at once, I am perfectly willing to lend you more — anything within reason. I don't fancy Rajan Mohan would be a patient creditor."

Max gave a laugh of exasperation. "What an old literal-head you are, Tom! Do you imagine that I should apply for a loan to a mere social acquaintance? — and a foreigner at that? No, old boy, I have less direct views than that. Rajan Mohan could— if he wished— give me a little inside information in regard to investments. I've long had a wistful eye on the ruby mines of Burma. You say he was confoundedly set about getting the lease of Rose Gardens and that Aunt Ell wouldn't give it up. Well then, if he can't be the lessee, there's no reason why he shouldn't be a guest at the house party."

Carrington knocked the ash from his cigar with deliberation. "Before you invite Rajan Mohan to Rose Gardens, suppose you ask him where he and his ruby were when Sir Robert Williamson was stabbed to death with a poisoned dagger in the library of that very castle."

Max rose with an indifferent shrug. "Hang Sir Robert Williamson! That little question is up to Scotland Yard. It's not my concern nor yours either, Tom. Well, I'm off to try my persuasive powers on Aunt Ell. I suppose if I invited the East Indian without her permission, she would turn him out of doors. But I think," with a confident laugh, "I can bring her around. If she proves too obstinate, I will threaten to make myself an ogre to the fair Helena. You see," with a twinkle in his eye, "I have surmised my respected aunt's little matchmaking plan. Oh, by the way, Tom, have you invited any guests as yet?"

Carrington, in his sudden displeasure at Max's unreasonableness, decided to break the news without preamble.

"I have invited one — Miriam."

"The heck you have!" Max's face hardened, the suggestion of a sneer about his mouth became pronounced. "Why the blazes did you do it, eh?"

Carrington told him.

Max gave a harsh laugh of irritation. "You're confoundedly soft! Oh, well," with a resigned shrug," I suppose she would have tracked me down wherever I went."

At that moment Carrington felt something akin to contempt for Max. "You're treating Mimi rather shabbily."

"Then let her keep away from me." Max's tone was expressive of that indifference, nothing short of brutality, which men display toward the woman of whom they have tired. "Look here, old chap, why didn't you invite Susanna instead? Then," with a mocking smile, "you would have pleased yourself as well as me."

Carrington stiffened. Max had never before appeared to him in so unlovable a light.

"It was Miss Flynn's express wish that I should not invite Susanna."

Max burst into a shout of amused laughter. "By Jove! Tom, I don't think the choice you have made will please Aunt Ell much more than if you had shown a little daring and invited Susanna after all. I wonder if I could coax her into giving an invitation to Susanna as well as to Rajan Mohan. It would be a jolly entertaining house party then. So long, Tom!"

Still laughing, Max went out.

4

ROSE GARDENS

Lord Carrington was awakened the next morning, unpleasantly early for a man of his easy habits, by the insistent ringing of the telephone. It was Miss Flynn calling. She desired to know if he could accompany her to Rose Gardens that very afternoon. Something had happened to her — she would explain on the train — it made her determined to take possession of the old house that night. She deemed it advisable for a man to accompany her — even a woman of her independent character was not averse to summoning a member of the dominant sex to her aid in a case of necessity — and as Max, because of a previous engagement which he thought could not be broken, was unable to play attendant squire, Carrington had occurred to her as being in every way a suitable escort.

Carrington, too, had a previous engagement for that evening, but he was too good-natured to refuse Miss Flynn's request, or rather demand, and so, after a vain attempt to induce her to give up the lease of Rose Gardens by a recital of Dickerson's colorful account of the crime that had taken place there and the apparent connection with it of some malevolent East Indian association, he assured her that he would be at King's Cross Station in due time for the train which she desired to take to Yorkshire.

He was as good as his word and was leisurely pacing the platform, scanning the passing throng of travelers and tourists with his monocled gaze, when Miss Flynn's tall, austere figure made its way toward him. That venturesome lady was followed by an elderly, worried-looking maid, laden down with boxes and bags, and by an indifferent-appearing porter, also burdened with luggage.

"Glad to find you on time, Carrington," was Miss Flynn's characteristically curt greeting. "Aeronwen," said to the distracted maid, then she added, "don't let that Morocco bag out of your hands for a moment. Carrington," as he was assisting her into a first class compartment, "what have you done with your luggage?"

"My man has charge of it."

"I hope," Miss Flynn paused on the carriage step, "you are not bringing anything of especial value?"

"Oh, no! I shouldn't say Rose Gardens was exactly a safe treasure-house."

Aeronwen gave a little gasp and dropped the Morocco bag.

"You are very clumsy today, Aeronwen," said her mistress severely.

Aeronwen hastily picked up the bag. "It's nerves, Miss Ellery, that's what it is. And why shouldn't it be when we're heading straight into danger?"

Miss Flynn's whole attitude was expressive of disgust. "I am sorry, Aeronwen, I showed you that note this morning, but I did not suppose a woman of your years would permit herself to be afflicted with nerves. Hand me the bag, Aeronwen, before you drop it again."

As the train left the great city behind and plunged on through suburbs and woodlands and queer, barely alive little villages on its way to the north, Carrington was shown the note which had upset the middle-aged nerves of Aeronwen. Miss Flynn drew from a pocket of the morocco bag a square, white envelope on which the address, "Miss Ellery Flynn, — Cavendish Square," was painstakingly printed in cramped characters. The postmark was "Kensington," and the date of posting the preceding evening.

"Read the enclosure, Carrington," bade Miss Flynn.

He took from the envelope a sheet of plain, white paper folded once. As he opened it, there was wafted to his nostrils the peculiar, subtle fragrance of some perfume which he had never smelled before, but which vaguely suggested to him strange, exotic blossoms, the storied Lotus Flowers perhaps. Across the middle of the paper was printed in the same laborious, cramped characters as those upon the envelope, "For pity's sake, do not go to Rose Gardens. Danger is there."

"It was that note," declared Miss Flynn, sitting very straight and stiff in her corner of the compartment, "which made me resolve to go this very night. I never allow myself to be deterred from a course of action by silly practical jokes."

Carrington refolded the paper and placed it carefully in the envelope which he gave back to Miss Flynn.

"You think it is no more than a practical joke then?"

"This is the twentieth century and a civilized country," she reminded him.

He nodded assent. But that faint, exotic perfume was still in his nostrils, strangely stirring his – up until now – stolid British senses and conjuring up the vision of a plaintive olive face and a pair of soft, dark eyes, shy and troubled as those of a frightened fawn. Nora Mohan, poor little transplanted lotus flower! Why should she not have sent this line of warning through terror of what her brother might do to the woman who had outwitted him in securing the lease of Rose Gardens?

Miss Flynn, however, refused to credit this belief. "If the note is more than a practical joke and was written by that poor shrinking child, then Rajan Mohan forced her to do so in the hope of frightening me away from Rose Gardens, but I am not to be frightened away as long as there is telegraph connection with Scotland Yard. It is unbelievable, Carrington, but Max actually begged me to invite that brown-faced adventurer to be my guest this summer — it seems he met him at some club. Of course I refused. Max then behaved very foolishly, displayed a little of his mother's temper, and even declared he would not come to Rose Gardens. You understand how essential it is that he should come and so I finally consented to his bringing down two or three friends with him. He forestalled the proviso I was about to add by informing me that Lady Susanna Helton intended to spend the summer in Scotland."

Carrington thought that Susanna must have changed her mind very suddenly for she had told him only the day before that she had declined Lady MacGowrie's invitation because Lord MacGowrie persisted in making love to her, but he wisely said nothing. He could not, however, help wondering if Max, the incorrigible, had some daring plan in his head. He had always taken liberties with Miss Ellery which no one else in the family would have ventured upon and yet had contrived to keep the lion's share of her favor by a successful blending of audacity, whimsicality and boyish charm of manner.

Carrington became aware that Miss Flynn's gray eyes were fixed upon him rather sharply.

"I was sorry," she remarked, "to learn that you had invited Miss Cramer to Rose Gardens. From what I have heard of her I judge she is not a guest whom I should have chosen. Her father was impossible, and she appears to have no established position."

"Her father was a rotter right enough, but Mimi herself — why she's just a forlorn little creature, rather a pitiful little soul when all is said and done. She's always been buffeted about from pillar to post and has had to fight for whatever she got. Her mother was never known to speak a kind word to her, and her father tolerated her and that's all. I doubt if she ever had a real friend in her life."

Miss Flynn's expression became slightly less severe. Her heart was kinder than she herself would admit. "Well, I dare say Miss Cramer will know how to make herself agreeable. You under, stand, Carrington, I will expect you to look after her. Max must be left free. Now there is another little matter. I received a communication from Cockerill and Waddington this morning which did not please me. I think they are not treating me quite fairly. Those East Indians have unquestionably offered them an even larger sum for Rose Gardens and they are adding all manner of conditions and stipulations, hoping of course to annoy me sufficiently to make me give up the lease. But they don't know me. I have signed that lease and will hold to it. Moreover, I admit I have a certain number of women's curiosity and am determined to find out why these East Indians are so desperately anxious to rent Rose Gardens. You are always complaining of being bored, Carrington, it might amuse you to turn into a detective and help me solve this mystery."

"By Jove! It might." He looked mildly excited. "What were Cockerill and Waddington's conditions, Miss Flynn?"

"That the woman who acted as housekeeper for Sir Robert Williamson, the late owner, and the man who was the butler should remain in the same capacities. It seems they have been caretakers of the estate since Sir Robert's — death. The man is an East Indian."

"And the woman?"

"She came originally from Australia, I believe."

Carrington passed his hand thoughtfully down the smooth back of his head.

"An interesting pair! I shouldn't wonder, Miss Flynn, if we found more or less excitement at Rose Gardens."

"I am prepared for it!" grimly. "I have Max's revolver in this bag."

Carrington smiled ever so slightly. The notion of Miss Ellery Flynn leveling a revolver at some housebreaker was not entirely lacking in humor.

"I believe," with a suggestion of a twinkle in the calm depths of his gray-blue eyes, "that Pearson thought it advisable to pack my revolver. I fancy we should be a match for the butler and the housekeeper — or even Rajan Mohan himself. Our first glimpse of the Yorkshire moors, Miss Flynn." He pointed to the huge expanses of moorland, flaming with the gold of the gorse and the broom, which now, as the train labored up the steep gradients northward, were replacing the farmlands, the wooded valleys and the green fields.

Miss Flynn looked with interest on the rugged Yorkshire scenery — the lofty shoulders of the moors, the precipitous ravines gorged out between fortress-like escarpments, again rolling masses of moorland, and beyond, as the train climbed ever higher, the sea, like a haze of pearly-blue, blending softly with the hard, rugged outline of the land.

As the sun was commencing to sink, the train drew up at a small wayside station and Miss Flynn and Carrington descended. Standing there on the platform in the waning light, while the tail-lamps of the train lost themselves in the distance, the Londoners felt very much alone, the silence of the countryside seemed oppressive and even formidable. Aeronwen shivered and drew close to her mistress.

A moment later a horse-drawn carriage with a pair of stout horses swung into view. The coachman, a hard-featured, thick-set fellow in a nondescript blue livery, saluted Miss Flynn with respect, mingled with curiosity, as he drew up at the edge of the platform. Miss Flynn and Carrington took the two side seats, facing each other, Aeronwen crowded in beside her mistress, and Pearson, Carrington's valet, climbed to a seat beside the coachman. A flourish of the whip and the stout horses started off at a smart pace along a wide roadway, bordered by strips of grass and indented on the left by a large pond which reflected the pale pink of the evening sky. Some ancient barns, a flock or two of geese, and a few whitewashed gables stood out against the deepening tones of the landscape, while beyond rose ever steeply the majestic shoulders of the moors, now merging into gloom. There was something soul stirring, awesome in the silence, the vastness of the moor spaces. It seemed almost a desecration to break the brooding quiet, and so the travelers rode on, without speaking, over the bare ribs of the hills where the heather, not yet awakened, slumbered snugly in its coat of chocolate-brown.

The horse-drawn carriage turned into a side road and curved upwards to towering heights where there swept down a cold, cutting wind that set the Londoners shivering. It needed but this chilling blast to complete the grim suggestiveness of the bleak waste, the darkening sky, and the mystery of that old castle toward which they were hastening. Aeronwen sat huddled against her mistress in a misery of loneliness and homesickness. Miss Flynn herself was strangely subdued. Carrington wondered if she was beginning to regret her venture.

As the horse-drawn carriage still pressed upward, the wind grew keener, whipping their faces with the sting of salty brine, the air became filled with the ceaseless thunder of the heavy waves of the North Sea, and beyond the bold headlands, shrouded in dusk, as they reared out towards to the west, there glimmered the harbor lights of Whitby.

Suddenly there rose before the travelers the ridge of a lofty promontory, on its crest, lashed by the winds of the North Sea, clustered a dark mass of buildings, which sent up into the evening sky two high, narrow towers. The driver pointed with his whip.

"Rose Gardens!"

Miss Flynn, with the spirit of adventure shining in her eyes, stared up eagerly at those two ancient, crenelated towers... waiting to see the famous rose bushes. Aeronwen regarded them with a sort of fascinated fear and pushed closer to her mistress. Carrington, too, his imagination excited by the long ride through the desolate grandeur of the darkening moors, felt that there was something almost sinister in the aspect of those twin relics of a bygone age, outlined with peculiar distinctness against the twilight glow. For centuries they had stood like sentinels, frowning down on stretches of sea and moor, grim guardians of the old house which, only a few short months ago, had been the scene of violent and unexplained death. Perhaps were those two hoary turrets magically endowed with the power of speech, they might have told what dark link it was which united this old Yorkshire castle to distant India — a link not severed by the mysterious death of its late owner, since the brown-skinned men of that occult land sought still to gain a foothold here.

It seemed that the old house meant to offer merely a sullen welcome to its new mistress, for its windows gave back darkness to the dark. Gaunt and silent and stern, under the desolation and terror of its solitude, it clung to the naked back of the promontory. On near approach the house showed itself to be composed of a central block of black granite, above which rose the Rose Gardens, battlemented and pierced with many loopholes, and from which, on the right and left, stretched more modern wings, outspread like arms, as though to make more secure the apparently perilous position of the old castle perched on the ridge of the promontory. The whole pile was singularly bare of ivy for so venerable a structure and this fact accentuated its gaunt and forbidding aspect.

As the horse-drawn carriage passed through a turreted gateway, one of the heavy mullioned windows in the central block suddenly showed forth a golden oblong, bordered with shadowy gray where the lamplight thinned the black of the wall. There was life then in that grave-like house, someone had been watching for the coming of the horse-drawn carriage. A moment later the massive entrance door swung open and a strange, fantastic figure was silhouetted against the yellow light of the hall. It was the East Indian butler in native garb. He stepped out into the night, making a graceful and dignified greeting.

"Welcome, Mem Sahib!" His voice had the same liquid quality as that of Rajan Mohan.

He opened the door of the horse-drawn carriage and held out a lean, brown hand to assist Miss Flynn down. But she ignored that hand and descended unaided. Aeronwen followed closely, her teeth chattering more from dread of the solemn-faced East Indian and that old house, secret and silent, with its one lit window than from the chill of the biting winds that swept straight from the sea, foaming at the foot of the promontory.

Deferentially the East Indian butler ushered Miss Flynn into the great hall, dim and somber in the subdued light of the central lamp. Carrington followed her, carrying the morocco bag which she would no longer entrust to Aeronwen, who was fairly treading on her mistress's heels in her determination not to be left alone and unprotected. Carrington's customary boredom had long since vanished and, as the outer door clanged heavily behind Pearson who was the last to enter, he felt extraordinarily wide awake and ready to encounter the mysteries of the old house which the very atmosphere of the hall seemed to suggest. Long shadows trailed down from the age-blackened oak rafters, dimming the richly carved pattern of the wainscoting which reached to the high ceiling, and blurring into a vague purplish gray the various tints in the stone-flagged pavement. Two noble staircases, curving upward on either side of the hall, lost themselves in obscurity and even the splendid old fireplace showed ever so indistinctly.

Carrington, as his eyes became accustomed to the dusk, looked about vainly for the stags' heads and the armored figures that usually adorn the halls of well-ordered old English houses. In place of these traditional relics, East Indian curios of every description were ranged about the oaken walls and the gloom lent them grotesque shapes. The hideous faces of idols grinned with unseemly mirth, and one in particular, a monstrous statue of three-headed Brahma, standing forth from a dim recess, seemed to mock and threaten.

Miss Flynn turned sharply from a scrutiny of those three leering idiot faces to meet the mildly questioning gaze of the East Indian butler, who was standing by her side in an attitude of respectful attention.

"What is your name?" she demanded curtly.

"Ahmed, Mem Sahib," with another deep salutation.

Miss Flynn jerked her shoulders impatiently. Her English straightforwardness revolted at the groveling obsequiousness of the East.

"Have no preparations been made for our arrival? Why is Mrs. MacDonald not here to receive us?"

The shadow of some emotion, quickly suppressed, flickered for an instant over Ahmed's inscrutable brown face.

"I will call MacDonald Sahiba," he said in his liquid, deliberate voice.

With slow dignity he advanced to the staircase on the left. As a matter of fact, he appeared to go with a purposeful slowness and at every step he seemed to be listening for something.

"Pull yourself together, Aeronwen!"

Miss Flynn gave her elderly maid a reproving shake. The latter was staring with fascinated horror at the triple-headed Brahma. Carrington's man, on the contrary, had preserved the detached imperturbability of the well-trained British Servant and apparently was supremely unconscious of such very nontraditional — in the sense that they were distinctly un-English — objects as the leering images of foreign gods.

Before Ahmed could mount the stairs, a figure grew out of the darkness above, a woman's figure, dressed in black.

Ahmed turned quickly. "MacDonald Sahiba is here to give welcome, Mem Sahib."

Again there was the momentary flicker of some emotion on the face of the East Indian.

5

THE FIGURE ON THE TERRACE

Mrs. MacDonald descended the stairs with nervous haste and moved toward the center of the hall where Miss Flynn awaited her in a silence which plainly spoke rebuke. As the housekeeper came into the small circle of lamplight, her face was illumined clearly, it was the face of a woman who had known mental suffering — and who still suffered.

She was of rather an unusual type, not beautiful, yet striking, with her heavy masses of bronze hair, her large, tragic eyes of the same color, and her singularly white complexion. She was of medium height, admirably developed, with slightly voluptuous lines. In age she might have been anywhere in the vicinity of thirty-five.

There was a stereotyped smile of welcome on her lips, but in her eyes fear — indubitable, anxious fear. She looked a little doubtfully at Miss Flynn's uncompromising countenance, read the disapproval there, and her smile grew somewhat tremulous.

"I am Edna MacDonald," she said, in a low and musical voice which had in it a note of sadness.

"I am sorry not to have been on hand to receive you, but there were some little housekeeping duties which I had not quite finished — You see, the only servants at present are Ahmed and one maid, so there was much I had to do myself. Cockerill and Waddington's telegram was — was rather sudden."

The severity of Miss Flynn's expression did not relax. "I instructed Cockerill and Waddington to tell you that I should not expect many preparations to be made for our reception on so short a notice. But nevertheless it seems to me that a few lights in the windows would not have put you to too much trouble and would certainly have given a more cheerful aspect to the house than absolute darkness."

Edna MacDonald bit her lip and flashed a peculiar glance at Ahmed, who was watching her intently, as though waiting for instructions. Perhaps he read some unspoken wish in her glance, for suddenly he turned and crossing the hall, sped up the stairway on the right with a sort of panther-like swiftness.

"I hope you will pardon the absence of lights," Mrs. MacDonald was saying in her soft voice. "I told Ivy Blake to put lamps in several of the windows, but she evidently forgot to do so. Probably," there was a hint of nervous tension in her manner, "you will wish to go to your rooms before having dinner."

In answer to her call of "Ivy!" a buxom young country lass, clear-eyed and rosy-cheeked, appeared from somewhere at the back of the hall, bearing a lamp which Mrs. MacDonald took from her hand.

"The maid at least is wholesome-looking," Miss Flynn remarked in an undertone to Carrington as they followed the housekeeper up the stairway on the left. The two staircases mounted and merged into a square balustraded gallery, from which two long corridors branched off on each side. The chambers opened off these corridors. Carrington's was in the same wing as Miss Flynn's and only three doors from it. The room was gloomy, as he had expected to find it, and when Pearson threw back the window sashes to dispel the musty odor that pervaded the chamber, the thunder of the North Sea fell on their ears and a sharp, penetrating wind swirled through the apartment, billowing the old tapestries and snuffing out the candles which Ivy had just lit.

Carrington hastily closed the sashes and sent Pearson for a lamp. A few minutes later he joined Miss Flynn in the dining-room which opened out of the hall. This apartment, long, low-ceilinged and heavily paneled in dark oak, was no less somber than the rest of the house and there was something unpleasantly incongruous in the contrast between the fine old monogrammed silver and the prim line of portraits on the walls — both so essentially English — With the Oriental curios and idols that stood about the room. Ahmed alone in his exotic garb seemed to fit in with the ever-present suggestion of the East — Ahmed with his peculiar, liquid voice, his impassive features, his observant eyes, and his catlike tread. He was perfectly trained, this East Indian butler, deft in serving, attentive to every want, and yet Carrington had the uncomfortable sensation of being near some secret menace every time the brown man approached him.

To divert his mind from this obsession, he began to study the stiff old portraits of the past occupants of Rose Gardens. One, in particular, held his gaze; time had effaced only a little of the brightness of its coloring and the swaggering, ribbon festooned knight of the days of the Second Charles laughed down at him with reckless, insolent eyes. Vivid as though fresh from the painter's brush, gleamed the red of the roisterer's brocaded suit, equally brilliant was the scarlet of the sweeping plumes that adorned the broad-brimmed hat. In fact, this Carolean rake stood forth like a single splotch of brightness against the surrounding gloom. But Carrington, who was strangely fanciful that night, took an instinctive dislike to the flaunting picture, it seemed to him more a thing of evil than the grinning Indian idols.

At this juncture the rigidity of Ahmed's attitude drew his attention. The East Indian, too, was staring up at the Crimson Knight, and his face was no longer impassive — it was filled with hate. Hate of a man dead these two hundred years? Carrington lifted the black ribbon of his monocle and, screwing the glass into his eye, gazed curiously at the East Indian.

Ahmed became at once conscious of his scrutiny. Instantly he lowered his eyes from the portrait, and his countenance was again inscrutable. He raised the silver cover from a dish which Ivy had just placed upon the table.

"I may serve you to rabbit pasty, Sahib?" Ahmed's tone was respectful and properly subdued.

But Carrington partook of the rabbit pasty with indifferent relish, and he was not sorry when the meal had ended and it was permissible to withdraw from the presence of Ahmed.

Miss Flynn, too, had not appeared to enjoy the dinner thoroughly.

"They're both uncanny — the butler and the housekeeper," she confided to Carrington as she led the way into the hall. "Mrs. MacDonald looks to me like a woman who has a past she doesn't know how to get rid of and a present she doesn't know how to manage."

Aeronwen, the picture of disconsolate misery, was awaiting her mistress in the center of the hall, that being the farthest point from the idols which terrified her.

"I couldn't stay in that room alone another minute, Miss Ellery! I could see images in every corner."

"Ridiculous!" said Miss Flynn unsympathetically. She plainly felt a desire to shake some courage and a little common sense into Aeronwen.

Mrs. MacDonald at that moment was gliding through the hall with a step almost as noiseless as Ahmed's. Miss Flynn called to her peremptorily and asked her to show them over the house before it grew later.

"At the same time," she added, "I can see that everything is properly locked up."

Edna MacDonald's features stiffened. "That will hardly be necessary, Miss Flynn. I have always had charge of the locking up."

"Henceforth I will relieve you of that duty."

A flush suffused Mrs. MacDonald's very white skin. "Sir Robert Williamson was content to entrust the locking up to me."

Miss Flynn stood her ground. "Sir Robert Williamson, Mrs. MacDonald, met with violent death in this house."

Edna MacDonald quivered as though she had been struck. Her sudden color fled and for a moment she presented the appearance of some hunted creature. Then, realizing that Miss Flynn was scrutinizing her with cold suspicion, she contrived to recover her poise.

"Of course," she said quite humbly, "if you prefer to see for yourself that everything is properly locked up, I can have no objection. I only wished to relieve you of what seemed to me an unnecessary responsibility." She called Ivy to bring a lamp.

Miss Flynn turned to her maid, who was staring at Mrs MacDonald with much the same terrified gaze as that which she bestowed on the idols.

"I suppose you will want to come with me, Aeronwen?"

"Oh yes, Miss Ellery." Aeronwen showed immense relief at finding she was not to be left alone. "And — and won't his lordship come too."

"Really, Aeronwen, you are behaving very foolishly. I presume Lord

Carrington will wish to see the house."

Carrington stepped forward. "Delighted, I'm sure."

He, too, was looking fixedly at Mrs. MacDonald whose extreme pallor was accentuated by the recent storm of emotion that had agitated her. Decidedly the housekeeper of Rose Gardens was an interesting study.

A lamp having now been brought by Ivy, Mrs. MacDonald conducted Miss Flynn, with Aeronwen again treading on her heels and Carrington following leisurely, from one end of Rose Gardens to the other. She led them through a large drawing-room and a smaller one, on to the modern billiard-room, and thence into a magnificent ballroom of immense size. Aeronwen slipped on the highly polished floor and fell in an ungraceful heap. Carrington gravely assisted her to her feet, but Miss Flynn, yielding to the desire that had possessed her the entire evening, gave Aeronwen a vigorous shaking, which made her so indignant that she forgot to whimper and tremble at every shadow as they passed through a long gallery into a splendid library, vaguely illumined by a few wax tapers in a candelabra pendent from the vaulted ceiling. Here again East Indian curios confronted them on every side.

The light of the lamp which Mrs. MacDonald carried flashed back in streaks of fire from the eerie collection of curious-shaped daggers, glittering on the dark oak wainscoting. Sir Robert Williamson had shown strange taste in the adorning of his castle. Carrington recollected that it was in this very room Sir Robert had met his death.

But Miss Flynn apparently had no thought, then, of the late occupant of Rose Gardens. As she passed from room to room, her appreciation of the old house grew. The passion of the antiquarian was in her eyes as she looked at the beautiful old brocades and embroideries on the furniture, the ancient oak-paneling, the rare china, and the priceless old tapestries. The sinister suggestion of India which everywhere protruded itself, she seemed resolved to ignore. Here in the library, with its mullioned windows, its oaken wainscoting and its rows of bookshelves, all so characteristically English, it was comparatively easy to banish the thought of that land of mystery, for the idols standing about were almost swallowed up by the shadows in the vast room, and the daggers on the walls, now that Mrs. MacDonald had moved her lamp to the middle of the apartment, no longer streaked the wainscoting with darts of fire.

The sashes of one of the deeply set windows were slightly thrown back and through it sounded the roar of the sea. A double door of leaded glass cut in the center of the north wall, between the rows of bookshelves, looked out upon a stone terrace. Miss Flynn advanced to this door to make sure that it was secure. At the same time she directed Mrs. MacDonald to close the window and extinguish the candles. Carrington drew the window to, while the housekeeper, reaching up on tiptoe, blew out the tapers.

Miss Flynn turned to rebuke Aeronwen who was trying to prevent her from approaching the door, evidently the maid was under the impression that her mistress intended to walk out upon the terrace. Suddenly Mrs. MacDonald's lamp was extinguished. Carrington, although he had not been watching her at that moment, would have been willing to swear that she had blown it out purposely. The library was instantly flooded with darkness. Aeronwen uttered a piercing shriek.

"Look there at the door, Miss Ellery!"

The sudden change threw the door, into relief — a long rectangle of grayish light — and showed a figure standing close, peering in. Before one could hardly visualize it, the figure darted across the terrace and vanished in the night.

6

THE BROKEN IDOLS

Aeronwen began to moan and cry out of nervous fear. Miss Flynn shook her again, but without the desired effect. "Give me the key to this door, Mrs. MacDonald," bade Carrington crisply.

"I — I haven't that key."

"Why not?" demanded Miss Flynn belligerently. "You have every other key with you, have you not?"

"That key is — lost I think, at any rate, mislaid." Mrs. MacDonald was plainly agitated.

Carrington felt his way, with numerous collisions, to the hall. "I am going outside, Miss Flynn, to discover, if I can, who that was looking in at the door."

Aeronwen raised a scream of protest. "Don't let his lordship go and leave us alone in the dark! That man might get in somehow and murder us all."

"Be quiet, Aeronwen." But Miss Flynn's own voice was almost shrill in the stress of her excitement. "It was only a woman — didn't you see the feathers on her hat? I wish you would go, Carrington."

"It was a man," insisted Aeronwen hysterically, "a man dressed very strangely."

As Carrington hurried along the gallery into the entrance hall, he heard Miss Flynn saying, "Don't be absurd, Aeronwen! Men don't wear feathers in their hats. Are there any matches in this room, Mrs. MacDonald, or have they too been mislaid?"

Carrington, however, thought as Aeronwen did that the person who had looked in at the door was a man. It was ridiculous, of course, but the transient impression he had gained on that shadowy figure which certainly had worn a hat with feathers brought to his mind the picture in the dining-room at which Ahmed had stared with eyes of hate — the flaunting picture of the Crimson Knight.

In the great hall Ahmed was busying himself lighting candles and he showed mild amazement — and a hint of some other emotion — when Carrington bade him undo the outer door. This usually deft servitor proved singularly clumsy in obeying, and when at length the massive door swung open, Carrington felt sure that the person in the feathered hat — whether man or woman — had by now put distance between himself and Rose Gardens.

As Carrington stepped out into the night, the wind, tearing like a tornado across the bare promontory, almost took away his breath, and the booming of the sea below was fairly deafening. The stars were creeping into the cloud-swept sky and by their light he made the entire circuit of the house, but found no trace of any person lurking about. Through the library door opening on to the stone terrace, he saw that one could gain a comprehensive view of the whole apartment. In fact, he stood for a few moments looking through the leaded panes, studying with interest the rather tragic face of Edna MacDonald. The wax tapers had been relighted and, as Mrs. MacDonald was standing directly under the candelabra, talking with Miss Flynn and evidently trying to conciliate her, he had opportunity for a prolonged scrutiny of the woman who had served as housekeeper to the late tenant of Rose Gardens, mysteriously slain in that very room not more than a year ago.

Her personality seemed to him baffling and consequently repellent. Women of this type had no attraction for him and when in their presence, he was always conscious of a desire to escape. Being of a frank and open nature, he hated mystery, and too, being also of an indolent temperament, the effort of trying to understand such women wearied and finally bored him. But in the case of Edna MacDonald there appeared to be necessity for trying to understand her. Her smooth manner very likely concealed hostility and certainly her agitation at mention of Sir Robert Williamson's death would hardly prejudice one in her favor. She began now to move about the library, pushing chairs into place and giving little housewifely touches here and there. Carrington was forced to admit that there was grace in her every movement, but to him it was a snake-like grace, and the curious contrast of her bronze-colored hair and eyes with her very white skin which would have aroused enthusiasm in an artist struck him as uncanny.

At that moment Aeronwen caught sight of him peering in. Mistaking him for that other who had so alarmed her, she gave vent to another scream. Carrington decided to go in and reassure her. Moreover it was beastly cold outside. The densest of London fogs was cheerfulness itself in comparison with the bleakness of this house on the North Sea.

Upon reentering, he found that Miss Flynn had recovered her equanimity to the extent of being able to discuss with Mrs. MacDonald the engaging of additional servants. The housekeeper did not show undue joy at the prospect of an invasion of new servants. As a matter of fact, she seemed to be endeavoring to conceal her unwillingness to receive them, although her own duties would thereby be greatly lightened. The mention of the arrival of guests the next day even caused her to exhibit dismay. But why should it? Guests would enliven the gloom of the old house and surely Edna MacDonald was not the type of woman who would be content to bury herself indefinitely in lonely monotony.

Carrington found himself longing for the sound of Max's irresistible laugh. He wondered now, how it was that he could have felt irritated with his friend the night before. Max, he felt sure, was too chivalrous to treat Mimi gentlemanly unless she fairly drove him to do so by her importunities. Well, he would try to amuse Mimi while she was at Rose Gardens and keep her away from Max. He owed that much to Miss Flynn and to Max since he had invited her against the wishes of both. He fell to wondering what guests Max himself would invite. It was useless to think of Susanna. Even Max would hardly dare to bring as his aunt's guest, a woman against whom she was so prejudiced.

Miss Flynn broke in upon Carrington's musings by suggesting that every one retire early in order to feel fresh in the morning when Max and her other guests should arrive. Mrs. MacDonald was quick to avail herself of the opportunity to escape to the seclusion of her own rooms, and Miss Flynn, after a second tour of the house to make herself doubly certain that everything was locked up as it should be, permitted Ahmed to extinguish the candles in the hall and mounted to her chamber. Aeronwen, who had finally secured permission to sleep on the couch in her mistress's room, besought Carrington in an agonized whisper to leave his door unbolted so that she could call him readily in case of need. He consented to this although he did not particularly like the idea of sleeping in an unlocked room at Rose Gardens. It would not be surprising if Ahmed of the furtive step were addicted to night walking.

However, once comfortably in bed with the window curtains drawn to shut out that vista of wild sea which oppressed him, his British stolidity reasserted itself and he forgot Ahmed and all the mystery of Rose Gardens. One face only, a charming, smiling face, remained before his mental vision and he fell asleep with the name of Susanna on his lips.

He was awakened by a hand clutching at his shoulder. A light flashed in his eyes and he blinked up into the panic-stricken face of Aeronwen. She was a queer-looking object to break in upon a man's dreams — her hair in hair curlers, a striped petticoat over her shoulders, and her color a greenish-white.

"Get up, my lord, do!" she begged. "Somebody's broken into the house and Miss Flynn's going down to see who it is. She'll be killed!"

Carrington was dazed with sleep, and his chief sensation at that moment was annoyance that the vision of Susanna should be superseded by that of Aeronwen in hair curlers.

"You have the nightmare, Aeronwen," he said languidly, preparing to turn over on his side. "Go back to bed."

"Please, my lord, get up!" Aeronwen's voice distressingly rang shrill. "There was an awful crash in the hall, my lord — Didn't you hear it? — it was like the crash of doom!"

Her words brought conviction. What he had taken in his sleep to be a clap of thunder might have been this crash she referred to. He sat up fully awake.

"If you'll kindly vanish, Aeronwen, I'll get up and investigate."

Aeronwen fled, and he, throwing a dressing-gown about him and pushing his feet into bedroom slippers which Pearson had hid in foresight to leave conveniently at hand, rapidly made his way along the corridor, which, of course, was dark, to the head of the double stair sweeping down into the great hall. On the right staircase he could distinguish the tall figure of Miss Flynn, resolutely descending. The blackness of the hall below was thinned by a glimmering light, and he heard the voice of Edna MacDonald, not quite so soft and well modulated as hitherto, asking if Miss Flynn, too, had been awakened by the crash.

The housekeeper came apparently from the back of the apartment where a gallery branched off to the servants' hall and the kitchens. She was attired in a negligee of Oriental design, which was knotted about her waist and did not appear to have been put on with any particular haste. The light of the candle she carried made the two long heavy braids of hair which hung over her breast shine like burnished copper and revealed the alarm in her eyes.

Miss Flynn, her usual dignity somewhat impaired by the unconventional arrangement of her own hair and a flannel dressing-gown, obviously put on in haste, was staring with disapproval and suspicion at Mrs. MacDonald.

"How did you get downstairs so quickly?"

Edna MacDonald braced herself to meet Miss Flynn's hostile gaze. "I sleep downstairs in a room off the servants' hall."

Carrington hurriedly descended. "Will you lend me your candle, Mrs. MacDonald? I should like to go through the lower part of the house."

Mrs. MacDonald yielded the candle readily, but, before Carrington could cross the hall an excited cry rang out, "Is it anoother idol brawken?"

Everybody turned in amazement. Ivy Blake, a night-lamp in her hand, was leaning tensely over the balustrade of the gallery above. Her comely young face was white and scared.

"Is it anoother idol brawken?" she repeated.

The alarm in Mrs. MacDonald's eyes grew. "I — I haven't looked to see."

Aeronwen, limp with fear, pressed down the stairs and huddled up to her mistress. Ivy followed her excitedly.

"Tha'llt not need to hoont for boorglars. I knaw — 'tis anoother idol."

"Is the girl crazy?" demanded Miss Flynn.

"Luke theer!" screamed Ivy, pointing to the corner where the statue of triple-headed Brahma had stood — it no longer stood there — "I knawed how it wor — t' third brawken idol."

She ran over to the corner and her lamp disclosed the triple idol lying broken on the flagstones. Carrington examined it with interest. The image was made of some kind of pottery gilded to represent bronze. One of the heads was crushed in as though by a heavy blow, the other two were simply cracked as from the impact of the fall. Carrington looked up at Ivy who was regarding the fallen Brahma with a kind of awe.

"What did you mean by the third broken idol?"

Ivy shivered. "This is t' third night theer's been a crash and av'ry time it's a brawken idol. knaw, it's t' ghost oh' Sir Roobert Williamson coom back an' now he caaun't abide thoose idols an' 'e brak's 'em."

Carrington turned to Mrs. MacDonald. "Is it true this is the third night an idol has been found broken?"

Miss Flynn seemed content that he should be spokesman.

"It is true, this is the third night." Mrs. MacDonald spoke slowly and as though with reluctance.

"How do you account for it?"

She shrugged her shoulders and smiled a little wearily. "I can't account for it. It's all a mystery."

"Nonsense!" broke in Miss Flynn. "Idols don't fall down without hands to push them."

"Where is Ahmed?" asked Carrington quickly. The absence of the butler was rather odd.

"He is probably asleep." Mrs. MacDonald apparently did not like the question. "His room is in one of the Rose Gardens and he could not have heard the fall of the idol."

"The dead could have heard it," snapped Miss Flynn.

"Pearson," said Carrington, addressing his valet who had joined the group in the hall, "go and ask Ahmed to come down here."

As a matter of fact, he did not expect that Pearson would find the butler in his room, and he was accordingly surprised when, a few minutes later, Ahmed glided down the stairs in Pearson's wake. Carrington fancied he detected a shade of triumph on Mrs. MacDonald's face at sight of the East Indian. Evidently she had read his mind. His dislike of her grew.

Ahmed approached with a mildly inquiring deference, as ever, soft of step. His eye sought Mrs. MacDonald's once and then he stood before Miss Flynn in his customary attitude of respectful attention.

"You send for me, Mem Sahib?"

But no amount of questioning on Miss Flynn's part, or Carrington's, could elicit from Ahmed any information that would tend to clear up the mystery of the three broken idols. At each occasion he had been asleep in his "so distant chamber" and had known nothing of the happening until Mrs. MacDonald had ordered him to clear away the wreckage.

Miss Flynn turned impatiently from Ahmed and proposed that they make another tour of the house to be sure that everything was as it had been when they retired. At hearing this, Mrs. MacDonald, who had been bending intently over the broken Brahma, straightened up. As she did so, some object slipped from the folds of her negligee and fell with a metallic ring on the flagstones. Mrs. MacDonald stooped quickly to pick it up, but Ivy's hand was already on it.

"Eh I but it's t' key to th' lib'ry doar," she cried amazedly. "I told yo I didn't lose it."

Mrs. MacDonald's face might have been a mask for all the emotion it betrayed. There was a faint smile of self-reproach on her lips.

"I am sorry I accused you unjustly, Ivy, but you know you are often careless about mislaying things. I found that key in my bureau drawer, Miss Flynn, when I was undressing tonight. I intended to give it to you in the morning."

Miss Flynn held out her hand. "I will take it now."

As Edna MacDonald passed her the key, the eyes of the two women met and the housekeeper's were clouded — unpleasant.

Miss Flynn decreed that Carrington alone should accompany her through the house — Aeronwen went along as a matter of course. They tried the key in the library door and found that it fitted. Miss Flynn then entrusted it to Carrington to keep for her.

As Aeronwen again, when her mistress's back was turned, besought him to leave his door unlocked it seemed to him that the safest depository for the key would be under his pillow where it could not be disturbed without awakening him. He had the notion that Mrs. MacDonald, for some purpose which he could not fathom, might wish that key in her possession again.

Since everything in the house appeared quiet and he was tired from the long railway journey, he soon fell asleep. As before, Susanna was the center of his dreams. Perhaps the bronze of Mrs. MacDonald's hair, recalling similar glints in Susanna's when the sun shone on it, was what brought the latter before him so persistently that night. However it was, he dreamed of Susanna again and even had the fancy that she was hovering about him. The warm touch of her hand on his was almost like reality.

When he awoke, the sun was forcing its way in cheerily through the worn old hangings. The dark paneling glowed in the golden rays, the roar of the sea outside had abated into a musical murmur, and the chamber no longer seemed gloomy. Carrington reached under the pillow for the key. He wished to examine in the daylight the peculiar chasing he had observed on it.

He drew forth his fingers in dismay. The key was not there. Perhaps it had slipped among the bedclothes. He got up and searched carefully. But it was useless — the key had disappeared!

7

GUESTS ARRIVE

When Miss Flynn learned of the disappearance of the key, her indignation was so extreme that she almost taxed Mrs. MacDonald with the theft of it. But the housekeeper's expression was so meekly innocent and her astonishment at hearing of its disappearance apparently so genuine, that Miss Flynn was mollified into making a half apology for her distrust.

With the matter-of-fact daylight courage had come back to both Aeronwen and Ivy, and the latter with an air of importance and shuddering delight was pointing out to Aeronwen the exact spot where the other two idols had fallen. Miss Flynn, irritated beyond words by this daylight bravery and this harping on what to her was an annoying mystery, went out upon the terrace with Carrington to watch for Max. Even Carrington was forced to admit that in the bright sunshine the rugged Yorkshire scenery was not without charm. The high escarpments of rock put forth striking colors and below stretched the wide sweep of the sea like a blue carpet edged with white where the waves were chafing against the cliffs. On the left spread a great expanse of smooth turf, and there rose the roofless arches of Whitby Abbey, standing out like a silhouette on the green horizon. Beyond, a staunch lighthouse showed itself a dazzling white against the azure of the sky. And over there, for an additional bit of color, clustered under the dominion of a sturdy Norman church the red roofs of Whitby Town.

Miss Flynn drew a breath of satisfaction. "Such a view as this is worth all the unpleasantness connected with Rose Gardens. Carrington, look! Is not that the horse-drawn carriage winding up the cliff?"

When they were alone together in the hall, Max slipped his arm persuasively through Carrington's.

"Tom, you'll give me free way with Susanna, won't you? I know you're a little soft on her yourself, but, old man, she's the one woman I ever was really mad about, probably because, unlike the others, she's a bit indifferent, elusive you might say — laughs at me when I make love to her. But I'm bringing her around, if you'll only keep Mimi off me, and yourself in the background. Do you know, I think she rather likes you."

"Only as a friend." Carrington's voice held a note of bitterness. "Don't worry, Max. There could never be any sentiment between us. As Susanna herself has told me, I am too hopelessly conventional for a woman ever to fall in love with."

At this moment Edna MacDonald descended the stairs and came straight toward Carrington. Her pallor was intense and there was trouble in her eyes.

"I beg your pardon, Lord Carrington, but will you tell me the name of that lady who has just arrived?"

"Lady Susanna Helton." Carrington could not repress the surprise in his tone. "Mrs. MacDonald, Mr. Flynn," he introduced perfunctorily.

Max bowed a little carelessly — and his glance was appraising. Mrs. MacDonald colored ever so slightly at meeting his almost insolently admiring eyes, but it struck Carrington that she did not Hush entirely from displeasure.

"Thank you, Lord Carrington," she said nervously, "I thought that I had seen Lady Susanna Helton somewhere before, but I — I was mistaken."

Max looked after her curiously as she hastily withdrew from the hall, there was a mocking twist to his mouth.

"Interesting type — Mrs. MacDonald. If it weren't for Susanna — " He broke off with a laugh. "I say, Tom, why do you suppose she was so confoundedly anxious to know Susanna's name?"

When Miss Flynn came downstairs again, Max made his peace with her by promising to call on Helena Dormont that very afternoon.

"You know, Aunt Ell," with a wink at Carrington, "I invited Susanna more or less on Thomas's account. He will need some occupation while I am playing squire to Helena."

"He could have occupied himself with Miss Cramer."

Max gave a soft laugh of mischief. "I think Tom can take care of two, if he can't — why I'll come to his aid."

Miss Flynn tried to look stern, but even she was not proof against the twinkle in Max's eyes and she smiled in spite of herself. He put his arm about her and kissed her lightly.

"We're friends again, eh, Aunt Ell?"

"Max, you're incorrigible! You know I can't be angry with you. You promise to be very agreeable to Miss Dormont?"

Max promised and went upstairs laughing. Ahmed followed respectfully, carrying his Gladstone bag.

An hour or so later Carrington found Max in the hall again examining the broken Brahma with minute attention.

"My word, Max, are you becoming a convert to Brahma?"

Max swung round hastily. "Epicurus — and Susanna — are my only idols." He spoke lightly, but his eyes were restless and his fingers worked nervously. "This old chap with the shattered head rather interests me; he's so ugly. What time does the ghost generally walk?"

"You mean — "

"What time do the idols fall?"

"This one fell about midnight." Max's harping upon the subject was beginning to puzzle Carrington.

Max stretched himself indolently upon the old settee by the fireplace. "I'll take only cat-naps tonight, Tom. 'Pon my word, I'd like to lay the ghost of this old house."

Soon after lunch Max set off obediently for Dormont Court. Miss Flynn accordingly unbent a little toward Susanna and invited her out upon the terrace. Carrington drew up a chair by Susanna's side and prepared to make the most of Max's absence which he suspected was partly due to a desire to be away when Miriam should arrive.

Miss Cramer made her appearance in the middle of the afternoon and Miss Flynn received her with much the same frigid politeness as that with which she had received Susanna. The latter was very cordial in her greeting. Miriam tried to reciprocate, but did not altogether succeed and her disappointment was obvious at finding Max gone. Carrington again felt sorry for her and mentally vowed that he would do his best to make her stay at Rose Gardens an agreeable one.

About four o'clock Max came strolling back, humming a cheerful little tune. At the sight of Miriam, who had hastened forward to meet him, his expression was not one of unalloyed delight, but he greeted her pleasantly enough and even took a chair beside her, after throwing a glance of whimsical reproach at Carrington who did not offer to relinquish his seat by Susanna. Max interrupted Miriam's voluble chatter by informing Miss Flynn that he had a piece of news for her. His eyes were full of mirth and the half-humorous, half-mocking twist of his lips was conspicuous.

"Prepare to write a note of felicitations, Aunt Ell. Helena Dormont is engaged to be married."

"What!" Miss Flynn could not have started up more suddenly if a bomb had exploded under her chair. "Who to?" in her agitation forgetting her grammar.

"Young chap by the name of Mountford — in the army, I believe. A good match for Miss Dormont, I should say."

Miss Flynn stood up abruptly. "The wind is growing sharp. Suppose we have tea in the hall."

Max's high spirits were infectious, and the gloomy old hall resounded to unwonted merriment. Miss Flynn alone had very little to say and sat stiff and for the most part silent with the massive tea-urn before her.

A ponderous knocking that for a moment checked the happiness felt by Miss Flynn's guests sent the attentive Ahmed to the entrance door. Max gazed after the East Indian with a kind of repressed eagerness. Several times Borrowdean had caught Max glancing at the butler in a curious way. What was on Max's mind? His merriment did not seem altogether spontaneous. Could it be that he attached something sinister to the fall of those idols and believed that danger was threatening Miss Flynn?

Ahmed now was gliding back with rather an undue rapidity toward the tea-table, bearing a calling card on a silver salver. He had evidently left the caller in the small entry-hall. It was apparent to all that the East Indian was laboring under extreme emotion. His face had gone a sickly hue, and his eyes were like those of a trapped animal and the hand that held the salver shook.

Miss Flynn bestowed upon him a prolonged stare of displeasure and took the card from the tray.

"Who is the visitor, Carrington? I haven't my reading-glasses with me."

The monocle dropped from his eye as he read aloud the name engraved upon the bit of pasteboard, "Prince Rajan Mohan."

8

THE CRIMSON KNIGHT

Miss Flynn rose precipitately. "I will receive Prince Rajan Mohan here, Ahmed." Max looked distinctly interested. Susanna glanced at him comprehendingly.

"Is it that same East Indian prince whom we met at the Ascot races and later at the Russian Embassy ball?"

Max nodded, a little jubilantly, it seemed.

"I have heard of this Prince," broke in Miriam eagerly. "They say he flaunts an immense ruby of priceless value at evening functions and yet has no detectives to guard him as most of these Oriental potentates have. He is fairly tempting Providence. I wonder — "

The approach of Rajan Mohan cut short her words. The East Indian as before, was correctly and quietly dressed in European clothes which bore the unmistakable impress of the West End tailor and he showed on his person none of that ostentatious display of jewelry in which Orientals commonly delight. In fact, his attire was precisely that of any well-born English gentleman, his only adornments being the unobtrusive pearl pin in his tie and his watch-chain of early Victorian design. He was rather handsome, this East Indian, tall, well-formed, with regular features, but there was an expression in his black eyes and a hardness about his smooth shaven mouth which did not attract.

Carrington found himself staring curiously at the East Indian's snakewood walking-stick — a vicious looking object with a cobra's head at the top from the open fangs of which protruded the tip of a dagger point in place of the serpent's tongue. With such a weapon as this within reach Rajan Mohan scarcely needed the protection of detectives.

The prince relinquished his hat and gloves to Ahmed, who received them with an exceedingly low salaam. The butler's face still showed the sickly hue of fear. Rajan Mohan did not glance at Ahmed, and he himself carefully deposited the snakewood walking-stick upon a chair nearby. He then shook hands gravely with Miss Flynn, whose greeting was the reverse of cordial and presented his sister. Nora Mohan's shrinking little figure had been dwarfed almost into invisibility behind her brother's imposing form. There was the same plaintive terror in her eyes that there had been two nights ago at the Carlton and she gazed up so appealingly at Miss Flynn that the latter was moved and spoke to her with unusual gentleness.

Miss Flynn, with the air of one performing an unpleasant duty, introduced the East Indian and hid sister to her guests. Max greeted Rajan Mohan with the cordiality of an old-time friend, but there was hauteur in the East Indian's bearing. It was not so when he held Susanna's hand for a moment in his. His brown face lit up.

"It is a great pleasure for me to meet again Lady Susanna Helton."

Susanna smiled charmingly and Carrington had for an instant a savage feeling against the East Indian. It was one thing to relinquish Susanna to the attentions of Max, his friend, but an entirely different matter in the case of an East Indian adventurer. Rajan Mohan appeared to harbor no resentment against Carrington for the curtness which he had previously shown him and his manner was courteous in the extreme. Of Miriam the prince took scant notice. In fact, his eager eyes scarcely left Susanna's face. She, for her part, seemed to derive considerable amusement from his obvious infatuation and turned aside his thinly veiled compliments in her usual bantering fashion.

Max, finding himself unappreciated, directed his attention to Nora. At first, she was too shy to answer in more than monosyllables, but gradually under the influence of Max's encouraging smile, she opened up and told him with a childlike eagerness of the wonderful sights she had seen in London — Evidently her first experience of life in a great city. In the daylight and dressed in tailor gown, she looked older than she had at the Carlton. Carrington decided that she was probably eighteen instead of sixteen as he had previously judged her to be. Yet she had the timidity and artlessness of a child — of a child who has always lived in seclusion and more or less under subjection. But Carrington was sure that it was more than awe— it was terror — with which her brother inspired her. So long as Rajan Mohan devoted himself to Susanna, Nora chatted away happily with Max, like a child who has found an appreciative listener, but, let the East Indian turn his glance upon her, she would stop talking in a curious, abrupt way, and it would require much encouragement on Max's part, to draw her out again.

In the course of the conversation, Rajan Mohan remarked with a faint smile at Miss Flynn that he had succeeded after all in leasing a house in Yorkshire — as a matter of fact in the near vicinity of Rose Gardens, for the grounds adjoined those of Dormont Court.

"By the way, Miss Flynn," he said, "have you heard that Dormont Court was broken into and — what do you English call it — looted last night? Many valuable art treasures were stolen."

"No! I had not heard." Miss Flynn evinced some agitation. "Have they caught the thief?"

Rajan Mohan shook his head regretfully. "They are not likely to. It is one of many mysterious robberies which have taken place recently here in the North Riding."

"Mysterious robberies! What do you mean?"

Rajan Mohan regarded her gravely. "Is it possible, Miss Flynn, you do not know that for the past few months there have been innumerable daring robberies in the North Riding? Last night was the most successful of all. Really, Miss Flynn, one must admire your courage in wishing to occupy Rose Gardens."

The East Indian's voice held a peculiar note and his eye swept the hall, embracing the Indian curios and idols. Several times Carrington had caught him glancing sharply at the mutilated image of Brahma.

Miss Flynn stiffened. "My intention to occupy Rose Gardens is hardly a matter of courage, I think. There is little here to tempt a thief unless he desires to make a collection of idols as Sir Robert Williamson did."

Rajan Mohan flushed darkly. "You English have no reverence — not even tolerance — For the gods of other peoples. But then" — he put restraint upon himself — "you do not understand. It is your misfortune. But I do not want to quarrel with you, Miss Flynn, because — it is best to be frank — I have a quite extraordinary proposition to make to you. It is a favor I would ask — a great favor you will say. It is not for myself," as her expression grew ever more foreboding, "it is for my sister."

Nora heard his words and looked up in her frightened way.

"My sister," resumed Rajan Mohan in his slow, liquid voice, "has not your courage, Miss Flynn. The robbery last night has excited her sadly. There are strange tales in regard to this robber who terrorizes the North Riding. The country folk are superstitious, they say that he is the ghost of some gentleman who was executed for his misdeeds two centuries or more ago — in fact an ancestor of the late Sir Robert Williamson. According to the peasants, he has reappeared from the grave — or the gibbet perhaps — every few years since his hanging and has haunted the moorland paths so that the natives do not dare to cross the moors at night. But this is the first year, I am told, that he continues the robberies for which he was hung so many long years ago."

Carrington listened with interest. He thought vaguely of the portrait of the roistering courtier in the dining-hall at Rose Gardens and of the figure in the plumed hat which had peered in through the library door.

"Silly, superstitious twaddle!" declared Miss Flynn. "I haven't a doubt that the face of this man who has been committing burglaries here is known to every official at Scotland Yard and it is only a matter of time when he will be arrested."

Rajan Mohan shrugged slightly. "It may be. You English have little belief in the occult. It is not so with us who are of the East. We have reason to believe in mysteries."

"How do those living on the moor describe this resurrected robber?" inquired Carrington, his voice losing something of its usual drawl.

Rajan Mohan turned politely. "He is said to wear always the costume of a knight of your merry King Charles II. I understand that Sir Gerald Dormont saw him last night fleeing from the house after the robbery and he swears to the same costume."

"Any particular color, this costume?" No one could accuse Carrington of looking bored as he put this question.

"A bright red — scarlet." Rajan Mohan's voice was almost a snarl.

Carrington nodded. "I thought so."

The tea-cup which Ahmed was passing to the prince fell with a crash on the flagstones. Murmuring profuse apologies, the butler stooped and with head lowered under Miss Flynn's reproving gaze, began carefully to gather up the shattered cup, bit by bit. Miss Flynn sharply bade him procure another cup and send for Ivy to sweep up the debris.

Rajan Mohan paid no heed to the little mishap, but he did bestow on Carrington a peculiar, questioning stare before resuming his conversation.

"You will wonder, Miss Flynn, what all this has to do with the favor I wish to ask you in behalf of my sister. As I said, she has not your courage, your disbelief in the occult. She is of the East, and you will understand that she must think as those of the East think."

Carrington observed Nora shiver under the glance which her brother directed at her.

"My sister," continued Rajan Mohan, "is terrified of this mysterious robber, she is delicate — Her health suffers under terror. She cannot live at the house I have leased, it is too near Dormont Court, the windows look out upon the spot where a page was shot down last night by the brazen robber whom he was pursuing. In short, my sister thinks that she can live nowhere except where she has lived ever since she was a little child — in sound of the North Sea here at Rose Gardens, Miss Flynn. It is evident you do not know," he added quickly, observing her utter amazement, "that my sister has lived in the household of Sir Robert Williamson ever since she was three years old. He was her guardian, one might say. Speak, Nora. Is it not so?"

Nora raised her head. Her eyes were shining. She met her brother's gaze now without flinching.

"Sir Robert Williamson was more than a guardian to me. He was like a kind and loving father. He would have made me really his daughter if— if he had lived a little longer."

"That is not to the point, Nora." Rajan Mohan spoke harshly. He seemed to resent her affection for Sir Robert Williamson. "Show Miss Flynn the letter you found in Sir Robert's desk after his death. It will prove to her that you have some right to regard Rose Gardens as your home and perhaps will make her more willing to receive you as her guest for a few weeks."

Nora obediently opened a small bag she carried and tendered to Miss Flynn an unsealed and partly finished letter, that was written to a prominent solicitor in Lincoln's Inn Fields. In the letter Sir Robert was making arrangements for a new will to be drawn up in favor of "my ward, Nora Mohan." He described Nora as having been entrusted to his care by her own father at the time of his death fourteen years previous when he, Sir Robert, had been traveling in India. The letter went on to state that it was his particular desire that Rose Gardens, in regard to which there was some legal tangle, should come unequivocally into Nora's possession.

Carrington read this letter aloud at Miss Flynn's request, and during the reading Rajan Mohan's face was a study in passion restrained. He seemed to hate the memory of the man who had been his sister's benefactor, and who would have made her his heiress had not death intervened. When Carrington had finished Sir Robert's letter, Rajan Mohan produced another from the solicitor in Lincoln's Inn Fields which substantiated Nora's claim of being the unofficial ward of Sir Robert Williamson. There was no doubt that the East Indian was exceedingly anxious for his sister to be received at Rose Gardens. But why? Carrington did not for a moment believe that it was out of consideration for Nora's mental or physical state. Nor did he believe that it was simply from a desire to be rid of the care of his sister. There was some deeper motive than this and Carrington felt convinced that it was connected with the death of Sir Robert.

On the other hand there was no doubt that Nora herself was anxious to come back to Rose Gardens, but whether it was from real affection for the old house which had been her home for so many years or a desire to be free from her brother's tutelage or some other reason not so innocent, Carrington could not make out.

Max suddenly spoke a word in Nora's behalf.

"I think, Aunt Ell, that Princess Nora Mohan would be a jolly little addition to the house party."

Miss Flynn yielded as she generally did to Max's wishes and when Rajan Mohan took his departure after assuring Susanna that he hoped for the pleasure of seeing her again shortly, he left his sister as the guest of Miss Flynn.

Max smiled quizzically at Nora. "Are you happy now, little Lotus Flower?"

Nora glanced up shyly into his half gentle, half mocking eyes and her dusky cheek flushed. "I am sure I will be, Mr. Flynn."

Max laughed and sauntered out from the hall. Susanna, in her frank, friendly way, bore Nora off to the terrace to watch the waves. Carrington went into the dining-room for another scrutiny of that picture which was constantly recurring to his mind.

He was surprised to find Max standing though fully before it. Max wheeled quickly.

"So you've come too for a glimpse at this Crimson Knight? The moment you asked Rajan Mohan the color of the robber's costume, I knew you were thinking of this picture. You hardly took your eyes off it during lunch. What do you think of this ghostly burglar, Tom? Does he step down out of the canvas — or what?"

"I think," answered Carrington with deliberation, "that it is worth our while to find out."

Max studied the handsome, reckless face of the Knight for a moment. "This chap is interesting, Tom. And so," he added with a laugh, "is the little Lotus Flower. What do you say to playing a string at billiards, old man?"

9

A NIGHT OF MYSTERY

That night Carrington, in view of the disappearance of the key to the library door, decided to sleep on the couch in that room so as to be ready for developments. He felt sure that the key had been stolen for some purpose and he intended to discover what that purpose was. Miss Flynn advised him to keep his revolver at hand and Max insisted upon sharing his vigil. Their intention to pass the night there was known only to Miss Flynn.

After every one else had retired, housekeeper, new servants, and guests, Carrington and Max went down quietly into the library where the latter calmly appropriated the couch and left Carrington to get what sleep he could lounging in a chair. But sleep would not come. He fell to wondering if Mrs. MacDonald, whose chamber was on the ground floor not far from the library, could have heard them enter. The more he saw of the housekeeper, the more he distrusted her, and her question in regard to Susanna's name puzzled and annoyed him.

Susanna too was puzzling him, or rather he was puzzled by the note which had been brought to her that evening when they were all out upon the terrace watching the moon rise over the sea. The note had been brought by a little country lad, and Susanna had not been the same since receiving it. She had gone into the house to read it and when she returned her face was troubled and her gaiety vanished. Could it have been a dunning letter from some creditor? Max, had she said had placed all hope of meeting her debts on Gypsy Queen, the losing horse?

The hours dragged by without incident and far away a clock solemnly struck two. Max was sleeping peacefully, the moon's rays falling caressingly on his chestnut head. No figure in plumed hat had yet peered in through the leaded glass door opening on the terrace, there was no sound of stirring in the old house, no crash of a breaking idol. An overpowering drowsiness crept over Carrington and he fell asleep to dream that the Crimson Knight was stepping out through the painted canvas. The dream was very real, the insolent, reckless eyes of the ribbon festooned rake laughed into his, the arrogant mouth mocked him with its jeering twist, he could even hear the cautious tread of his buckled shoes as the courtier stole away to nocturnal adventures.

Suddenly Carrington sat upright in the chair, wide awake, someone was stealing across the floor. He rubbed the sleep from his eyes. There at the outer door was a woman's figure! A click of the lock and she was gone, hurrying across the terrace. He sprang to the door; it was locked behind her, and she had disappeared into the night which the moon, buried in scurrying clouds, no longer lit. He had merely caught a transient glimpse of the woman, wrapped in a long mantle and with a scarf or veil floating about her head, but he knew she was Edna MacDonald. It was she then who had taken the key from under his pillow.

As he turned from the door, he made another discovery. The couch was vacant and Max was gone. He struck a match and lit a candle to make sure that his friend was not playing any trick on him. But no, he was alone in the room. He looked out into the corridor and called Max's name softly. There was no response.

Carrington then blew out the candle and settled himself in his former chair prepared to wait for Mrs. MacDonald's return. As a precaution against dozing off again, he lit a cigarette and resolutely kept his thoughts fastened on the mysteries that troubled him. He did not regard Max's disappearance as one of them. Max had probably found the couch uncomfortable for an extended nap and had gone up to bed, doubtless laughing to himself at the surprise he should cause Carrington.

The minutes dragged by, the pulsing, of the sea outside, the only sound audible now, was dangerously soothing, and Carrington, for all his efforts to awake, was growing sleepy again, when on a sudden the hush that held Rose Gardens was broken by a peculiar, drilling noise. It was not loud, it was subdued, cautious, as though the maker of it feared that someone would hear. Yet the noise went on steadily, resolutely, purposefully.

At first Carrington was at a loss to locate it, then he decided that it must come from the great hall. He hated to leave the library even for a moment in case Mrs. MacDonald return in his absence, but he must find out what that drilling was. Halfway to the hall, he was checked by a low, startled scream. Then a familiar voice said softly.

"Don't be alarmed, little Lotus Flower. It is only I, Maxwell Flynn."

Carrington hurried into the hall. The dawn which was just sending its pale light through the high windows revealed Max in his dressing-gown as Carrington had seen him last, and at the base of the double stair Nora in negligee, her dusky hair falling like a cloud about her shoulders and her eyes more than ever like those of a frightened fawn.

"By George! Tom," Max called out, "did you hear the noise too? I was just about to get into bed — forgive me for deserting you, old chap, but that couch was never meant to spend the night on — when I heard a jolly queer noise. At first it was very faint, and I thought I was imagining it, but it grew louder and I ran down to investigate. When I got here, the ghost had vanished. Then her little highness" turning with a half tender, half mocking smile to Nora, "came down, too, and mistook me for the ghost. Didn't you, little Lotus Flower?"

"I — I was all dazed," she faltered. "I think I am hardly awake even now."

"It's a sleepy little Lotus Flower, eh?" Max spoke very gently. "You had better go back to bed, little princess."

"I must find out first what that noise was," demurred Nora anxiously. "I think — I think the statue of Brahma has been moved."

She ran excitedly across the hall. The idol surely had been pulled out a little from the recess in which it stood. Nora stooped and raised some object from the flagstones.

"See! Could not this have made the drilling sound?"

"By Jove! It could." Max took the object from her hand and passed it to Carrington for inspection.

"It's a gimlet, Tom, and a strong little instrument too."

Nora uttered a cry of consternation. "There is a hole straight through one of Brahma's faces, big enough to put my finger in!"

Carrington took down a candle from a silver sconce on the wall, lit it, and examined the idol. Someone had indeed bored a hole through one of the two remaining heads of the image.

Carrington looked kindly at Nora. "Don't be too upset over it, little girl. It's only an idol after all. The old fellow himself — your god I mean — isn't actually injured."

Nora smiled tremulously. "It isn't that. I am not a worshiper of Brahma as my brother — but why should any one — " she broke off pitifully from Carrington to Max.

Max put his arm about her shoulder slightly caressing gesture as though he was assuring a frightened child. "You run off to bed, little Lotus Flower, and leave the worry to Lord Carrington and me."

Nora hesitated. There was a haunting, doe-like look in her soft, dark eyes raised to his.

Max smiled banteringly. "Can't you trust us to do the worrying, eh?"

Nora let her cheek rest a brief instant against Max's arm. "I am not going to think any more about it, Mr. Flynn. I will go directly to bed."

Max laughed and released her. "A sensible decision, isn't it, Tom?"

Nora ran lightly up the stairs. "Goodnight, Mr. Flynn," she called softly, leaning down from the balustraded gallery.

"Goodnight, Princess Nora." Max made her a mock, ceremonious bow.

"Coming up, old man?" He turned to Carrington who was studying the mutilated idol.

"No, I'm going back to the library."

Max stifled a yawn. "Suit yourself, you old night-owl. I'm off to bed. I don't believe the ghost will get in any more work tonight and I'm beastly tired."

Carrington returned immediately to the library. Everything appeared exactly as he had left it and he did not believe that Mrs. MacDonald had come back. But as time went on and still she did not come, he began to fear that he had missed her after all. The room was almost light now and he ensconced himself in a big morocco chair, the back turned toward the outer door so that she should not see him through the leaded panes and take alarm.

The question of who had drilled a hole through the head of Brahma was troubling him now. And why had it been done? It was rather strange that the sound of the drilling had been loud enough to call Max and Nora down from their chambers, and yet had been audible to no one else on the upper floors. Of course Max had not been asleep. He had he said was about to get into bed when he had heard the noise, but Nora — how did she happen to hear it so distinctly? Her chamber was somewhere at the farther end of the west wing. She must have singularly acute hearing unless she had already been up and about the house. Still, it was difficult to imagine a timid creature like Nora wandering aimlessly at night through such a ghostly old place as Rose Gardens. If she had been wandering about, she had done so with deliberate purpose. He recalled how shocked and alarmed she had been at discovering the fresh mutilation of the idol, but her agitation had not been due to religious scruples or to any feeling that sacrilege had been done to the East Indian god. What was the mystery surrounding these mutilated idols?

The sound of a key furtively turning in a lock startled him, he almost forgot exercising caution and sprang up from the chair in his relief that the wearisome vigil was over at last. When a rush of cold, salt air wafted through the library and the gentle closing of the door told him that the one he had waited for so long was in the room, he rose quickly to his feet.

"Mrs. MacDonald, I think I must ask you how you got the key to that door."

The woman turned swiftly and the veil fell away from her face.

Carrington started back with an exclamation of amazement.

It was not Edna MacDonald — it was Susanna!

10

ANOTHER MYSTERY

Susanna stared at him unhappily. "I was hoping you had gone upstairs." She was pale and looked intensely miserable, as though she had come face to face with sordid tragedy and felt herself cheapened, humiliated, crushed down by it.

Carrington was deeply moved to see her like this — she who had always hitherto, no matter what worries beset her, contrived to appear light-hearted and full of joy. He drew a chair forward for her, and she sank into it dejectedly, with a sigh of utter weariness, more of mind than of body, it seemed to him.

He stood looking down at her awkwardly, longing to offer sympathy but not knowing what to say.

"Susanna, old girl," he blurted at length, "you're in some trouble. Can I do anything to help you?"

She glanced up at him with a faint smile of appreciation. "You are awfully kind, Tom, but there is nothing you can do. I must fight this out myself."

"Susanna," he laid his hand gently on her shoulder — his voice was a little husky — he meant to play fair with Max, to give him "free way" with Susanna, but he could not be expected to remain entirely passive at sight of her distress, "Susanna, if it's — if it's Gypsy Queen that's worrying you, I should like — that is, I — oh, hang it all I you know what I mean, I've got more money than I know what to do with."

Susanna caught his hand and pressed it in both her own. Her eyes were suspiciously bright. "Dear old Tom, it is not Gypsy Queen and I cannot permit you to help me. I can only tell you that something happened tonight... something that makes me wonder if there is such a thing in the world as happiness — for me, at least."

"Oh, I say, Susanna — " It was so unlike her to talk in this way.

She rose suddenly. "Tom, I must see Rajan Mohan tomorrow — alone. But I don't want any talk about it — any gossip — if I were to write a note asking him to meet me somewhere on the cliffs tomorrow, would you see that it was delivered to him? I don't want to trust a servant — they talk too much."

Carrington again was conscious of a savage feeling against the East Indian. "If that chap is bothering you in any way — "

"No, no, Tom, it is strictly a matter of — of business." But her eyes, always so frank, avoided his.

A miserable suspicion seized him. "Susanna," he said desperately, "promise me that you will accept no loan from that brown fellow — nothing that will put you in his power."

"Why, what an absurd idea, Tom!" She gave a little forced laugh. "If I will not accept money from you, my old friend, surely I will not do so from one who is almost a stranger to me. You will take my note, Tom?"

He had a struggle with himself, but he could not resist her appeal. "I will take the note. And, Susanna, remember, you can always count on me. If you won't let me help you in dealing with this matter; I wish you would with the Gypsy Queen. I know that's worrying you, too."

"It is worrying me, but I can't quite bring myself yet to letting you help me. I've just a little pride, Tom, and then — I know how generous you have been to Max. You mustn't allow all your friends to bleed you, dear old boy."

"Susanna, I want you to promise me something else — that you won't let any one except for me to help you with Gypsy Queen."

She laid her hands on his shoulders and smiled at him almost maternally. "Dear old boy," she said again, and her voice was very tender, "you actually beg people to take advantage of your goodness. Well, I promise. I will let no one help me but you. Now I want you to promise me something, too. No matter what happens, don't fail me with your friendship. Just now I need it even more than I do money — and Heaven knows I need that badly enough. But your friendship I can't do without. You're sane, conventional, respectable, and you're wholesome for me."

He felt an almost irresistible desire to draw her into his arms — she looked so absolutely wretched.

Loyalty to Max alone restrained him. His emotion repressed made him seem a little brusque in manner as he said, "You ought to know I'm not just a fair-weather friend."

She gave a little sigh, almost of exasperation.

"Of course I know that and I know, too, that you are horribly, hopelessly literal."

Carrington stared after her thoughtfully as she hurried from the room. He did not altogether grasp her meaning, but he was a man, and being such, was not too self-depreciative to speculate on what she might mean. At any rate he wished fervently that Max had chosen to bestow his volatile affections in some other quarter.

Susanna excused herself from coming down to breakfast on the plea of "a shocking headache," but she met Carrington on the terrace later and gave him her note to Rajan Mohan. She looked rather a wreck in the pitiless sunlight, but assured Carrington that another nap would freshen her up.

By tacit consent no mention was made of the fresh mutilation of the three-headed idol save to Miss Flynn and she appeared more annoyed than alarmed.

Carrington did not perform his duty of messenger to Rajan Mohan in a very tranquil frame of mind. He could not conceive what business Susanna could have with the man, and he could not but wonder where she went last night and what had happened to upset her so. Then, too, how had she gained possession of the key to the library door? It must have been Mrs. MacDonald — or Ahmed perhaps — who had taken it from under his pillow. But why should either of them give it to Susanna? It was another of the mysteries so rife at Rose Gardens, but this one touched him more nearly because it concerned Susanna. He resolved to think of it as little as possible. She had practically asked him to trust her, and he would do so in face of everything.

As he walked on over a stretch of brown moorland starred with the gold of the furze and the broom, he came upon a little group of shepherds and rustic folk discussing the latest exploit of their favorite goblin, the Crimson Knight — namely, the robbery at Dormont Court. The cold-blooded pistoling of the page lent an additional thrill to this escapade and the simple-souled country folk were thoroughly enjoying the retelling of the tale. To satisfy something more than curiosity, Carrington approached the little group and asked if anyone of them personally had seen the brazen burglar.

One old shepherd proudly declared that he had and the others listened with awe and envy to what they must have heard countless times before — the garrulous and colorful account of how this old shepherd one night some few weeks previous had been forced to cross the moor in order to fetch a doctor for "t' missus" and how on one of the moorland paths there had suddenly sprung up before him, apparently from the heather, the figure of the phantom knight.

"Ah wor thot freetened Ah couldn' run nor shout fer halp. Ah joost staared an' staared an' 'e staared baack wi' his crool, spittiful eyes, an' then he laughed, eh, how he laughed, crool like his eyes. For tree neets aafter Ah couldn' sleep for hearing thot laugh."

"But what did this person look like and how was he dressed?" questioned Carrington with some impatience.

The shepherd shivered impressively. "He looked like t' owd devil. He wor tall an' thin an' dressed varra straange wit' feathers in his 'at an' a queer coot an' short breeches an' mony ribbons arl over him."

Carrington found this description sufficiently illuminating and continued on his way. The old shepherd had described to the letter the leering rake in the picture-gallery at Rose Gardens.

Arrived at Rajan Mohan's house which bore the wholly English name of Lancaster Manor, Carrington was ushered by an East Indian serving-man into a long, low-ceilinged drawing-room whose stiff, mid-Victorian furnishings in no way suggested the vivid luxury of that land where its new tenant had come. Through the open French windows was wafted the scent of wholly English flowers and the sight of the white-bearded Gupta Singh, stately and dignified in his native garb, solemnly promenading between the beds of roses, mignonette, pansies, and larkspur lent the only incongruous note to the essentially English setting.

Rajan Mohan appeared almost immediately, greeting his visitor with polite hospitality. Carrington in return was correctly civil but found it difficult to remain so when he observed the eagerness, barely suppressed, with which the East Indian opened Susanna's note. The contents seemed to amaze him greatly, to puzzle him not a little, but on the whole to please him.

"Would you be so kind, Lord Carrington, to carry back from me a little note to the Lady Susanna?"

Carrington did not like the ardent gleam in the East Indian's eyes nor the soft, caressing tones of his voice as he spoke Susanna's name.

Carrington's back stiffened. "I was prepared to bring back a reply," his drawling enunciation was exaggerated almost to the point of insolence.

There was a slight darkening of Rajan Mohan's face, but he seemed determined not to take offense. "I will consider that a great kindness," he remarked smoothly.

Pulling the bell-rope, he requested the East Indian servant to bring him letter-paper and writing materials for his own use and cigarettes and liqueur for his guest. Carrington, however, declined both. He had come to feel such dislike for Rajan Mohan that it was impossible for him to accept even conventional hospitality at his hands.

The East Indian looked at him a little curiously but did not press his hospitality. Seating himself at a remarkably handsome Jacobean writing-table, he penned, with much painstaking thought, a rather lengthy epistle to Susanna.

When this was finished, Carrington rose instantly. Although by no means a man of passions, he would have liked to tear into bits the note, written on strange, foreign paper, which Rajan Mohan, with a few courteous words of thanks, put into his hand. There was an air of confidence, of assured power about the East Indian which particularly irritated him. Then, too, he felt a ridiculous resentment against him for the simple fact that he wore the clothes of an Englishman and wore them also with correctness and ease as though he had never known any different garb. To Carrington, who, perhaps, was too insular in his prejudices, this seemed nothing short of usurpation. Moreover, if this handsome, arrogant East Indian could in this way readily usurp the dress and bearing of an Englishman might he not also usurp the privilege of taking an Englishwoman to be his wife? Carrington caught a glimpse of his own face in a wall-mirror and was dismayed by its expression of obvious rage. He had always prided himself on his self-control and never in the company of casual acquaintances had his features betrayed a stronger emotion than good-natured boredom. But now here was this brown man in whose veins surged the hot blood of an alien race, only superficially civilized, putting to shame in the matter of courtesy and self-restraint one who was a descendant of generations of conventional living, cool-blooded Saxons.

Carrington took hold of himself. His face no longer expressed anything but the impassivity of high-bred indifference.

"Pray don't mention it, Prince," he drawled. "It gives me pleasure to carry your note to Lady Susanna."

Rajan Mohan, with an air of amiable condescension, accompanied his visitor to the porch.

"I suppose there were no unusual occurrences at Rose Gardens last night — no visit from the Crimson Knight, as the country folk call this picturesque North Riding robber?"

Carrington lifted the ribbon of his monocle and stared deliberately through the glass at Rajan Mohan. "You take a tremendous interest in Rose Gardens, don't you?"

"But naturally, Lord Carrington, since it has been the home of my sister for so many years."

The calm demeanor of the East Indian's answering stare stirred Carrington to anger. For an instant his eyes blazed, but almost immediately a bored look filmed over them once more.

"You will be glad to hear, Prince Rajan," his voice drawling and polite, "that your sister is well and happy this morning. I dare say it is the North Sea air."

The East Indian nodded gravely. "Without doubt it is the North Sea air. For my sister it is always a tonic. Lord Carrington, may I trouble you to convey my respectful good wishes to that intrepid lady, Miss Flynn?"

Carrington found Rajan Mohan's tone as he uttered these last words particularly objectionable and he walked quickly away from Lancaster Manor in case he again lost control of himself.

Susanna was awaiting him on the terrace, and she received the East Indian's note with a feverish eagerness which served to increase Carrington's resentment against the East Indian. She went up to her room to read the reply. She was a few minutes late to lunch, but seemed to be unaware of Miss Flynn's displeasure and entered at once into a lively skirmish of words with Max. But her happiness was fitful and now and then Carrington would see the shadow of some trouble darkening her eyes.

After lunch she contrived to escape from Max and disappeared without any one knowing where she went. But Carrington knew that she had gone to meet Rajan Mohan and his heart was heavy. He felt utterly unequal to the task of trying to keep Miriam away from Max as he had promised to do — in his present mood her in consistent chatter would be maddening, so he, too, wandered off alone. Some irresistible impulse drew him to the cliffs. He did not intend to spy upon Susanna, but he distrusted Rajan Mohan as much as he disliked him and he knew that the East Indian was capable of violence if any purpose of his were thwarted.

As a rule Carrington was not in the least addicted to the exercise of rock climbing, but this afternoon he scrambled zealously over great masses of the cliffs until he reached a lofty limestone outcropping which offered an almost limitless panorama of sea, sands and cliffs. The waves were breaking all around the jagged limestone outcropping, filling the air with their booming, while a strong wind blew the white spray high above the foaming crests and Carrington, as he lay stretched full length upon the promontory, resting after his unwonted exertions, felt his face sting from the salty moisture. The sky was sharply blue, but the sea was full of shadows, of vague, weird colors, grayish green, purplish-blue, gold-flecked where the sun danced upon the waters, and again dusky violet like Susanna's eyes.

That distant figure in white coming lightly over the rocks, was it Susanna? Raising himself on his elbow, he gazed intently at the graceful figure. As it came nearer, he saw that it was Susanna. She stood now in indecision upon a bare, black nab of rock, the wind blowing her skirts bewilderingly about her. She had the little Pomeranian tucked under one arm, the pink of his bow matching exactly the parasol which she carried unopened in the other hand.

She made so alluring a vision outlined against the blue of the sky in her picture hat and her filmy frock that Carrington was about to get up and go over to her, even should he be requested to hold the snappish Pompon, when he saw a man making his way toward her with eager haste. It was Rajan Mohan elegant and imposing in his English garb. He was using his snakewood walking-stick to facilitate his progress over the rocks.

Carrington settled down again, but he did not remove his eyes from those two standing together now on that black nab of rock. Susanna's greeting had been cordial, but a little restrained, the East Indian's distinctly ardent. Carrington had a struggle with himself to remain passively on the limestone outcropping. Never had Susanna seemed more desirable, nor Rajan Mohan more objectionable.

Neither were aware of his proximity and they stood looking out to sea, talking very earnestly. They were too far away for him to watch their expressions, but he judged from Susanna's gestures that she was making some appeal. The East Indian appeared obdurate at first, then he too, seemed to be making an appeal. From the East Indian's fervor Carrington suspected that it was a declaration of love. At that moment he would have felt little regret had Rajan Mohan lost his footing and slipped into those angry waves churning around the nab. But nothing of the sort happened, nor did Susanna repulse the East Indian or even laugh at him as Carrington expected her to do. Instead, she continued to gaze out to sea, evidently thinking seriously. After a few moments she spoke to Rajan Mohan and then they walked away together, with him carrying her parasol and assisting her over the rocks.

It afforded Carrington some slight consolation to observe that Pompon shared his dislike of the East Indian and was giving vent to his feelings in sharp little yelps which his mistress was trying in vain to check. The sound of a familiar laugh, joyful and full of fun... and yet with a hint of mockery in it, drew his gaze from the retreating figures of Susanna and Rajan Mohan and turned it to the long strip of yellow sand curving like a crescent on the right of the limestone outcropping.

Max and Nora were strolling along, laughing and talking. There was no trace now of worry or fear on the beaming face of the little East Indian girl. She was like a happy child off for a rare holiday. She was hanging upon her companion's jesting words and gazing up into his face with shy but wholehearted admiration. Every now and then she would stop to pick up shells, exclaiming eagerly over their beauty and holding them to her ear to hear the sounds of the sea. At such times Max would regard her with a smile of cynical amusement.

Somehow Carrington felt a little angry with Max. If he were really in love with Susanna, why should he trifle with this little East Indian girl, as unsophisticated as a child in the nursery? Was it all in line with his expressed desire to be on terms of friendship with Rajan Mohan because he represented the fabulous wealth of the East or was it merely from a wish to find some amusement on an afternoon when Susanna was not available? In any case it was not fair to Nora. Max's interest in things East Indian was somewhat puzzling. Those ugly Indian idols seemed to exercise a sort of fascination over him and he was unable to keep away from them. Nora represented that land from which they came but could this fact explain his interest in her? Simple childlike girls were not the type of women which generally appealed to him.

Carrington remained on the limestone outcropping, staring out over the sea and thinking rather bitter thoughts until long after Max and Nora had gone from sight and the wind had grown uncomfortably keen. Then he rose and made his way back to Rose Gardens. The old house, clinging there to the promontory, seemed more than ever grim and sinister in the mood that held him then. As he entered the great hall, the sound of music led him to the smaller drawing-room.

Nora, her hair blown from the walk on the sands, her face still that of a happy child on a holiday, was seated at the piano. Max was leaning gracefully against the instrument, watching her with that same amused, cynical smile. Nora had been playing a little timidly, but under Max's encouraging words, she gained confidence and the music swelled beneath her fingers. Strange chords crashed and broke, the mystery and the haunting sadness of the East alike brooded in the weird notes. The wild, quivering melody evoked all manner of extravagant, impossible dreams.

Carrington was conscious of a sense of unutterable depression, but Max still wore the smile of the cynic. One last shivering chord and Nora's fingers dropped from the keys. She looked up at Max, half in doubt, half in hope.

Again he put his arm lightly about her shoulders and patted her on the arm. "Bravo, little Lotus Flower!"

She thrilled under his touch; her eyes shone, her dusky cheeks were aflame.

Carrington turned away abruptly. That evening he spoke to Max.

"I hope you'll play fair with the little East Indian girl. She's only a child as far as worldliness goes. She might take you seriously."

Max's easy laughter bubbled up. "My word! Tom, what a long face. Now don't worry over the little Lotus Flower. Such exotic blossoms are not for my garden, but you know I am bound to be decent to her since she is Aunt Ell's guest."

11

THE COSTUME BALL

Carrington looked down without enthusiasm upon the ancient suit of armor in which he was imprisoned. "Pearson, do you think it possible for me to dance in this steel box?"

Pearson paused in his task of encasing Carrington in the shining coat of mail and surveyed him rather dubiously, "It might be possible, my lord."

"I expect I am making a jolly ass of myself tonight, Pearson."

The valet remained discreetly silent. Carrington pushed up the steel visor with some disgust. This costume ball, Max's idea to enliven the gloom of life at Rose Gardens, found as little favor with him as it did with Miss Flynn. A ball was well enough, but let it be a properly conducted affair in conventional, sensible evening dress, not a sort of Bohemian function where the guests appeared in the fantastic costumes of other ages and other countries — costumes which they could not hope to wear with proper effect and which consequently made them seem ridiculous.

Carrington had not particularly enjoyed his visit at Rose Gardens, especially during the last ten days. Rajan Mohan had been in constant attendance upon Susanna, Max as a result had been moody and irritable, and during one occasion there had been almost a scene between the two men, the East Indian's anger having been aroused by some mocking words of Max's in regard to the idols, which were holy in the eyes of Rajan Mohan. Susanna and Nora, too, had intervened, a semblance of peace had been brought about, and

Rajan Mohan was among the guests invited to the ball. As a solace for the loss of Susanna's society, Max continued to amuse himself with Nora, leaving Miriam to depend entirely on Carrington for her entertainment.

As a prelude to the ball, the one intact head remaining to the statue of Brahma had been broken the night before by a blow from some heavy implement and the crash had again roused the household. Ivy Blake chose to consider this as an omen of impending evil. As a matter of fact, Carrington was inclined to agree with her. The atmosphere of Rose Gardens on the eve of the ball was charged with unpleasantness and mutual distrust; someone of the household must be responsible for the breaking of the idols. But who was it and how much longer would this person be content simply to shatter images for the furtherance of some unknown design?

Carrington's musings were interrupted by the sudden opening of the door. At sight of the scarlet-clad figure which entered, he remained a moment astounded. It was as though the Crimson Knight had stepped out of the frame which held his painted likeness. There was the roistering blade to the side, with his plumed hat, his resplendent, ribbon festooned suit, his flowing wig, his reckless eyes and his mocking smile. Then the knight burst into a cheery, audacious, boyish laugh, and the spell was broken.

"Max! Why the heck are you dressed up in this fashion?"

Max's laughter bubbled forth again. His eyes now were teasing, the curve of his lips wholly humorous.

"Gave you rather of a start, eh, Tom? The guests should be arriving soon. Let us come down and see how they will welcome the famous Crimson Knight."

Forthwith they went downstairs where Max's costume provoked the amazement he desired and brought him a rebuke from Miss Flynn, who disapproved, as Carrington did, of his impersonating the North Riding robber. Max's appearance in this garb had an astonishing effect upon Ahmed. On the way to the ballroom, he passed the East Indian in the hall. The butler started violently and let fall with a crash the tray of glasses he was carrying. His features were convulsed with conflicting emotions — hate, fear, and incredulity.

"Look closer, Ahmed," Max urged pleasantly. "You'll see I'm not the chap you took me for."

For some reason it gave Max infinite satisfaction as well as amusement to observe the effect of his costume on others. But no one betrayed more agitation than did Rajan Mohan who was among the first of the arriving guests. His emotions were no less acute than Ahmed's, but in place of fear he showed rage. And when, at a second glance, he recognized Max, he was able to call up no saving sense of humor, but exhibited anger and resentment.

The East Indian's own appearance was somewhat startling, due not so much to the full native garb which he wore with a princely dignity, but rather to the enormous ruby — a ball of crimson fire set in dull gold — which ornamented the breast of his silken robe.

"The Surya's Eye ruby!" Susanna murmured in Carrington's ear. "Think what a fortune that the jewel represents — and see how boldly he flaunts it!" There was an undertone of bitterness in her voice.

Carrington surveyed her gravely. "I hope you will not permit that East Indian to monopolize you tonight."

Susanna laughed but not quite naturally. "You absurd fellow 1 I believe you're jealous. I have promised Prince Rajan several dances, but I have saved two for you. Well!" as he remained silent, "have you nothing to say. Can't you thank me, at least?"

He smiled painfully. "No end kind of you, I'm sure, to save me Prince Rajan's leavings."

"Tom, I never saw you ill-natured before. I suppose I ought to feel complimented, for I believe you are jealous." She gave a little nervous laugh. "By the way, dear boy, you haven't said how you like me tonight."

He viewed her critically. She was wonderful as Cleopatra, in a diaphanous robe of violet-blue, glittering with gold spangles. A diamond asp sparkled about her throat and the glow of the hundred wax candles in the crystal luster above her brought out the rich, auburn glints in her hair.

Carrington's eyes lit up. "You look — ah — ripping!"

The approach of Rajan Mohan, who came to claim Susanna for the dance which was just commencing, cut short her jesting words of gratification. Carrington was obliged to call to the fore the full strength of his conventional training in order to return the East Indian's polite salutation. Not only the arrogant, dominating personality of the East Indian, but that blazing jewel, like a splotch of blood, upon his breast, affected him most unpleasantly. Moreover, the East Indian's air of proprietorship toward Susanna was insufferable.

He turned away abruptly as Rajan Mohan led Susanna into the center of the great ballroom where already more than fifty couples in fancy dress were dancing. He had no heart to seek a partner. Everything, for him, was colored by the fierce, red light of the Surya's Eye ruby, and he felt the presentiment that something was to happen which would make this brilliant ball seem like a mockery.

Unnoticed in the excited whirl of the dance, he passed through one of the long French windows and stepped out upon the terrace to be alone with his thoughts. But even here on the terrace, swept by the ever keen winds from the sea below, he could not find the solitude he sought. The moon, riding high among a few white clouds, disclosed the figures of a man and woman standing together, on the edge of the promontory, cut clear as silhouettes against the silver sheen of sky and water. The fantastic costume of the man startled him for a moment — it was Max in his courtier's dress. The woman without doubt was Edna MacDonald. She was of course not in fancy dress and was easily recognizable from her general appearance and the arrangement of her hair in heavy braids twisted about her head. It was strange that Max should desert the ball for the purpose of coming out on the cliffs to talk with the housekeeper. Did he mean to solace himself for Rajan Mohan's monopoly of Susanna by a little affair with Edna MacDonald? To some she might seem an attractive woman, in spite of her air of mystery. Carrington shrugged and reentered the house. In any case, it was not his concern.

Miriam, in the guise of Empress Poppaea, and looking not unlike that very earthy divinity with her fluff of golden hair, its hard shade softened by the moon's rays, and her big blue eyes with their expression of artless appeal which struck the observant as being not entirely sincere, stepped suddenly through the French window.

"I saw you come out here, Tom. I want to talk to you. I happen to be partner-less, too, for this dance." She tried to laugh, but the attempt was not altogether successful.

Carrington glanced hastily toward the edge of the promontory. He was relieved to find that Max and Mrs. MacDonald were no longer there. Perhaps Miriam had not seen Max, and he hoped not.

"I want to speak to you about Susanna," Miriam was saying. "Miss Flynn is extremely displeased with her, and one can hardly wonder at it. You spent the afternoon taking a nap, I believe, so of course you did not see the visitor she had. He was a distinctly unpleasant-looking person, a Hebrew and quite obviously a money-lender — one gets to know that type. His manner was insufferable, bullying even. Susanna went out on the cliffs with him and was gone over an hour. When she came back, her expression was quite desperate. I never saw her like that before."

"Why have you told me all this, Miriam?" Carrington's voice held a curious hard note.

Miriam looked at him innocently. "Why, you're such a friend of Susanna — it's evident she's in a tight place — And I thought you might advise her for her own good. It is equally evident that Rajan Mohan is infatuated with her —
"

"But she will not encourage him if my influence is of any avail," Carrington broke in sharply. He understood Miriam's purpose and knew that she would go to any lengths to remove Susanna from her path. "I am going back to the ballroom. Are you coming?" .

Miriam smiled reproachfully. "Why are you in such a hurry, Tom? You'll not find Susanna there, you know. Just before I stepped out here, Ahmed came to her with a note. She stopped in the middle of her dance with Prince Rajan — made some hurried excuse and left the room. If any other woman than Susanna had abandoned her partner so abruptly, one would have called it a gaucherie, but Susanna has a way of making everything she does seem right. No doubt it was necessary for her to leave the ballroom as she did. I suspect the note was from the money-lender."

Carrington stepped through the French window as quickly as his casing of armor would permit. Miriam's words were rousing him to an unusual state of exasperation. A careful scrutiny of the crowded ballroom failed to reveal Susanna in her gold-spangled dress. She had not returned then. Rajan Mohan, too, had disappeared — he probably had gone in search of her. Carrington was surprised to observe Max in his ribbon festooned scarlet suit among the dancers. Max must have reentered the house while he, Carrington, was talking with Miriam. Max was easily the most graceful male dancer on the floor, and he was in high good spirits as he whirled past Carrington with Nora, in East Indian costume, on his arm. He was chatting merrily and looking down with teasing eyes into Nora's flushed, innocently adoring face. Carrington, watching him, wondered if Max were not, after all, a bit of a Lothario at heart. Perhaps this was Nora's first ball. At any rate, she yielded herself to the excitement of it with the soulful enjoyment of a child, her young figure swaying to the music with all the charm of unconscious grace. She seemed that night to have shaken off the influence of her brother.

By the way, why did not Rajan Mohan return? He pondered for a moment. It annoyed Carrington that he should be gone so long in search of Susanna. If that note which had called her away, was from some dunning moneylender, as Miriam had suggested, Susanna in the stress of the moment might turn to the East Indian, might listen to his suit. The dancers came and went between the ballroom and the terrace, but neither Rajan Mohan nor Susanna were among them. Miriam did not come in for over an hour after Carrington himself had entered and she looked chilled and miserable from her long stay in the cool night air. Carrington danced with her twice because Max did not seem inclined to do so. Her hand was cold and trembling and her face intensely white save for a bright pink spot on each cheek. Carrington felt very sorry for her and a little indignant with Max. He need not utterly ignore her!

Miss Flynn, naturally, was both amazed and incensed over the continued absence of Rajan Mohan and Susanna. She considered it an affront to her hospitality and to her other guests. Carrington, however, thought it unfair that she should lay the entire blame on Susanna. As time wore on, others began to comment audibly on their unexplained absence. There was a general atmosphere of unpleasantness, and guests began to take their departure. Max had lost his gaiety and Nora her look of a happy child reveling in the excitement of her first ball. As a matter of fact, Nora began to appear, as she invariably did when in her brother's presence, as though she were under the obsession of some fear.

It was an immense relief to Carrington when Max, after one of his numerous excursions from the ballroom brought Susanna back with him. To Carrington's surprise Rajan Mohan did not accompany her. Susanna's appearance was such as to create more comment. Her hair was wind-blown and damp with the moisture from the sea, her eyes shadowed, her cheeks flushed. She apologized to Miss Flynn for her absence, alleging as an excuse an unexpected business engagement which had to be attended to that night. Miss Flynn received her apology with a frigid air of disapproval and disbelief.

"Did you see anything of Prince Rajan Mohan during the course of your 'business engagement'?"

Susanna's coloring waned. "I have beef! Down on the cliffs," she said faintly. "Prince Rajan Mohan was not there."

At this juncture Ahmed entered the ballroom and came swiftly toward Miss Flynn. There was terror in his face.

"Mem Sahib," — unlike his wont he spoke quickly and jerkily — "is it by your order the lights in the library are gone out and the door locked?"

"Certainly not." Miss Flynn's voice, too, was slightly agitated. She crossed the ballroom in haste, bidding Ahmed accompany her.

Carrington followed them, drawn on by that presentiment of evil which had oppressed him throughout the evening. Something made him glance back at Susanna in her spangled dress. Her color had entirely forsaken her now, and she put out her hand to steady herself against a chair.

Miss Flynn stopped short before the closed door of the library. There was no light under it, no sound from within. Miss Flynn grasped the handle, it yielded.

She turned suspiciously to Ahmed. "What did you mean by telling me this door was locked?"

"But — but, Mem Sahib, it was locked!" Ahmed's teeth were chattering.

Miss Flynn grunted incredulously and pulled open the door. The rush of cold salt air which greeted them signified that the door onto the terrace was open, which it had not been at the commencement of the ball. The moon had sunk behind clouds, and the darkness in the library was absolute.

Carrington interposed as Miss Flynn was about to cross the threshold. "I think you had better let Ahmed bring a light."

But the East Indian had already gone for one. It had seemed an eternity before he glided back, bearing a triple-branched candlestick. Carrington took it from his shaking hand and stepped into the room.

The light of the three candles was almost lost in the huge apartment, but their wavering glow revealed enough to cause Carrington to motion Miss Flynn back. She was not to be deterred, however, and precipitated herself toward the stone-pillared fireplace where a long, shadowy object lay outstretched on the floor. Carrington held the candles above it and their flames flickered on the brown, rigid features of Rajan Mohan and glinted back from the stained dagger at his side. This had been taken from the wall above him as an empty space in the collection of daggers showed. Even in that first paralyzing moment of horror, Carrington noted that the crimson splotch on the East Indian's breast was no longer from the red fire of the Surya's Eye ruby. The jewel he had flaunted was gone.

Ahmed, who had pressed after them into the library, gave utterance to an inarticulate cry. Miss Flynn, her face white and grimly set, hurried to the door to intercept the excited guests brought from the ballroom by Ahmed's cry.

Carrington stooped suddenly and with a quick, furtive movement, picked up from the floor near the body of Rajan Mohan a small, glittering disc.

It was a gold spangle.

12

GOLD SPANGLES

Miss Flynn with admirable presence of mind, calmed her guests by telling them simply that Rajan Mohan had met with an accident. She then cleared the house of all who were not staying there, dispatched a servant for the nearest doctor and sent a telegram to Scotland Yard. Having done all that could be done, the strain of inaction proved too much for her. She collapsed and had to be put to bed.

Carrington, meanwhile, ignorant of the proper course of action in cases of violent death, closed the terrace door of the library and locked it with the new key which Miss Flynn had had made. Who had possession of the original key was a problem. He had last seen it in Susanna's hand some ten nights previously. He next surreptitiously picked up from the floor two other glistening spangles, laid a curtain of ancient tapestry over Rajan Mohan's body and withdrew softly from the library, closing the door after him. He would have locked this door, too, could he only have found the key. He then went upstairs and had Pearson get him out of his imprisoning suit of armor.

How especially flat and silly the costume ball seemed in the light of what had occurred! The remembrance of Susanna in her glittering frock brought him bitter thoughts. He sent Pearson from the room on some pretext and, drawing out the spangles he had picked up in the library, examined them minutely. They had certainly come from Susanna's dress. He refused to harbor for an instant the ugly suspicion which those three little gold discs provoked, but he hid them away in the inner pocket of his Gladstone traveling-bag, for he feared that, were others to see them, they might not be so conservative in their judgment.

It was almost dawn now, and he glanced out of the window to see if there was any sign of the doctor coming. The sight of a figure in a plumed hat stealing along the cliffs filled him with a sense of annoyance. Why should Max keep on that absurd costume and go prowling about in it?

The crunch of carriage wheels on the pebbly driveway drew Carrington from the window and sent him in haste to the great hall to receive the doctor. The physician had brought him the coroner of the shire and a detective from Scotland Yard who, he explained, had been working in the North Riding for some days on the trail of the Crimson Knight.

While the doctor and coroner were busied in the library, the detective — Inspector Rathbone he was called — rounded up the servants and plied them with questions. Ahmed appeared to be of particular interest to him. He even insisted that the shrinking butler accompany him into the library. Inspector Rathbone, with keen, aggressive eyes and a tenacious set to his jaw, seemed like a man who, once he had resolved to follow up a certain clue, would not permit himself to be affected by any human power. Carrington was thankful that it was he and not Rathbone who had picked up the gold spangles.

At this moment Max ran down the stairway on the right, with springy, boyish step, head up, mouth smiling. To see him in this way, apparently without a care in the world, one would never imagine, in a room not far distant, lay the victim of violent death.

Carrington stared at him in amazement. Max was now in conventional morning garb.

"How on earth, Max, did you get into the house so quickly and into those clothes?"

It was Max's turn to look amazed now. "What the heck are you talking about, Tom? I haven't been out of the house since you discovered Rajan Mohan in the library."

"But I saw you on the cliffs in your Knightly costume not more than fifteen minutes ago."

Max smiled sympathetically. "Old top, you've taken too much of something. You never could stand wine, you know. I haven't been out of the house, I tell you. I sat with Aunt Ell until she got calmed down. Since then I've been in my room dressing."

Carrington considered. "Then it must have been the real Knight I saw."

"Sure it wasn't too much wine, Tom? I don't put much faith myself in that mythical robber."

The library door opened suddenly and the coroner and detective came out. Ahmed, quite limp with fear, followed them.

Max addressed Carrington in a quick undertone. "Suppose you don't mention the fact, if you can help it, that I dressed up as the Knight last night. I have asked the others to forget it."

Carrington looked at Max curiously. It was a singular request, and yet — in view of the notoriety of the Courtier in Knightly garb — perhaps it was advisable.

The coroner, it seemed, had a few questions which he wished to ask the members of the household. He held this preliminary inquiry in the hall. Miss Flynn had recovered her usual composure and came down, with Aeronwen shuddering after her. Miriam was the next to appear. Carrington was struck at once by the change in her bearing since last night. Then she had been a rather pitiful little object, unable to conceal the wound which Max's indifference caused her. Now she carried her small figure with a queenly air, her eyes no longer held appeal, they were almost commanding, and her over-red lips had lost something of their baby-like curves and were hard and tight-set. Even in the ghastly light of candle-glow and struggling dawn, she was neither tired nor colorless, her complexion still delicately pink and white, suspiciously perfect.

Max sauntered forward and drew up a chair for her. "You're looking uncommonly fit, Mimi," he remarked with what toward her, was unwonted affability on his part.

She seated herself with elaborate precision. "I am glad you think so, Max" a faint, confident smile on her lips.

She directed her attention then to the coroner who was putting a few questions to Miss Flynn. Max remained, leaning with indolent grace, against the back of Miriam's chair and did not abandon this attitude when Susanna and Nora came down the stairs together.

The young East Indian girl appeared now like a very unhappy and terrified child and sat close to Susanna, as though hoping to gain some assurance from the strong personality of the older woman. Susanna was gentle and tender with the girl, evidently trying to sink her own troubles in the effort to console and reassure Nora. Susanna, unlike Miriam, did not look "uncommonly fit" in the wan light of dawn. She was frankly tired and soul-weary and had scorned artificial means to conceal the fact.

Mrs. MacDonald, who was keeping herself persistently in the background, was no more colorless than customarily, but her eyes had gained a hunted expression which did not tend to raise Carrington's estimate of her. Neither did he like the glances which every now and then she flashed at Susanna. It was almost as though she hated Susanna and at the same time feared her. But why should she have these feelings toward one who was practically a stranger to her? To be sure, her eagerness to learn Susanna's name argued some previous knowledge of her, but when he had mentioned this to Susanna, she had said, as Mrs. MacDonald had, that she must have mistaken her for someone else. But who, if not Mrs. MacDonald had given Susanna the key to the terrace door and where had she gone that night? Carrington was angry with himself because these doubts of Susanna kept recurring, and more persistently than ever since his discovery of those three gold spangles near Rajan Mohan's body.

The coroner, having ascertained that Carrington was the one responsible for closing both doors of the library, inquired severely if in doing this, he had been aware that he might be destroying some valuable clue. Carrington, mindful of those spangles, flushed uncomfortably, glanced hastily at Susanna and answered that his only thought in closing the doors had been to keep the servants out of the library and he had not done this until everyone else had gone upstairs. He observed that Rathbone the detective followed his glance at Susanna and a sense of disquiet came over him.

The coroner diverted his attention by another question. "Where did you find the key which you put in the lock of the hall door?"

Carrington adjusted his monocle in amazement. "I beg your pardon? I put no key in the lock — saw none there. In fact before discovering the — ah — unpleasant occurrence in the library, we supposed the door was locked and the key missing. The butler gave us to understand this."

The coroner eyed him reflectively. "So I have heard. But the key is in the lock now. Are you certain you did not put it there?"

"Absolutely certain."

There was a little commotion among the servants huddled together at the back of the hall. Ivy Blake started forward as though she wished to say something, then lost her courage and retreated.

The coroner, observing this, addressed her peremptorily. "You know something about this key, my girl?"

Ivy looked ready to cry with terror and embarrassment. "Ah doan want to maake trooble for onybody."

"You will not make trouble for anybody by telling the truth," said the coroner uncompromisingly. "Now then, do you know who put the key in the lock?"

"Ay, Ah knaw."

"Who was it?"

Ivy hesitated. Then she flung up her head defiantly. "Ah doan see th' use oh' so mooch talk about an owd key. It wor Lady Susanna Helton put it in t' lock."

All eyes turned on Susanna. She flushed slightly, but met the coroners' gaze without flinching. In fact, it seemed to Carrington who happened to glance also at Edna MacDonald, that she betrayed far more consternation than did Susanna.

"Is this girl's statement true — er — Lady Susanna?" demanded the coroner.

"It is true." Susanna's voice was even and composed. "I saw the key lying in the hall near the door and I picked it up and put it in the lock."

"When did your Ladyship do this?"

"Why, shortly after the — murder was discovered."

"Before or after Lord Carrington closed the library door?"

"After. I remember that the door was closed."

"Then," said the coroner with deliberation, "you must have come downstairs again later. Lord Carrington says that everyone had gone upstairs before he closed the door."

Susanna bit her lip. "I may have been mistaken about the door being closed. At such a time as this one's mind is not very keen in regard to trifles."

"Then you did not come downstairs later?"

"No." Susanna spoke rather sharply.

"I should like to ask," suddenly interposed Rathbone, "if anyone else noticed the key lying on the floor."

There was a general dissent. Mrs. MacDonald watched Susanna nervously. The latter, however, had turned her attention to Nora and seemed to be unaware of the portent of the detective's question.

Rathbone suddenly addressed Ivy. "When did you see her Ladyship put the key in the lock?"

Something in his manner or the bullying note in his voice antagonized the girl. She threw back her head with a defiant gesture. "Why does tha ask me? She told tha man it wuss — afore she went oopstaares."

"Was the library door closed or open?" persisted Rathbone.

"Ah doan knaw," stolidly. And that was all Ivy could be brought to say.

The coroner, after a few more questions by means of which he elicited from Mrs. MacDonald the information that the body of Rajan Mohan had been found in practically the same position as that of Sir Robert Williamson one short year before, took his departure, setting the public inquest for the following Monday, thereby leaving five days for further investigation. This statement by Mrs. MacDonald gave a new aspect to the death of Rajan Mohan, which, at first, had seemed to have as motive simply robbery, in that the Surya's Eye ruby was missing. But now it seemed that the previous murder must have some bearing on the recent one.

This was Carrington's reasoning, but it struck him that Rathbone was inclined to view the two murders as separate units, and he did not at all like the way in which the detective's gaze lingered on Susanna. He appeared to attach little importance to the incident of the broken idols, which Miss Flynn related to him in detail, but related back again to the matter of the key.

Susanna grew a little impatient of his continued questioning. "Really, Mr. Rathbone, you would almost harry one into admitting things which one did not do."

Rathbone favored her with a sour smile and changed the trend of his inquiries. This time he addressed Miss Flynn.

"Do you happen to remember which one of the ladies at the ball last night wore a costume covered with gold spangles?"

Carrington felt himself grow cold. He dared not look at Susanna, but he caught the suggestion of an unpleasant smile on Miriam's face and heard a smothered ejaculation from Max, who was still leaning over Miriam's chair.

Miss Flynn sat up stiffly at Rathbone's question. "Is this an official investigation of an unexplained crime or merely an interview for the society column of a newspaper?"

"I have a serious object in asking this question, Miss Flynn," Rathbone answered in his drawling, yet hectoring voice. "I must insist on knowing which lady wore a gold-spangled gown."

Miss Flynn bridled. "I do not recognize your right to insist, and I have nothing to say in regard to my guests' costumes."

Susanna rose from her chair. "I wore a gold spangled gown, Mr. Rathbone." Her tone and manner were calm and collected as though she were merely stating a fact of little import to any one.

The detective wheeled upon her and, plunging hist hand into his pocket, drew out and flashed before her eyes a bit of gauzy material, sewn with gold spangles.

"Then perhaps you will explain how this came to be clenched in the right hand of Prince Rajan Mohan."

Susanna quivered. Edna MacDonald drew a convulsive breath.

But almost instantly Susanna recovered her poise. Her lips even smiled, though her eyes remained shadowed.

"I am afraid that is one of the little mysteries which Scotland Yard must ferret out for itself."

13

A MATTER OF OPINION

That afternoon Gupta Singh came to claim the body of his compatriot. The shock of the tragedy had aged the old East Indian, but the emotion he displayed when he looked on the dead features of Rajan Mohan had little of the personal note, it was rather regret for what India had lost.

"He was the hope of the house of Mohan," Gupta Singh said in a stern, measured voice. "He should have restored the former glory of his race, that was his destiny — Not to perish here in this insidious Western civilization which, like a poison in the veins of the men of the East has made them weaklings and slaves. But it is for Brahma to judge — for Brahma to punish."

Nora shuddered at the words of the old East Indian. She looked in a curious, pathetic way at Max, but he avoided her glance and, with his air of careless gallantry, replaced the scarf that was slipping from Miriam's shoulders.

Gupta Singh gazed searchingly into Nora's downcast face and his expression grew sterner and more forbidding.

Nora Mohan, you are a daughter of India, you know your duty, you know that sacrilege was done when the Surya's Eye ruby was stolen from your brother. Will you join with me in the search for that sacred stone and aid by every means in your power the mission which brought me over the seas? — the mission which your brother was under oath to fulfill? Will you do this, Nora Mohan, or will you earn the punishment which Brahma metes out to those who are faithless to his teachings?"

Nora quailed under Gupta Singh's scrutiny, but, after a moment, she flung up her head and confronted him with the desperate courage of an animal brought to bay.

"The teachings of Brahma are nothing to me! I have been taught to worship the god of the English, and England, not India, is my country now. I have a horror of that cruel three-headed god whose priest you are and I would forget if I could, that I am of East Indian blood and that my ancestors worshiped such a savage being. I will not help you, no, I will not!"

Gupta Singh turned from her with a majestic movement of contempt. "Your faithlessness to the god of your forefathers cannot go unpunished."

Nora fled out on the terrace to escape the oppressive personality of Gupta Singh and remained there during the removal of her brother's body to Lancaster Manor. She exhibited no sorrow at his death — only a kind of dazed horror.

Susanna went out on the terrace to talk with her and Carrington followed. He could not rid his mind of the accusation in Rathbone's face when the detective had flashed before Susanna's eyes that bit of spangled gauze found clenched in Rajan Mohan's hand. Without a doubt she could explain, quite satisfactorily, how it came to be there, but the fact remained that she was unwilling to do so, and naturally this aroused suspicion. It was hardly to be wondered at that Miss Flynn already treated Susanna almost as though she were a self-confessed criminal, and yet he found himself bitterly resenting her attitude. She might, at least, waive her judgment until after the inquest.

"Susanna," he said abruptly, "I wish you had explained to that detective chap how a piece of your dress came to be in Rajan Mohan's hand."

Nora started and glanced apprehensively at Susanna. Susanna herself smiled a little wearily.

"What was there to explain, dear boy? It is obvious that I must have been in the library with Rajan Mohan."

Her indifference to the suspicion with which the general run of people would regard this interview was staggering to Carrington.

"But, Susanna, don't you see, it looks as though there had been — ah — unpleasantness — between you?"

"There was unpleasantness, Tom."

Carrington felt helpless before her calm admission of this damaging fact. "But you must not let this be known! Don't you know, can't you see? — "

"I see quite clearly, Tom. But what is the use of denying that my interview with Prince Rajan was exceedingly unpleasant? Mr. Rathbone is already assured of that."

"Then you must explain further. You must absolve yourself from doubt."

Susanna shook her head. "I can explain nothing, to no one, Tom. But you — you trust me, don't you?"

He gripped the hands she held out to him. "You know I do!"

"Dear old Tom!" She laughed a little unsteadily.

"I say, let me come in on this, too," exclaimed a jaunty, buoyant voice, and Max, with his confident air, his mocking smile, strolled toward them. "Don't overwhelm Tom with your gratitude, Susanna, as though you hadn't another friend in the world. Don't I count a little, eh?"

Susanna laughed with something of her usual gaiety. "Silly fellow! Of course you do. I will be lonely without your championship."

Max laughed back at her with ardent, confident eyes. "You know it's more than championship, Susanna."

Nora suddenly pressed forward. Her face was full of trouble.

"Lady Susanna, do you think that one ought to keep to a promise — a very solemn promise — which they did not want to make and which will injure someone they are fond of, but who is not — not quite an honorable person?"

Susanna looked at the girl very kindly, but before she could answer Max spoke for her.

"Do you know what I should do, little Lotus-Flower," his voice held a caressing note, "I should forget that promise which I did not want to make and I should do exactly as my heart dictated."

Nora kept her gaze lowered. "Sometimes," she said sorrowfully, "one's heart does not dictate what is right."

"But you have said, little Lotus-Flower, that your promise was not right — that it will injure someone."

Nora regarded him in wistful silence. There was hopelessness in her young face.

Susanna impulsively put her arm about the girl "Max! You must let Nora decide this problem — whatever it may be — for herself. It is not for you to find a solution with plausible words that are worse than platitudes."

Max looked at her with a face of whimsical reproach. "Oh, I say, Susanna, that's hardly kind of you when I am only trying to make Nora feel easier in her mind." He smiled at the young East Indian girl with a mingling of tenderness and banter.

Susanna gently pinched Nora's cheek. "My dear, you tell Mr. Flynn that you don't need his advice, that you are quite capable of deciding this matter for yourself."

But Nora broke suddenly from Susanna's embrace. "No, I'll not tell him that! I think I'll— I'll take his advice."

Max gave a soft laugh of triumph. "You're beaten, Susanna! Nora esteems my judgment even if you don't. What do you say, little Lotus-Flower, to a walk along the sands? It will brighten you up wonderfully?"

Nora's dark eyes shone. "I should like to go down on the sands, Mr. Flynn, near the sea."

"Come along then!" He caught her hand and pulled her down the steps of the terrace. "As a punishment for your unkind words, Susanna," he called back happily, "I will not ask you to come with us, nor you either, Tom, such a long face as you're wearing would make you a dismal third."

Susanna looked after Max with an indulgent smile. "He's a dear fellow, Tom! But I wonder," — her expression grew serious — "if one ought not to tell that little East Indian girl — she's such a child — that Max doesn't mean all he says. And I don't think I should take his advice on a momentous question, should you, Tom?"

"No." Carrington spoke with emphasis. "And in this matter I am not sure that his advice is wholly disinterested."

A little distressed pucker gathered on Susanna's forehead. "Tom, I have noticed lately that you and Max are not quite as good friends as you used to be. I should feel dreadfully if I thought I was in any way the cause of this. Your friendship is as good for Max as it is for me, even his aunt admits that he needs a steadying influence. Don't deprive him of it, Tom. I know you're both rather fond of me, and I think the world of both of you, I don't see why we shouldn't all three be good pals together as we always have been, do you?"

Carrington lit a cigarette reflectively. "I don't see exactly," he said slowly. "But I don't think we can be."

"Why not?" she entreated. "You seem to distrust Max. It's quite noticeable. Doesn't it occur to you that you may be doing him an injustice? I am sure you are generous and fair-minded enough to trust your friends even if some of their actions do appear a little peculiar. You have said that you trust me, now why not Max?"

In her earnestness she leaned toward him so that her hair almost brushed his cheek. He flung his cigarette away.

"Can't you understand" — his voice was hoarse, even a bit savage — "that it's different with you?"

Susanna drew back abruptly, watching him curiously for a moment. Then she laughed, and her laugh had a happy ring in it.

"I don't believe you are absolutely emotionless, after all, Tom!"

Then, even as he stared at her, again not altogether certain of her meaning, a shadow fell across her face. The laughter died on her lips, the light went out from her eyes.

The crunch of steps on the graveled path made Carrington turn. A man, dressed in flashy but seedy, clothes was advancing with a swaggering assurance. He was obviously an oaf and of a most unpleasant type.

"This man has a message for me," Susanna said in an utterly weary tone. "You'll have to excuse me, Tom."

Carrington went slowly into the house. There was a deadness at his heart.

14

THE RUIN ON THE CLIFFS

An hour or so later Carrington wandered out toward the cliffs. Aimlessly following a grassy footpath which skirted the edge of the rocks, he roamed on until the Rose Gardens, as he glanced back toward them, were only thin black lines cutting the ruddy gold of the sunset sky. The sudden restless energy which had impelled him to lay aside his leisurely habits and set forth on this long, rough walk by the cliffs deserted him now that he found how far his wanderlust had carried him. He became conscious of fatigue and lowered himself wearily into a little ravine between two high escarpments, tempted into this gully by the sight of a chair-shaped boulder wedged there which would offer a support for his tired back.

Once established upon this rock, he looked about him with a sigh of content. The cliffs here were lower, smoother and more regular in formation than those in the vicinity of Rose Gardens. In the golden light of the late afternoon the blueness of the sea seemed almost unnatural and the waves, lacking the irritant of high winds and jagged spurs, rolled in with rhythmic calm. On the pebbly beach below a flat-bottomed red rowboat — or coble in Yorkshire parlance — grated gently, as the water lapped its keel. Above a wide expanse of grass and bracken stretched away from the cliffs and a hundred paces or so distant rose the column of a small stone tower, its single window facing out to sea.

Suddenly Carrington's eye was caught by the figure of a woman coming swiftly through the grass and bracken toward the tower. He recognized her at once by her tall, graceful form and the dark cloud of her hair, for she wore no hat. It was Susanna. When she came nearer, he drew out his handkerchief and flapped it to attract her attention.

But she was in too great haste to observe the flutter of white between the rocks and by the time Carrington had scrambled up the side of the escarpment, she had reached the tower and was knocking on its closed door. This was opened immediately and Susanna passed inside, after which the door was closed quickly again.

Carrington stood on the scarp, staring dubiously at the stone shaft which had engulfed Susanna. Whom could she have gone to meet there? He was convinced that she had gone in answer to the message brought her by that villainous-looking person in the flashy clothes. The man was undoubtedly hounding her and she had been driven by some stress to come to the tower. Perhaps she was in danger there. The fear of this possibility sent him hurrying forward. Then a thought stopped him. She might have come of her own free will on a matter of private business. If this were the case, would she not resent his interference, would, she not believe that he had doubted her and was spying upon her?

He decided to wait nearby and watch. But if she did not come out soon, he would feel justified in forcing his way in. Now that he was, close at hand; he studied the tower critically. Built of small, irregular stones crudely cemented together, it stood not more than forty feet high and, with its broad circular base and walls narrowing only slightly toward the apex, it presented a queer, squat appearance. It was possessed, as aforesaid, of a single window overlooking the sea. This was hardly more than an aperture between the stones, and the dingy panes were shrouded by a curtain of coarse cotton which successfully balked any intrusive gaze. The low, narrow door of stout oak also seemed designed to repel intruders. The more Carrington surveyed the tower, the less he liked the idea of Susanna being within.

The minutes dragged by and still she did not come out. He was growing apprehensive and was about to approach the door and pound for admittance, when it suddenly swung open and a slender, wiry man in an inconspicuous tweed suit stepped out, glancing about him in a quick, furtive way. At sight of Carrington, he closed the door sharply and started running toward the cliffs with long, reaching strides, like one trained and practiced in running.

Carrington, forgetting his love of ease, ran valiantly in pursuit, but, though his wind held out, the other readily maintained his advantage and sped over the cliffs and down to the beach below, leaping the gullies and ravines with the unerring step of an adept at rock-climbing. While Carrington was scrambling and slipping down the side of a scarp, this man had reached the red rowboat and was pushing it into the waves, grown hungry to receive it. A moment more and he had sprung into the coble. Bending to the oars, he was borne out to sea, the boat rising and falling on the billows. By the time Carrington had gained the beach, the coble, seeming hardly more than a red speck dancing on the water, was rounding a distant nab and was shortly lost to view.

Carrington stood a moment in perplexity, staring after it. Although his glimpse of the fugitive's face had been merely a transient one, he was sure that he had seen the man before, but where and under what circumstances he was puzzled to know. As the man had hesitated a second in the doorway before starting into flight, Carrington had gained a vague impression of a pair of steely gray eyes, delicately chiseled features, and a sneering mouth, the whole countenance suggesting some unpleasant memory which he was at a loss to classify. Now that this man had successfully eluded him, Carrington scrambled up the cliffs again and hurried back to the tower, Susanna uppermost in his mind.

Why had she remained after the person she had gone to meet had come out? There was a horrible fear at his heart, and his hand shook as he pounded on the door. There was no response, no sound of stirring within, utter silence save for the mournful wash of the waves below. The screaming of a pair of gulls which rose from the sea and circled over the tower made Carrington shudder. He tore open the door and stepped in.

His relief was boundless. Susanna was seated on a rough wooden bench. Her back was toward him, her head dropped dejectedly in her hands, she did not look up.

"I though you had gone," she said bitterly. "Why work yourself into a passion because I did not hurry to open the door for you? Weren't you afraid that someone would hear your pounding? You're rather famed in these parts, you know." There was a world of contempt in her voice. "Well, why don't you speak? Why have you come back? I told you I could do no more for you than I am already doing, and I shouldn't advise you to push my patience too far."

"Susanna, old girl!" interposed Carrington pityingly.

She sprang to her feet, staring in blank astonishment. "Thomas!"

Carrington, flushed and uncomfortable, stood looking at her in helpless silence. He had always found it impossible to express himself when emotion overmastered him. It was doubly so now that sentiment was a factor.

"I — I hope you won't think I followed you here," he stammered at length. "I was sitting on the cliffs when I saw you coming toward the tower. I waved my handkerchief, but you didn't notice. You went inside and I — well, this tower seemed a jolly queer place for you to come to — and I — I got nervous. I was poking around here when the door opened and a man came out. When he saw me, he ran for the cliffs — and did so quite lively, too. He was not a good runner — and I'm not in training — so he got down onto the beach and went off in a red rowboat. It made me beastly nervous wondering what — What you were doing in here alone. So I — I just burst in. I beg your pardon; I'm sure."

A very gentle smile played about Susanna's lips. "On the whole, I'm rather glad you burst in, Tom. I was in the mood when everything looked black and hopeless and the sight of your dear friendly face is like a — well, like an antidote. You don't mind my considering you an antidote, do you?" She moved toward the door. "Let us walk back to Rose Gardens, Tom. I know you won't plague me with questions."

Carrington thrust his arm protectively through hers. "Come along, old girl. It's an uncommon fine evening for walking."

"Does your Ladyship often visit this tower?" suddenly spoke up a drawling yet peremptory voice.

A man had come quietly toward them from the direction of the cliffs. It was Rathbone the detective.

Carrington felt Susanna's fingers grip his arm convulsively. But she turned a composed face toward the detective, her expression showing only a natural surprise and a little annoyance that he should address her so abruptly.

Rathbone repeated his question and his tone was trenchant.

"Do I often visit this tower?" Susanna echoed lightly. "Why should it matter to you, Mr. Rathbone? You are not by any chance its owner, are you?"

Rathbone scowled. "Neither its owner nor its casual tenant. What I want to know — and I have authority for asking — is who the man is you came here to meet."

The detective's bullying manner angered Carrington, but Susanna only shrugged her shoulders and smiled a trifle wearily.

"Really, Mr. Rathbone, aren't you just a little impertinent?"

Rathbone's aggressive eyes held a threat. "I represent Scotland Yard, my lady."

Susanna gave a little exasperated laugh. "My dear man, suppose you do! Does that license you to pry into my private affairs?"

"They cease to be private, my lady, when they have to do with a rotter like the one you came here to meet."

Carrington could restrain his choler no longer. "By Jove, if you can't keep a civil tongue — "

Susanna pulled him back. "It isn't worth while to lose your temper, Tom! Mr. Rathbone rather amuses me — he is so direct in his attacks."

Rathbone eyed her sourly. Her insouciant good humor, appearing to him like a challenge, aroused his bull-dog instincts, and made him willing to sink professional caution in an effort to break down her defenses.

"You'll have a chance at the inquest, my lady, to explain among other things the nature of your connection with the Crimson Knight."

There was a moment's curious silence. Carrington felt unaccountably cold. All manner of surmises and wild suspicions began to formulate in his mind. Susanna was watching the detective with the faint beginnings of a satirical smile on her lips.

"I am sorry to disappoint you, Mr. Rathbone, but the man I met here did not in the least resemble the descriptions I have heard given of the Crimson Knight."

Rathbone's scowl deepened. "I didn't suppose he would wear his attire in the daytime. It's no use, my lady. I'm on his track, and I think," he added significantly, "that it will prove to be a double track."

Susanna remained unshaken. Her sang-froid was magnificent.

"You interest me, Mr. Rathbone. I had no idea detectives in real life possessed so much imagination. I will want to know how you progress with your theories. Come along, Tom, or we will not have time to dress for dinner."

15

BULLETS OF SALT

Miss Flynn stared amazedly across the dinner table at the young East Indian girl, who, in the act of seating herself, had uttered a little smothered cry and caught at the chair for support. Her eyes, fixed upon her plate, were wide with terror. Yet seemingly there was nothing terrifying on the plate, only salt — though in the shape of a bullet.

"What is the matter, Nora? Are you ill?"

"Who — who put this on my plate?" Nora gasped at length.

"By Jove!" Max exclaimed suddenly, "someone has been salting my plate, too."

Sure enough on Max's plate lay another bullet of salt.

Nora looked at him for a moment with an expression of pitiful despair, then she sank into her chair and covered her face with her hands. Max with his careless, mocking smile continued to examine the bullet before him. He, apparently, took it for a joke.

Miss Flynn turned accusingly to Ahmed who, to all appearances, unconscious of the little scene, was noiselessly and deftly arranging the dishes on the table.

"What is the meaning of this nonsense? If you have so much leisure that you can find time to mix up salt in absurd shapes, I will dismiss the new servants and give you more occupation."

"Pardon, Mem Sahib, but I did not place the salt on the plates."

"Then who did?" with increasing sharpness.

Nora uncovered her face and gazed with a breathless intensity at Ahmed's inscrutable features.

"I do not know, Mem Sahib."

"You mean you will not tell."

There was a flicker of an emotion on the East Indian's brown face, the shadow of fear in his eyes.

"I do not know, Mem Sahib."

Nora rose precipitately. "You will excuse me — please, Miss Flynn. I am going to my room. My head pains."

"Why, surely," objected Miss Flynn kindly, you are not taking seriously a silly practical joke. Sit down, child, and eat your dinner. Ahmed, remove that plate and bring another. Remove Mr. Flynn's too."

"You don't understand!" protested Nora. "I — I couldn't eat now." She crossed swiftly to the door, and the shadows seemed to steal forth from the dark wainscoting and enshroud her young figure as she shrank past the Indian curios and idols that stood about the walls.

"Could I help you in any way, Nora?" Susanna called after her gently.

"No, thank you, there is nothing you could do." Nora's voice trailed back faintly from the great hall.

Max rose nonchalantly. "Perhaps I can persuade our exotic little guest to come back and finish her dinner." He spoke with easy confidence.

"I don't think even you could do that," interposed Miriam in a tone of certainty which held a ring of authority. "She doesn't make as light of the bullets of salt as you do. She knows what they mean."

Ahmed set down some silverware with a little clatter and murmured a suave apology. Max surveyed Miriam, his lazy eyelids stretched wide, his smile gone. She, on the contrary, wore a baffling, assured smile. She appeared distinctly pretty as she sat leaning forward slightly, looking up at him. Her bright hair gained a softer shade in the subdued light of the lamps, her complexion an added delicacy, but the blue of her eyes was of a cold, hard clearness, and her little hands, heavily ringed, and hardly larger than a child's, were clasped tensely on the table.

Max grew manifestly uncomfortable under her prolonged gaze. "What are you driving at, Mimi?"

"Why, simply that these bullets of salt have some significance which Nora perfectly well understands. The salt sign is frequently used in India to convey some communication — generally a warning or threat. "Am I right, Ahmed?" She suddenly directed the battery of those hard blue eyes of hers upon the butler who stood behind Miss Flynn's chair in an attitude of rigid immobility.

The East Indian slightly altered his position, but his countenance remained impassive. "It may be, Sahiba. There are many signs used in India."

Miss Flynn viewed Miriam disapprovingly. "How does it happen, Miss Royden, that you are so well-informed in regard to the melodramatic intrigues of the East?"

Miriam laughed — but without mirth. "After I had left boarding-school, I spent two years in India with my father. One learns a good deal in two years." She glanced up again at Max who was standing by his chair as though in indecision. "Now don't go and leave us to imagine all manner of horrible things about those salt bullets. I dare say in this case they don't mean much, but, coming so soon after Rajan Mohan's — death — they are, to say the least, suggestive. Sit down, Max, and tell us one of your amusing stories." Her tone was pleading, but her eyes compelling.

Max's debonair smile returned, and he slipped again into his seat at her side. "Did I ever tell you the funny mess Charlie Fallowfield got into at the last polo match?"

Carrington watched Max curiously. The latter, bending tenderly over Miriam as though no other woman in the world occupied his thoughts for a moment, began to tell, in his inimitable way which drew a smile even from Miss Flynn, of the trick played upon Charlie Fallowfield, a trusting youth with more money than brains. Susanna had spoken with truth when she said that he and

Max were drifting apart. And jealousy was so slight a factor in the widening breach as to be practically a negligible quantity. Carrington was generous-hearted and could have borne to see Max appropriate Susanna as his right and calmly ignore anyone else's sentiments in regard to her, but what he could not bear was to see him monopolize Susanna and at the same time trifle with other women. He did not like Max's attentions to Nora — did not think them fair to the girl — and, moreover, he was beginning to feel a vague distrust of Max — in just what particulars it was hard to say, but the distrust persisted nevertheless.

He observed that Susanna's attention wandered more than once during the account of Charlie Fallowfield's misadventures, but immediately she would force herself to listen again and would look at Max, smiling, boyish, and full of joy, with that indulgent expression with which she frequently regarded him. Tonight it annoyed Carrington as did, for the first time, Max's careless gaiety. It seemed almost heartless after the tragedy which had taken place in the house only the night before. Yet he would have given much to possess Max's boyish exuberance of spirits, his undeniable charm of manner. In comparison with his friend Carrington felt himself old, dull, and ineffectual. No wonder Susanna looked on Max with eyes of indulgence. But, after all, was it more than this? Did she really love him or did she consider Max as she did him, simply as a friend, a 'good pal'? Sometimes it seemed to him that Susanna's unhappy marriage had crushed all sentiment in her and made it impossible for her ever again to feel more than friendship for a man.

He pulled up his thoughts abruptly. What had he, a prosaic, conventional-living bachelor nearing forty, to do with sentiment? It had passed him by in his youth? Why should he welcome it now and allow it to make him ridiculous in the eyes of the very woman whose esteem he wished most to have? Susanna was clever — of course she guessed his passion — And it amused her in her lighter moments to fan it into flame. But what she really wanted of him and needed — had she not said so — Was friendship in the true sense. He would conquer this absurd sentiment — he could not hope to compete with Max in the field of romantic love — and he would give her what he was growing daily more certain that Max could never give her — the unselfish friendship that she craved.

He stole a glance at Susanna. She was very beautiful that night, but quieter than usual. As she turned her eyes full upon him with a jesting remark, he felt, in spite of his resolutions, something warmer than friendship stirring in his veins.

When he looked her way again, he was struck by the bitterness of her expression. She was staring up at the painted face of the Crimson Knight and her own had grown hard and rebellious.

Ahmed glided toward her. "Sahiba, I may serve you to cherry glacé?"

Susanna abstractedly accepted the iced fruit "Ahmed, did you ever hear from your late master the true story of that ancestor of his, that man in the crimson suit?"

Ahmed darted a swift glance of hate at the ribbon festooned Knight, then instantly lowered his gaze to the tray of ices he was carrying.

"The Sahib told nothing to his servant, Sahiba," his voice smoothly liquid as always.

"For my part," spoke up Miss Flynn tartly, "I am tired of mysteries and red robbers and East Indian idols that bore holes into themselves in the middle of the night. Rose Gardens in itself is all that could be desired, but — these East Indian appendages that go with it — " her gesture and her glance as it landed on Ahmed, said volumes.

The butler hastily approached her. "The Mem Sahib will have a second glacé?" he begged deferentially.

Miss Flynn frowned and shook her head. "I do not believe," she said severely, addressing Carrington, as he accepted her rejected glacé which Ahmed absently set before him, "I do not believe in eating a hearty meal, and then making an ice-box of one's stomach. Max," abruptly turning to her nephew, "what do you think of this Rathbone fellow as a detective? It seems he has spent some weeks trying to capture this Scarlet Chevalier — or whatever his ridiculous appellation may be and hasn't succeeded yet — so I don't believe he is at all likely to find out who killed Rajan Mohan. In fact, I have almost made up my mind to send for a private detective on my own responsibility."

Max pushed away the glass of vintage claret with which he had been toying. "Oh, give the chap a fair chance, Aunt Ell. Rajan Mohan hasn't been cold twenty-four hours yet."

Dinner over, they all moved to the terrace for a short while, but the recollection of the horror that had ended the ball the night before hung upon them and all were glad to escape to their rooms early. Nora had not appeared again.

Carrington went at once to bed, but found it impossible to sleep. His mind persisted in reviewing with painful clarity all the unpleasant incidents of the past day and a half, and they all seemed to center about Susanna, her inexplicable absence during the greater part of the ball, the finding of spangles from her dress near the body of Rajan Mohan and even clutched in his hand. And next, her visit to the ruined tower on the cliffs to which she had gone, according to Rathbone's assertion, to meet the notorious robber of the North Riding. What hold could this man have upon her? A sudden vague suspicion made Carrington spring out of bed. The memory of the insolent, devil-may-care face of the Crimson Knight flashing before his mental vision, filled him with resentment.

As he could not banish, that pictured face, and the bed had become a place of torment, he proceeded to dress himself partially and then, in his dressing-gown, sat down by the open window and lit a cigarette for company. The wind came to him with a brackish flavor, salt from the sea, and the booming of the waves sounded preternaturally loud in the hush of night. Across the dim waters, merged in the black, of the starless sky, glimmered the harbor lights of Whitby, eyes of hope for weary mariners. Carrington stared unseeingly upon the shadowy seascape, his cigarette burned out unheeded on the window-ledge.

Suddenly the strident hoot of an owl startled him. The cry, breaking in upon his thoughts, annoyed him, and when it was repeated several times in succession with almost a human note of impatience in the piercing call, he got up to close the window. It was then he caught sight of an indistinct figure on the promontory below, blurred against the dark background of sea and sky. At first he took it for a woman but when it stole swiftly toward the house as though some answer had been given to the owl signal, he saw that it was a man dressed in the garb which had come to be associated with the North Riding robber.

Carrington seized a box of matches and hurriedly opening the door of his chamber, stepped into the corridor. He was reasonably certain that someone in the house had responded to the Knight's signal and was about to admit him into the house. As he hastily groped his way through the unlit corridor, he tried not to think that this person might be Susanna for, in any case, this man must be prevented from rifling the house of their hostess. As Carrington reached the double stair leading down into the great hall, he started and stopped short in amazement.

Along the corridor from the opposite wing, a figure in white was advancing with a peculiar, slow, studied motion. There was something ghost-like in the shadowy, gliding form, but Carrington, sane and matter-of-fact, did not expect to meet ghosts even in a house like Rose Gardens, so he calmly waited until the wraith drew nearer and then he struck a match. The light flickered on the wan face of Nora Mohan. Her eyes though open, were set and unseeing, and she did not blink as Carrington held the match before them. She was in her night robe and barefooted. Without checking her slow, measured glide, she passed by him and descended the stairs, not even touching the rail to guide herself.

Carrington followed her, a great pity in his heart for the young East Indian girl. Those bullets of salt must have had some terrible significance to call her forth from her bed at midnight and send her sleep-walking through the house — or was it the Knight's signal she was going to answer in this subconscious state? Nora had reached the foot of the stairs now and the darkness in the great hall almost swallowed up her little white-clad form. Carrington struck another match. There she was, gliding with certain step, her hands outstretched now, toward the huge, stone pillared fireplace. Reaching upon tiptoe, she commenced to run her fingers searchingly over the Eastern curios on the mantel.

Apparently she did not find what she sought, for, with a little sigh, she turned away and glided toward the back of the apartment. As Carrington followed, the feeble glow of a candle caught his eye. Edna MacDonald, a lit taper in her hand, was just entering noiselessly from the servants' hall. She stared sharply at Carrington and there was antagonism and defiance in her look. The candlelight brought out the copper fire in her heavy braids of hair, intensified the whiteness of her skin and showed up in relief the grotesque figures worked in gold thread on the flowing sleeves of her Oriental negligee.

Carrington made a sign to her not to address Nora, but she evidently had no intention of doing so. She stood, uttering no word or sound, watching the girl's movements with a feverish eagerness. Nora's fingers were fluttering now over a hideous little idol suspended from the wall. Suddenly she gave a sobbing cry of relief. The head of the idol fell to the floor and from its misshapen body she drew a folded strip of paper.

Edna MacDonald sprang toward the girl.

16

THE PAPER IN CYPHER

Before Mrs. MacDonald could snatch the paper from Nora's hand, Carrington quietly took possession of it. Mrs. MacDonald confronted him, a tiger-like gleam in her eyes, her customary smoothness of manner gone. "That is my property, Lord Carrington."

"I was under the impression," he drawled, "that it was the property, temporarily at least, of Princess Nora Mohan."

"It belongs to me!" Mrs. MacDonald's voice rose hysterically. "I have a right to that paper."

Carrington seemed hardly to hear her words. He had turned solicitously to Nora. Mrs. MacDonald's excited voice had pierced the subconsciousness that en-wrapped the girl. A tremor shook her and her eyes, no longer unseeing, looked now with questioning fear into Carrington's.

"Where am I? What has happened?" she asked dazedly.

"You have been walking in your sleep, little girl," he answered soothingly. "There is nothing to be afraid of. Mrs. MacDonald will take you up to your room."

"Mrs. MacDonald" faltered Nora, for the first time observing the housekeeper. She met the latter's unfriendly gaze and shivered. "Oh, what has happened?" she moaned. "Who broke that idol?" She pointed to the head of the image at her feet.

"I will tell you what has happened," said Mrs. MacDonald in cold, incisive tones. "You yourself in your sleep removed the head from that idol and drew out a slip of paper — I think you know what paper."

For a moment Nora looked utterly bewildered, then comprehension dawned in her face. "You mean — the paper?" tremulous joy, mixed with awe, in her voice.

"I mean the paper to which I have every legal right," replied Mrs. MacDonald, fiercely.

Nora drew a convulsive breath. "I think — that is not so. The paper was meant for me, and I found it." She looked very young and pathetic in her white robe with her loosened hair and her little bare feet as she stood defying the older woman.

Edna MacDonald towered above her in the strength of her anger. "It makes no difference whether you found that paper or not. It belongs to me by every legal as well as moral right."

Nora held her ground. "I do not think so!"

Suddenly she looked about her anxiously. "But where is the paper? Have you — did you take it, Mrs. MacDonald?"

"I took the paper," said Carrington quietly.

Nora turned to him hopefully. "You will please give it to me."

Mrs. MacDonald laid her hand compellingly on his arm. "I can convince you, if necessary, that the paper is legally mine."

Carrington gently freed his arm. "You can try to convince Miss Flynn in the morning. I will keep it until then."

Edna MacDonald broke forth into angry protests, insisting that she be allowed to have the paper.

Carrington shook his head firmly. "I will ask Miss Flynn in the morning to decide what is to be done with it."

Nora, during Mrs. MacDonald's protests had remained mute. She now looked up appealingly at Carrington. "If you knew," she said in a low, earnest voice, "what that paper means to me, I think you would give it to me now."

"Run along up to bed, little girl," he adjured kindly, "and don't worry about that paper. I will keep it safely."

Nora studied his face with pitiful intensity. Her eyes were like dark wells of tragedy. "Will you promise not to give it to her?" indicating Mrs. MacDonald who stood regarding the paper in Carrington's hand, still with the tiger-like look of a woman who sees herself robbed of her dearest possession.

"I will give it to no one except Miss Flynn," he assured her. "Now, do run up to bed, or you'll catch cold in your — ah — the way you're dressed."

For the first time Nora appeared to become conscious of her night clothes and her bare feet. She gave a little gasp and fled up the stairway on the right, just as Miss Flynn, bearing a lit lamp and closely followed by the shivering Aeronwen, descended the stairs on the other side.

"What is all this commotion down here?" Miss Flynn demanded severely. "A broken idol or another murder? And who was that running up the stairs — was it Nora — what ailed her?"

"It was Nora and she had been sleep-walking," Carrington answered. "We waked her and — "

A smothered scream from Aeronwen interrupted him. She was pointing with a shaking finger at the head of the small idol on the floor.

"It's the ghost at his work again, Miss Ellery!"

Miss Flynn whirled upon her and because her nerves were completely unstrung, she shook the maid until every separate hair curler stood up on end.

"If I hear another word about ghosts, I will lock you up in the library and make you stay there until daylight!"

This threat had the desired effect. Aeronwen lapsed into shuddering silence.

The voices in the hall had roused the other guests and Max, in a very handsome dressing-gown, his chestnut hair carefully brushed, and his expression singularly alert for one suddenly awakened, was the next to appear.

There was an aroma of cigarettes about him which suggested that he, like Carrington, had found sleep impossible. Miriam, in a highly artistic blue silk negligee, pressed after him. Susanna followed more leisurely. She still wore her dinner gown and looked exceedingly weary.

Miss Flynn was just listening to Mrs. MacDonald's rather hysterical account of how Nora had drawn the paper from the body of the idol and her own claims to its possession.

"You may believe that you have a right to this paper," said Miss Flynn tartly, "but I will not be convinced until I have heard Princess Nora's story, and I don't propose to remain up all night listening to it. I have always hitherto been a respectable-living woman and have kept respectable hours. The whole matter must wait until morning. I will take charge of the paper, Carrington, Probably it is not in the least worth all the fuss made over it."

"On the contrary, Miss Flynn," said Mrs. MacDonald in a voice of repressed passion, "that paper is of inestimable value to me. You do very wrong to withhold it."

Miss Flynn glanced sharply at the housekeeper. She was trembling with the passion that consumed her.

"I should like to know in what the value of this paper consists, Mrs. MacDonald?"

The housekeeper tried vainly to modulate her voice. "It is of value only to one who can read the cipher in which it is written."

"You think you can read it?"

"I am sure of it! The paper was intended for me. It is my right. Every spare moment for the past year I have spent in the study of cryptography so that I might read this paper when it was eventually discovered. You see how cunningly — how cruelly — it was hidden, but the malice that put it there has been thwarted and I ask you, I beg you, to give me what is rightfully mine. Miss Flynn!" as she remained unmoved, "what if I tell you that that paper has direct connection with the murder of Sir Robert Williamson and of Rajan Mohan, too."

"In that case," said Miss Flynn with decision, "I will consult Scotland Yard before I surrender it to any one."

A light of desperation kindled in Edna MacDonald's eyes. "If you do that, Miss Flynn, you will regret it."

She turned abruptly and walked from the hall.

"In the morning," said Miss Flynn grimly, "I will send for that Rathbone fellow. I will also write to Cockerill and Waddington and ask them if it is necessary to keep that woman here indefinitely. Now I suggest that we all go to bed and try to get a little sleep before another idol breaks. Come, Aeronwen! Well," as the maid hung back, "what is the matter now?"

"Surely, Miss Ellery, you're never going to take that murderous paper up to bed with you?"

Max burst out laughing at Miss Flynn's look of exasperation. "I'm inclined to agree with Aeronwen, Aunt Ell. A mysterious document in cipher is not a proper bedfellow for a respectable Englishwoman. Better let me take charge of it."

"I do not intend," responded Miss Flynn uncompromisingly, "to humor Aeronwen' silly, superstitious fears. Are you coming, Aeronwen, or are you not?"

"If that paper is in the room; I will not close my eyes for one second," whimpered the maid.

"Then keep them open," snapped Miss Flynn, and began to ascend the stairs.

"Oh, I say, Aunt Ell," laughed Max, "don't condemn poor Evan to hours of mental torment. I'll keep the paper safe enough."

"Please, please, Miss Ellery, let Mr. Flynn have it!" Aeronwen was reduced almost to tears.

"Why don't you humor your maid, Miss Flynn?" suddenly spoke up Miriam. "You'll have no peace if you don't."

"That is very true." Miss Flynn looked down on Aeronwen as though she wanted to shake her again, but she restrained herself. "This once I will give in to your silliness, Aeronwen, because I must get some sleep — I am sure I wasn't allowed to last night — and I know just how you would carry on if that paper was in the room. Take it, Max."

"And hold on to it," admonished Carrington gravely. "It seems to be a very much desired object."

"Oh, I'll hold on to it right enough," said Max with his easy confidence. "Coming up, old man?"

"Not yet. Think I'll stay down here a while and smoke. I'm not in the mood for sleep."

Max regarded him curiously a moment. "You inveterate old smoker!" he exclaimed and ran lightly up the stairs after Miss Flynn. Miriam went up too, but Susanna lingered.

"I wonder why sleep has so suddenly become distasteful to you, Tom."

"Oh, I don't know," evasively. "I dare say I've had too much sleep in my life."

"No, Tom," she said slowly, and her voice had an anxious note. "I don't think it is that." She turned and dragged wearily up the stairs.

Carrington stared after her gloomily until the graceful form in the elaborate dinner gown was merged in the darkness above. Then he crossed the hall and entered the library. Everything was quiet and undisturbed there, but matter-of-fact as he was, he could not repress a slight shudder at the recollection of what had occurred in this room the night before. He went to the terrace door and tried it. It was locked and there was no sign of any figure in Courtier's Knightly dress lurking about. It did not seem probable that this man had been admitted, for — Carrington had to grant it — the person who would have been most likely to admit him had been under his own observation until a minute ago.

Unless — a sudden suspicion came to him. He hastened from the library and groped his way in the dark along the corridor leading to the servants' hall until he came to a closed door which he judged to be Mrs. MacDonald's. From within rose a sound of sobbing, low, fierce, and despairing. Carrington listened abashed to that heavy, deadly sobbing, the outpouring passion of a soul-wrung creature. For the first time pity began to stir in his breast for Edna MacDonald, strange and incomprehensible personality though she was. With a sense of having committed almost a desecration in hearing these sobs of heart agony, he stole away on tiptoe. He was practically convinced now that the North Riding robber had not been admitted.

When he re-entered the great hall, he was surprised to see Susanna ensconced in a high, carved chair near the stone fireplace. She had lit a single taper on the mantel and its glow shone softly on her face, smoothing away its lines of weariness and enhancing its beauty. She smiled faintly as Carrington approached.

"Do you object if I keep you company, Tom? I am not in the mood for sleep either. I don't want to talk, just to sit here with you. There's a restfulness about you, dear boy." She leaned her head back and closed her eyes with a sigh of content.

Carrington, looking down upon her, felt a wild impulse to stoop and kiss the slightly parted, red lips. He pulled himself together sternly, forcing himself to remember that it was only friendship she wanted of him — let Max play the lover. He walked over to the oak settee on the other side of the fireplace, stretched himself out upon it, and lit a cigarette. As most men do, he found a kind of subtle consolation in watching the blue smoke curl upward to the ceiling.

After a long silence Susanna opened her eyes and glanced at him with a smile of reproach. "You might offer me a cigarette, Tom."

"I beg your pardon. I didn't think." He jumped up, tossed his cigarette case into her lap and struck a match.

She made a careful selection, took the match he held out to her and lit the cigarette with a little gesture of relief. Then she leaned back again in the chair, sighed luxuriously, and blew out a little cloud of smoke.

After a moment she sat upright and flung away the cigarette. "It has lost its flavor, Tom — like everything else. Listen, dear boy, Fm worried, horribly worried over the inquest. What will they ask me?"

Carrington carefully knocked the ash from his cigarette before replying. "I suppose they will ask you about your — ah — interview with Rajan Mohan."

"Then," said Susanna with calm conviction, "I will have to commit perjury or plead guilty to having killed him."

Carrington stared at her aghast. "What the heck do you mean, Susanna?"

She rose with a reckless, desperate air. "Just what I said, Tom. I know it will be hard, but I am going to hold you to your promise of friendship in spite of everything. Mind you don't fail me!"

Carrington laid down his cigarette and rose too. "Susanna, whatever comes out at the inquest, I will be your friend — and will believe in you."

"Thanks, dear old Tom!" She turned and ran up the stairs with a little hysterical laugh that was almost a sob.

17

ONE MYSTERY FOR ANOTHER

Max, to everybody's surprise, was punctual to breakfast. It was apparent at once that something had happened to upset his careless equanimity. He looked serious and a little worried. Susanna's attempted raillery hardly provoked a smile and neither Lorna nor Miriam, both watching him with intentness, appeared to exist for him.

"Aunt Ell," he said directly, "you have steady nerves and so I am going to tell you without any beating about the bush that I have reason to believe Rose Gardens had a visitor last night — after we went up to bed the second time."

Miss Flynn set down her cup of coffee hurriedly. "If you are trying to be facetious, Max — "

"But I'm not," he declared. "In fact, I am sure this person attempted to pay his visit earlier in the evening, not long before our little Princess" — he turned with a slightly caressing smile to Nora — "started out on her sleep-walking tour."

Miss Flynn stiffened with impatience. "Will you speak plainly, Max! Who paid a visit?"

Max looked across at her with solicitude. "Now take it easy, Aunt Ell. It was that chap they call the Crimson Knight."

There was a moment's complete silence. Then Susanna laughed nervously.

"Of course you don't expect us to believe that."

"But it's a fact, Susanna."

Carrington moved uneasily. Miss Flynn caught her nephew up sharply.

"Will you have the goodness to speak plainly and not make us drag every word out of you!"

Max nodded affably. "I'll do my best, Aunt Ell, but it's a long story and almost an incredible one."

Forthwith he launched into an account — the beginning of which Carrington, too, could vouch for — of how, as he sat smoking at his window before going to bed, he had heard the hoot of an owl. The persistent repetition of this cry, which had struck him also as singularly piercing, had caused him to glance from the window and he had seen there below a man in the now notorious costume of the Crimson Knight. This man had approached the house as though to enter it and Max had started to go down stairs to prevent this. In the subsequent excitement in the great hall over the ownership of the paper in cipher, the Knight had slipped from his mind and had not occurred to him again until shortly before dawn when he had awakened with the vague sensation of there being someone in his room. It was too dark to see, and he had no notion where the matches were and, though he listened intently, he could hear no further sound of any one moving. Being unconscionably drowsy, it was easy to persuade himself that his imagination had run riot, and almost immediately he had fallen asleep again.

But when he next woke up in the full daylight, he found that his night visitor had been no trick of the imagination. A chair pushed out of place had first aroused his suspicions. Next he discovered that the door was ajar, although he had been careful to lock it in order to insure the safety of the paper entrusted to him by Miss Flynn.

"And what of the paper?" broke in Carrington. "That, I hope, is safe."

"The paper," said Max regretfully, "has disappeared."

Nora uttered a cry of apprehension. "Was that the paper you would not give back to me, Lord Carrington?"

He nodded gravely.

Nora's young face grew pitifully wan and despairing, her eyes looked bitter reproach at Carrington.

"You have made me lose," she said in a choking voice, "the one thing which might have brought me a little happiness."

Carrington, before her despair, felt himself culpable and could find nothing to say. In fact, he looked almost as wretched as she.

Miss Flynn took pity on his distress. "The loss of that paper is most unfortunate, but Lord Carrington did only what he thought was right. He gave the paper to me as a disinterested party and I entrusted it to my nephew to keep until morning."

"We are none of us exactly to blame, little Lotus-Flower," said Max gently, "because the Crimson Knight chose to steal it,"

"It was not the Crimson Knight." Nora spoke with hopeless conviction. "It was Mrs. MacDonald who stole it."

"But Mrs. MacDonald did not know I entrusted it to my nephew," objected Miss Flynn, bound to be just to the woman however much she disliked her.

"Mrs. MacDonald stole that paper," reiterated Nora with unshaken conviction. "She would do anything to get possession of it."

"I think it is time," observed Miss Flynn, "that we should be told what was written on that paper."

"It was taken from me before I could even unfold it."

"But you know more or less what it said."

"Yes! But I cannot tell."

"Mrs. MacDonald," pursued Miss Flynn relentlessly, "declares that this paper has some connection with the murder of Sir Robert Williamson and of your brother also. Is this true?"

Nora quivered. "Please! you must not ask me that."

Miss Flynn was silent a moment. "At least you can tell who hid the paper inside that ugly little idol."

"No! No! I cannot tell that either." Nora fixed her eyes with a pathetic appeal upon Miss Flynn. "They will not ask me these questions — will they — at the inquest?"

Miss Flynn's own eyes grew suspiciously bright The little East Indian girl had such a hopeless, hunted expression.

"I am afraid it is rather likely," she answered in a softened tone.

Nora gave a little moan and dropped her face in her hands.

Carrington turned to Max. "Where did you put the paper for safekeeping?"

"In the pocket of my dressing-gown."

"Not an especially secure hiding-place, was it?"

Max made a wry face. "Not especially. But how the heck should I know that this Courtier nay Knightly chap would unlock my door and walk in?"

"As a matter of fact," spoke up Miss Flynn, "I do not believe that he did. Nor do I believe that he entered the house at all. I have discovered nothing missing, not even out of place. It is not likely that he would break into the house simply for the purpose of stealing a paper the existence of which he could not even have known."

"Unless," suggested Max, "someone in the house informed him of it." He glanced up lazily at Ahmed who, while attending to his duties as butler, was obviously interested in the conversation.

There was a curious light in the East Indian's eyes as he met Max's gaze. It was not a pleasant expression.

Max looked away, a cold smile on his lips. "If the Knight did not steal the paper, Aunt Ell, who do you suppose did?"

"Ahmed," said Miss Flynn abruptly, "we will not need your services any more for the present. If there is anything required I will ring."

Ahmed made his Eastern obeisance and noiselessly withdrew.

"I will tell you now, Max," resumed Miss Flynn, "that I really think there may be some truth in Nora's suspicions of Mrs. MacDonald. After she left the hall last night, she may have been eavesdropping and in this way have learned that the paper was given to you. It is not improbable that she possesses duplicate keys and so was able to enter your room."

"I am sure that is what happened," declared Nora. "Mrs. MacDonald would stop at nothing to get that paper. She thinks she has a right to it, but oh, it is not so! Miss Flynn, won't you make her give it back to me?"

"It is my intention," said Miss Flynn, not unkindly, "to put the matter in the hands of that detective fellow, Rathbone. The paper must first be found, it is useless to tax Mrs. MacDonald with the theft of it. Naturally she will deny it and we have no proof. Moreover, it is surely the province of the police to take charge of a paper which appears to be involved in two murders. They can decide to whom it will be given."

At mention of the police Nora sprang up evidently frightened. "I had as soon Mrs. MacDonald had that paper as — as the police. They will never give it to me and I — I must have it!" She became conscious of Max's half amused, half cynical scrutiny and her distress turned suddenly to anger. "Gupta Singh was right. The English are cruel — cruel and bad to the people of India. Perhaps," she flung up her head with childish defiance, "I will answer questions at the inquest."

Max looked up at her with his expression of whimsical reproach which few women were proof against. "Oh, come now, little Lotus-Flower, you don't class me among the cruel and bad English, do you?"

Nora stood silent, staring at him. Slowly the anger died from her eyes and tears gathered.

"I think it would have been better if Sir Robert Williamson had never brought me from India." She turned and went swiftly from the room.

After breakfast Carrington again went out on the cliffs alone. Max was just starting for a walk over the moors with Susanna and Miriam. They had asked Carrington to join them, but he felt a singular distaste that morning to taking Miriam for his charge so that Max might be free to devote himself to Susanna. He was becoming tired of playing second to Max. Susanna could not mean to Max with his volatile affections what she meant to him. Why then should he continue to efface himself? From the cliffs he watched them set out, and it afforded him a kind of grim satisfaction to observe the proprietary fashion in which Miriam possessed herself of Max's arm. He would have small opportunity for love making this morning.

After the little party had gone from sight, Carrington sat a long time in thought. Here was another mystery to puzzle over — the theft of the paper which was of such inexplicable value both to poor little Nora and to Mrs. MacDonald. Every circumstance connected with it held mystery. What communication could it contain that must be written in cipher and hidden away inside an East Indian idol? And who had hidden it? One thing, at least, seemed reasonably certain, the explanation of the broken idols might be found in somebody's search — probably Mrs. MacDonald's — for this very paper. But what connection could this have with the murder of Sir Robert Williamson and with that of Rajan Mohan? Again, who had possession of the paper now? Mrs. MacDonald, it was likely. He, too, did not believe that the Knight had entered the house. As Miss Flynn had said, the fact that nothing else had been stolen argued against this.

Above all these questions and surmises, the coming inquest loomed dark. In what sort of a mess had Susanna become entangled? If she persisted in silence, Rathbone's suspicions would grow into certainty. Everything was against her, her interview with Rajan Mohan, which she frankly admitted had been unpleasant, the bit of her spangled dress clutched in his hand, her visit to the tower on the cliffs, and her persistent, reckless silence in every regard. Who was the man she had gone to meet at the tower? Was he the Knight, as Rathbone declared, or was he — Carrington lit a cigarette in desperation. What the heck did the man's identity matter in comparison with the damning evidence against Susanna of that fragment of her dress in Rajan Mohan's hand?

Susanna's own words pounded through his brain. "I will have to commit perjury or plead guilty to having killed Rajan Mohan."

Ah! But she was not guilty. He would not believe even her self-accusation and his blood surged with the desire to protect and defend her against the world. He would fight for her against herself as well, and perhaps some day — who knows — Her frank friendliness might turn to that warmer emotion which, at last, was kindled in his own phlegmatic veins. Again he forcibly checked his thoughts. He, Thomas Carrington, growing sentimental! He who had always viewed the vagaries of love with a bored tolerance, not unmixed with contempt, that men and women otherwise sane should lend themselves to the absurdity of considering each other divine products, set above the general run of human beings. He and Susanna had been good friends, good pals, for years with never a hint of sentiment between them, and then, suddenly and without warning, the madness had seized him. Yet — he had to admit it — He would not have wished this madness away. When it began, he could not tell. He only knew that now life was no longer empty for him — it was incarnate in Susanna, whether she ever returned his affection or not. If only Max would bestow his attentions elsewhere! Or Miriam succeeds in bringing him back to her!

What made Miriam so assured now in her bearing toward Max? This had been noticeable ever since the death of Rajan Mohan, and Max no longer treated her with scant courtesy, instead he even paid her little gallantries. What was the secret of her hold over him? Carrington, with a sense of self-shame, indignantly rejected the suspicion that assailed him. Max was easy living and his code of morals elastic, but he was no murderer.

The sight of a youthful figure in a thin, white frock, standing on the verge of a limestone outcropping and staring out to sea, drew away Carrington's thoughts. Poor little transplanted Lotus-Flower, in what a hopeless attitude she stood, gazing out over the gray, turbulent sea! There was a storm brewing, leaden clouds, bursting with rain, hung low on the horizon, and the heavy wind blew Nora's skirts about her graceful young limbs and played wild gambols with her loosened hair.

Carrington was beginning to feel uncomfortably chilly, and it made him colder to look at Nora in her thin muslin frock. Getting on his feet he clambered over the rocks to the little East Indian girl and advised her to come back with him to the house before she caught cold.

Nora shook her head. "I will not catch cold. I want to watch the storm sweep on."

Her olive cheeks glowed with the sting of the salt air, but there was no glow in her eyes — only gloom.

Carrington tried persuasion, but without avail. She was not cold, and she wished "to see the storm sweep on."

Reluctantly he left her and made his way to Rose Gardens. When he reached the terrace, he turned and looked back.

Nora still stood on the edge of the cliff, her white frock showing clear against the dull gray of sky and sea— a slight, ineffectual little figure buffeted by the onrushing storm.

18

WHERE IS NORA?

Nora did not appear at lunch. Ivy Blake, who had been sent by Miss Flynn to call her, reported that she was not in her room nor anywhere in the house. At Carrington's suggestion, Ivy went out on the cliffs in search of her, but Nora was no longer there.

"Probably she is down on the sands gathering shells," remarked Max indifferently, and resumed his bantering conversation with Susanna.

Miriam was watching them with narrowed eyes.

"Nora should learn to be punctual to meals," observed Miss Flynn severely. "Punctuality is a duty which a guest owes to his host."

"But there is some excuse for her this time," interposed Carrington. "The poor little girl is no end upset over the loss of that paper."

"By the way," Miss Flynn lowered her voice so that Ahmed, who was busied at a side table, should not overhear, "I sent for Rathbone this morning and gave the matter into his charge. He seems fairly intelligent, after all, and certainly is energetic. He searched the house very thoroughly to see if there were any further indications of a burglar having entered. He found nothing to suggest this even and next he interviewed Mrs. MacDonald. Naturally he got nothing out of her — the woman is a living enigma — but it is plain to be seen that he suspects as we all do that she is responsible for the theft."

Max threw Miss Flynn a comical glance of deprecation. "Speak for yourself, Aunt Ell, and allow us the same privilege. For my part, I still believe the Knight is the guilty one."

"And I," said Miriam in a clear, cold voice, "believe that it was neither the Knight nor Mrs. MacDonald."

Max turned to her with his mocking smile. "You speak like a prophetess, Mimi. Who is the guilty one in your opinion?" He laid his arm carelessly over the back of her chair, his teasing eyes laughing into hers.

Miriam interlaced her little fingers. She did not respond to his smile.

"For the present I will keep my suspicions to myself."

Miss Flynn surveyed her, frowning. "If you have reasonable suspicions of any particular person, Miss Cramer, I should say it was your duty to state them. But of course you will do as you think best."

It had been noticeable for some days that Miss Flynn had less liking for Miriam than she had for Susanna, in spite of the latter's apparent connection with Rajan Mohan's death. Probably Miriam's obvious efforts to keep Max in attendance upon her had something to do with this.

Miriam gazed back at her hostess with hard, unflinching blue eyes. "I think it best to say nothing as yet." She turned to Susanna. "You have not told us whom you suspect."

Susanna gave a little hurried laugh. "Oh, I don't believe in suspecting people."

"Sometimes," Miriam's expression was not friendly, "it is impossible not to suspect."

Susanna bit her lip, but there was no rancor in the frank look she gave Miriam. "But why not allow them the benefit of the doubt?"

Miriam elevated her carefully arched brows. "There is not always a doubt. What do you think about it, Tom? Miss Flynn might like your opinion."

"I agree with Susanna," a stern note in his voice.

"Naturally you would." Miriam laughed sarcastically.

When lunch was over, the threatened storm was raging in its full fury; the wind had risen to a gale and the rain was beating down in torrents. Nora had not yet returned. Miss Flynn, muttering something about the trouble and worry certain guests caused her, came into the hall carrying her own gossamer and galoshes.

"I am going to send Ahmed in search of Nora. She must be drenched to the skin. The idea of her staying out in such a storm! We will have her sick on our hands next."

Carrington got up with resolution from the comfortable chair in which he had been trying to content himself. The thought of Nora wandering in the wind and rain, bareheaded and in a thin, muslin frock tormented him.

"I'll take those things to Nora, Miss Flynn."

Max, who was stretched in graceful ease upon the settee, talking to Miriam, but gazing at Susanna, broke into an incredulous laugh.

"Good Lord, Tom, you go out in a storm like this! Why, a London fog always kept you indoors."

"Well, this storm isn't going to," said Carrington curtly.

Max's unconcern over Nora aroused his indignation.

"I'll go up and put on a heavy ulster," he said to Miss Flynn. "I'll be down directly."

Miss Flynn looked dubiously at the perfection of Carrington's clothes. "You'll get drenched too! I can send Ahmed just as well."

But Carrington was already half way up the stairs. He had a fancy that Nora would prefer him for an escort back to Rose Gardens rather than Ahmed whom he certainly suspected of having put on her plate the bullet of salt which had so alarmed her.

When Carrington came down wrapped in a long, thick coat, he was amazed to see Susanna in a tweed ulster, motoring hat and veil, waiting at the foot of the stairs.

"I'm going with you, Tom. I want to get out and battle with the storm."

"But — but it isn't prudent, you know." Carrington felt it his duty to object.

Susanna laughed. "I'm never prudent, Tom. It's no use; you can't dissuade me, even if you say you don't want me. I am a very determined person when I make up my mind. Come along, Tom."

"Hope you'll have a pleasant stroll, you two," Max called after them lazily. "I really think Nora deserves a little scolding when you find her. I'll hold you to that game of billiards this evening, Susanna, if you are not entirely washed away."

As they stepped outside, the massive entrance door of studded oak slammed behind them and the violence of the wind almost took Susanna off her feet.

Carrington looked at her anxiously. "Upon my word, you ought not to be out in this."

Susanna laughed again. "I'm just in the mood for it! Give me your arm to steady me a bit. Now then, where will we look first for the little girl?"

They battled their way to the cliffs, Susanna holding close to Carrington's arm, and he, trying to shield her as much as possible with his body from the wind and the lashing rain. The great rocks, wind-swept and dripping, stretched themselves above the raging sea, void, as far as the eye could reach, of any human presence save their own. Wild as the North Sea always was, it was now like a frenzied monster unchained. The vast expanse of the ocean was white with the foam of the waves, which hurled themselves in thunderous bombardment against the jagged scarps. Tempests of spray were dashed into the faces of the two on the cliffs. Susanna's veil was soaked and flapping limply.

Carrington pulled her aside as a higher wave boomed against the limestone outcropping on which they stood and broke over it in torrents of foam. "I wish you would let me take you back to the house."

Susanna shook her head. "This is too glorious to miss! Besides, we must find Nora. Where can the poor child be? Come down onto the sands, Tom. There is a cave along there where she might have taken refuge."

Susanna scrambled down the steep escarpments with grace and light-footedness as though she were accustomed to rock-climbing. Carrington, naturally less agile and, in addition, hampered by the gossamer and galoshes he was carrying, came down more slowly and rather awkwardly.

At last they reached the drenched sands over which the sea was rushing ravenously. Susanna stood close to Carrington, her hand pressing his arm.

"This storm is wonderful, Tom!"

"I say, won't you take off that silly veil?" he asked irrelevantly. "I can't see you at all through it."

She gave a little low, amused laugh. "You'll have to untie it then. The knot is in the back, stupid!"

She turned her head, and he awkwardly fumbled at the knot. Her near presence, the little intimate act of untying her veil, intoxicated him. He caught her by the shoulders.

"Susanna — I can't help it — I love you!"

She gently freed herself. "Not that now, Tom!"

He drew back abruptly. "I didn't suppose you could care for a commonplace chap like me."

"Dear boy, don't be absurd!" Her fingers jerked the knot apart, and she tore off the veil. There was more than rain moisture in her eyes. "Do you imagine I could permit you to speak of love to me while I am under suspicion of being concerned in a man's death? Oh, I know what you would say, how generous-minded you are, but I know, too, what the world will say — after the inquest."

"I don't care a hang for the world, Susanna!"

"But I do — for your sake. I'm too fond of you; you've been too good a friend for me to allow you to mix your name with mine at such a time as this. We will limit ourselves to friendship, Tom. It will be the best for us both."

Carrington surveyed her gloomily. "And what about Max?" he could not refrain from asking.

Susanna smiled indulgently. "Max is delightful, but — one could hardly take him seriously. No, Tom, I feel too sore and bruised and crushed — yes, and desperate — to love any one at present. And really," with a rueful laugh, "this is rather an inopportune occasion for discussing sentiment. I'm blown to pieces, and I'm drenched. I am sure no one else would dream of making love to me in this bedraggled state, you dear, foolish boy! But come, we must find Nora. I am worried about the poor little girl."

They fought their way along the sands in the face of the furious wind until they came to a natural cave penetrating deeply the high cliffs. Nora was not there. Carrington was becoming genuinely alarmed. He thought of her as he had seen her last — a lonely, dejected little figure poised on the edge of a limestone outcropping, watching the storm sweep over the sea. Had she slipped and fallen into the angry waves, or, driven to despair by brooding over the loss of that paper which meant so much to her, had she deliberately thrown away her young life? He should have insisted upon her accompanying him back to the house, in any case, he should not have left her alone on the cliffs in the mood she was in.

"Susanna," he said suddenly, "if you will wait here in the cave, I will push on to the nearest coastguard station. It may not be too late to — to recover her."

"You are getting morbid, Tom," declared Susanna briskly. "Don't allow yourself to imagine that anything like that has happened to Nora, We will go back to Rose Gardens. I am sure she will have returned by now, or if not, she must have gone to Lancaster Manor to see that old East Indian — what's his name?"

Carrington shook his head in dissent. "She would not go there. She stands in fear of the old chap."

"But he is of her race. She might think it necessary to tell him about that paper — That is, if it really is connected with her brother's death. In any case, Tom, the coast-guards could not launch a boat in such a storm as this. Look at those waves — and that wind, if anything, is increasing! I feel almost certain we will find Nora at Rose Gardens."

Nora was not there, however, and a message of inquiry dispatched to Lancaster Manor brought back the information that neither was she there and that Gupta Singh had gone to London that morning with the body of Rajan Mohan, preparatory to sending it to India for burial. It was the old East Indian's intention to return in time to be present at the inquest.

Nora's disappearance cast an added gloom over the atmosphere at Rose Gardens. Max alone was unaffected.

"Oh, I daresay she'll turn up in a day or two," he remarked easily. "More than likely she has run up to London to meet this old priest and pay the last rites to her brother's memory."

Carrington surveyed him coldly. "What! Go up to London hatless?" More than ever Max's unconcern roused his resentment.

Max smiled with lazy insolence. "My dear fellow won't your insularity permit you to remember that Oriental maidens are not so bound down to hats as your own countrywomen are?"

Miss Flynn, meanwhile, had notified the nearest coast-guard station and a thorough search of the cliffs and sand was being carried on. Up to dinnertime no trace of the missing girl had been reported. But a discovery made at the commencement of the meal increased the general apprehension that the young East Indian girl had not simply wandered off of her own free will.

On the plate set before Nora's empty chair lay another bullet of salt. Max, this time, was not favored in like manner. This second warning or threat had been intended for the girl alone. Ahmed, as before, denied all knowledge of the salt signal and Mrs. MacDonald, too, when questioned, made denial, but she betrayed agitation at sight of the white bullet. Evidently she knew its portent.

Carrington felt assured now that Nora had either been driven to seek death as a solution to the problems that beset her or else had been forcibly carried off.

19

THE CURTAIN RISES

The day set for the inquest arrived, and still no trace of Nora. When the storm had subsided, the coast-guards had dragged the sea within a radius of five miles of Rose Gardens but, if the young East Indian girl were within its waters, the sea would not yield her up. The entire moor-side, too, had been searched without avail. A wire had been sent to Gupta Singh in London. He, it seemed, knew nothing of Nora, but offered a fabulous reward for information concerning her whereabouts. "She must be found," his telegram had ended.

However, the fact remained that she had not been found up to the time when it was necessary to set out for the Bay Town — the little fishing village on Robin Hood's Bay — where the inquest was to be held. Carrington's apprehensions as to the outcome of the inquest grew as the horse-drawn carriage wound among the steep narrow streets of the old town, famed as a former haven for smugglers. But Susanna, the object of his apprehensions, apparently did not share them. There was a vivacity about her — a trifle feverish perhaps — which drew upon her disapproving glances from Miss Flynn and she showed an interest so intense as to be rather peculiar in the queer, tall houses so closely wedged together and built down to the water's edge, practically into and on top of one another, thereby giving the whole town a consciously guilty air as though it were endeavoring to conceal itself. Curious passages and little courts like cul-de-sacs intersected the huddled houses and must have afforded the smugglers of other days excellent means of escape from pursuing excise officers. It would be as impossible to trace a fugitive through this labyrinth of intricate little passages as to chase a rabbit in a warren.

Susanna was studying with especial intentness the old houses near the water's edge. They were almost identical in appearance, their dark stone walls enlivened by newly painted doors and windows, their doorsteps brightened by ocher-colored hearthstones, the scrapers sleek with black lead, and the windows shaded with spotlessly clean curtains. At the sound of the stout horses' hoof-beats in the quiet little street, one of these immaculate curtains was slightly drawn aside, and Carrington caught a vague, momentary glimpse of a man's face peering out In an instant the curtain was drawn to.

Something impelled Carrington to glance at Susanna. She was staring up at that window; her brows were contracted, her lips pinched, her whole expression bitter.

Max, too, was observing her with a cynical smile. "Jolly queer houses along here, Susanna," an odd intonation in his voice.

Susanna's features relaxed. She smiled lightly. "Immensely interesting, I think. I should like to go through some of them."

Carrington, without knowing exactly why he did so, made a mental note of this particular house which had held Susanna's attention. He had occasion later to be thankful that he had done so. It was the last house except for one other, upon the seawall. As it was built almost on top of its neighbors and towered two stories above them, the windows must have afforded an uninterrupted view of the entire sweep of Robin Hood's Bay. Carrington had no further time for observation. The horse-drawn carriage stopped before the small inn built on a bastion against which the waves were breaking hungrily.

Max, never to be outdone in little gallantries, sprang from the horse-drawn carriage and, with a filial deference, assisted his aunt to descend. Miss Flynn, dignified and severe, in austere black, unbent a little at Max's attentions and looked at him with eyes of pride and affection as he stood before her, handsome, debonair, and faultlessly dressed.

"Just one thing, Max," she said in a softened voice, "do be serious at the inquest and don't mock at the coroner even if you do think him stupid."

A whimsically tender smile played about Max's mobile mouth. "My blessed Aunt, I promise to be on my very best behavior."

His eyes, however, were full of teasing mirth and Miss Flynn looked a little dubious as she took his arm and let him lead her into the inn. Carrington followed with Susanna and Miriam. The two latter were obviously dressed with a view to the impression they should make. Susanna wore a golden-brown summer silk, the waist cut in a V to disclose her full white throat and neck, a smart Paris hat of the same golden-brown shade, dainty gloves and bronze high-heeled shoes. Under one arm she carried the inevitable Pompon, his absurd little body surmounted by a monstrous golden-brown bow. The ensemble of Susanna's costume with its harmony of burnished gold set off her brunette beauty to particular advantage. Miriam, too, had counted upon uniformity of coloring to lend charm to her own appearance, but the blue she had selected was of too vivid a shade and the contrast between this and the brightness of her hair was harsh and unpleasing. Her eyes also, sharply blue, heightened the severity of the contrast and in no way blended with her costume, made in the extreme of fashion as all Miss Cramer's clothes were.

Susanna, on the contrary, though always following strictly the prevailing modes, never went in advance of them and her gowns invariably expressed individuality, were graceful, becoming, and comfortable to her type. Miriam, during the entire drive to the Bay Town had been painfully aware of Susanna's superiority of taste and of Max's admiring consciousness of this fact. Consequently the glances Miriam bent on Susanna were appraising and unfriendly. They did not, however, disturb Susanna in the least — Carrington thought it doubtful if she even noticed them — there was nothing petty about her and she would not think it worth while to notice envy.

As Carrington, silk hat in one hand and Malacca stick in the other, ushered them ceremoniously into the inn parlor where the inquest was to be conducted, Susanna caught Miriam's arm in her friendly, intimate way.

"I do hope Pompon will behave himself," she said with a nervous laugh.

Miriam twitched away. "Why did you bring the little beast?"

A shadow settled over Susanna's face. "I thought poor Pompon might divert my thoughts a little."

Miriam looked at her sharply. "Do they need diversion so badly?"

Susanna returned Miriam's look steadily, but she did not reply. In silence they followed an usher through the crowded parlor, packed with the usual incongruous gathering at such occasions, gentry from the neighboring estates, sensation-seekers from the cities, journalists and gaping country folk, to where chairs had been reserved for them immediately in front of a long table littered with writing-materials and bundles of varying size tied up with pink tape. The coroner was already seated at this table, on each side of it were a half dozen shabbily upholstered chairs of early Victorian design. Toward these a dozen men, representing as many professions and walks in life, were pompously making their way. Carrington surveyed them without enthusiasm — some intelligent-looking, some obstinate, even surly, some eager, others bored, and still others merely stupid. These were the men who were to decide today how Rajan Mohan, a prince of far off India, had come to his death.

Involuntarily Carrington took Susanna's arm with a protective gesture as he handed her into a chair beside Miss Flynn. With punctilious politeness he would have had Miriam follow her but Susanna decreed that he himself should sit next to her.

"Mimi will like to sit with Max," she said in an excuse.

Miss Cramer had the grace to give a slight nod of appreciation, but Max looked positively ill-natured when he found himself relegated to the end chair with two persons interposed between himself and Susanna. Miss Flynn glanced scathingly at Pompon huddled in his mistress's lap and looking up at her with plaintive, wondering eyes.

"If that ridiculous dog should commence to bark — "

"Oh, but he's too tiny really to bark. He never does more than yelp." Susanna's tone was innocence itself, but there was a faint twinkle in her eye. "If he yelps too badly, I will ask Tom to carry him out."

Carrington flushed uncomfortably. Sensitive as he was to ridicule, the notion of pushing his way through the crowded room with an absurd, yelping little dog in his arms, made him writhe inwardly. Why, indeed, had Susanna insisted upon bringing the silly little creature? Miss Flynn stiffened with disapproval and drew as far away as possible from the unappreciated Pompon. Susanna's levity at such a time grated upon her sense of propriety. Could she not realize the serious position in which she stood through the discovery of a fragment of her dress in the hand of the man whose death was about to be investigated? — or the still more serious position in which she was likely to stand when the inquest was over?

But Susanna's levity was as fleeting as it was ill-timed. After all, it was nothing more then the pitiful effort of a naturally joyous and healthy soul to shake off the burden of bitterness and horror that oppressed it. She threw a hasty, but embracing glance about the improvised courtroom, and instantly the amused sparkle died from her eyes and lines of anxiety settled over her features.

Carrington, following her glance, discovered that the venerable East Indian, Gupta Singh, was seated on their left and was scrutinizing Susanna with an expression of merciless hatred on his harsh old face. Carrington's indignation rose and his own expression as he stared at the East Indian was fairly ferocious for a man of his easy good-humor.

Susanna touched his arm. "Don't look so savage, Tom. That old man can hardly help hating me. You see" — with a sigh — "he blames me for Rajan Mohan's death. He knows Prince Rajan rather — well rather lost his head over me and everybody, I warn you, Tom, is not as charitable as you are."

"Confound the old chap!" muttered Carrington uneasily. "Why couldn't the precious pair have stayed in India?"

"Well, I am sure I wish they had," said Susanna fervently.

The whispering in that packed little parlor rose now and then to loud murmurs in spite of the usher's rapping for silence. There were many familiar faces in that heterogeneous assembly and Carrington found himself resenting the offhand manner in which the men bowed to Susanna and the cool, supercilious nods of the women. The newspapers, he knew, had been hinting rather broad things against her and of course these society puppets, only too avid for a breath of scandal, or worse, in connection with the beautiful divorcée who had always frankly and openly scorned trivial conventionalities, had mentally tried and condemned her. If Susanna was aware of their hostile attitude, no trace of it showed in the persistently smiling countenance with which she greeted acquaintances. But when she thought herself unobserved, she dropped the mask and her face was that of a weary and despairing woman.

Carrington caught sight of Edna MacDonald seated near the door. She was dressed in unrelieved black which, of course, accentuated her extreme pallor, but offered an effective setting to her curious copper-colored hair and eyes. She was watching Susanna in an unfriendly, almost fearsome way. Several times at Rose Gardens Carrington had observed Mrs. MacDonald watching Susanna in this same fashion and he was at a loss to account for it. Surely generous-hearted, laughter loving Susanna was the last person in the world to inspire fear. Yet there was undoubted fear in Mrs. MacDonald's eyes turned upon her. The mystery of this enigmatic woman was again beginning to irritate him and the sympathy which the sound of her agonized sobbing had called forth was becoming blunted.

Ahmed, like Gupta Singh, a strange, unreal figure in Eastern garb, stood over her chair, his lean arms folded across his breast and his brown face under the bright-hued turban singularly alert to every movement and every person in the room. At that moment the back of Gupta Singh's powerful, grizzled head was the focus of the butler's attention and there was awe, reverence and a kind of cringing fear in his restless black eyes. He stooped suddenly and addressed Mrs. MacDonald in a furtive whisper. She replied in the same manner. Seeing this, the conviction Carrington had long held that there was some bond, some secret understanding between the housekeeper and the East Indian butler became strengthened. It seemed to him that it might very well date back to the murder of their former master, Sir Robert Williamson. He distrusted them both.

Carrington had no opportunity for further surmises. The usher rapped again for silence and the physician who had been summoned on the night of Rajan Mohan's death was called to the stand. In the hush of expectation that ensued while the physician somewhat impatiently pushed his way through the compact crowd of spectators, the waves beating against the bastion outside sounded abnormally loud and menacing and brought to Carrington a disturbing memory which he could not rid his mind of — The memory of Nora as he had last seen her standing hopelessly on the edge of a limestone outcropping staring into a wild and ravenous sea. What fate had befallen her? An even crueler one perhaps than that which had overtaken her brother? Those threatening messages in the shape of bullets of salt would seem to indicate this unless — the sea had saved her.

The physician now had reached the witness-stand. The spectators craned their necks eagerly. No need now to cry "Silence!" The curtain was about to go up on the first act of an absorbing play in which, they had no doubt, the beautiful woman in golden-brown, fondling an absurd little Pomeranian, would play no small part. Not a word must be lost, not even dry medical terms.

As the coroner put the first question to the physician, Susanna drew a convulsive breath. Then she straightened in the chair as though bracing herself for what was to come.

20

THE INQUEST

The physician, who was also medical officer of the North Riding and had performed the postmortem examination, gave his testimony at great length as to the cause of death. Technical terms were used in plenty and puzzled the elegant folk who had come to be entertained. In brief, the testimony amounted to this:

Rajan Mohan had come to his death by a thrust through the breast, effected by means of a long, narrow instrument with two sharp edges, such as a dagger or stiletto. This instrument had entered the thorax between the third and fourth ribs to the left of the sternum and had penetrated the left ventricle of the heart. Death must have been practically instantaneous. As regarded the nature of the wound, the possibility of suicide might be considered. But the fact that the instrument of death had been withdrawn from the wound and found on the floor by the dead man's side would seem to argue against the theory of suicide. For since the wound was such as to cause almost instant death from shock, it was hardly likely that the dying man could have had the time or the requisite strength to draw out the weapon from so deep a cut.

The coroner was about to dismiss the physician, when the latter asked if he might state a fact which appeared to him relevant to the inquiry and, in any event, was a striking coincidence.

"A little over a year ago I performed a postmortem examination on the body of Sir Robert Williamson, who was also found dead in the library at Rose Gardens. Sir Robert, too, had met his death by a thrust through the breast made by a dagger or stiletto."

There was a little stir at the back of the parlor. Mrs MacDonald seemed to be faint and a glass of water was brought her. When quiet had been restored, the coroner turned again to the physician and asked in his deliberate, emotionless voice:

"You wish us to understand, Dr. Blair, that you see or suspect connection between these two deaths because of certain similar features in both?"

The medical officer hesitated. "I don't want to commit myself too far, but — Well, yes, it is my personal opinion that there is connection between the two deaths. Of course," he added slowly, "some of the sensational elements, present in the earlier — er — death were absent in the one now being inquired into. I refer to the highly melodramatic sentence printed in red ink on a strip of paper pasted on the wall above the body of Sir Robert. I cannot now recall the exact wording, but it was to the effect that Sir Robert's death was due to his having incurred the enmity of some association or criminal society called the Surya's Clan — or some such weird name."

The coroner consulted his notes. "The Surya's Eye is the name of the colossal ruby reported to have been stolen from Prince Rajan Mohan either directly before or directly after his death. I think it well. Dr. Blair, that you have called attention to this fact. Now, if I remember rightly, it was a poisoned dagger with which Sir Robert was slain. Is the same true in the case of Rajan Mohan?"

"It is not. Chemical analysis has failed to reveal any trace of poison either on the blade of the dagger or in the wound itself."

The coroner was again about to dismiss the physician, but Dr. Blair clearly had something further to say.

"Mr. Coroner, at the risk perhaps of harking back too much to the past, I should like to bring out a little point which was hardly more than touched on at the inquest on Sir Robert's death. It may, or it may not, shed light on the present inquiry."

The audience was alert at once. Carrington, glancing back, saw that Mrs. MacDonald was leaning forward tensely in her chair and that Ahmed had shifted his curious, cringing gaze from Gupta Singh to the physician.

"Kindly proceed, Doctor," the coroner said.

"The poison on the dagger which killed Sir Robert," the doctor began, "was discovered by analysis to be a little known, but very deadly, East Indian poison. The dagger itself was usually carried by Sir Robert on his person as a protection against some enemy or enemies of whom he was always in fear. I was Sir Robert's physician, and I know that this fear dated from the time of his return from India where he had spent several years — I cannot say how — but he had learned many Eastern secrets, among them how to distill poison from an apparently harmless flower of India. The blade of his dagger had been dipped in this poison."

The coroner viewed the physician with interest "But if Sir Robert, as you state, died from the thrust of his own dagger which he himself had dipped in poison, does not this suggest suicide?"

Dr. Blair shook his head emphatically. "Not at all. While Sir Robert's wound from its nature might have been self-inflicted, he was not in the least a man who could have taken his own life under any circumstances whatsoever. As a matter of fact, he had a horror and a fear of death which amounted almost to a mania. But it always seemed to me that there was reason for this obsession — as though he might at some time have committed a deed because of which he rightly feared to meet the judgment of his Maker. He was a hard, bitter, self-centered man and was never known to show affection or even consideration to any human being, as far as I have heard, except to his ward, the young East Indian girl, Nora, who has turned out to be the sister of Rajan Mohan. To her, I believe, he was invariably kind."

The coroner considered a moment, "You have then no other cause for supposing connection between these two deaths except that in the former there were East Indian features or elements and that in the latter the victim himself was an East Indian and died by an East Indian dagger?"

The physician nodded. "That is so."

The next witness called was Miss Flynn. Carrington, who had been fairly easy in his mind during the medical testimony, commenced to feel a sense of disquiet for he knew that the questions asked now would be of a personal character and would tend to enlarge and emphasize any little incident which could have even the most remote bearing on Rajan Mohan's death. Miss Flynn was not in sympathy with Susanna and so could hardly be expected to shield her by glossing over her rather extraordinary conduct on the night of the costume ball, namely, her long and unsatisfactorily explained absence.

The coroner, however, got little enough out of Miss Flynn. As a well-born, well-bred English woman she very, properly resented the notoriety thrust upon her by being summoned to testify as to her knowledge of a vulgar, sordid murder, and she meant that the coroner and all concerned should feel the weight of her displeasure. She made it plain too, that the man who had brought all this notoriety Upon her by allowing himself to be killed in the house she had rented shared her displeasure to no small degree, and she laid stress upon Rajan Mohan's efforts to induce her to surrender the lease in his favor. But, in regard to the events directly preceding his death she was — for the coroner — provokingly uncommunicative. The matter of the library door being locked or unlocked, with or without a key, she refused to discuss, summarily dismissing the whole question as the figment of imagination or hysteria. She did, however, condescend to state that the terrace door had been found open in spite of the fact that she herself had locked it and retained the key in her possession before the commencement of the ball. The library that evening had not been prepared for guests, "and," she added severely, "had her guests confined themselves to the rooms laid open for them, this unfortunate tragedy might not have occurred."

Here Rathbone, whom Carrington had not observed before, stepped up to the table and handed the coroner a card. That official read it slowly, then turned again to Miss Flynn, standing stiff and straight before him — she had declined a chair.

"The guests, I suppose, were coming and going between the ballroom and the terrace?"

"I suppose they were." Miss Flynn's tone was sharp. "Dancers do not ordinarily remain in a heated ballroom the entire evening."

The coroner looked apologetic. Miss Flynn was a little formidable. His sense of official duty, however, would not permit him being long intimidated and he pressed another question upon her.

"Was any other guest or guests, with the exception of Prince Rajan Mohan, absent a markedly long time from the ballroom?"

Carrington felt himself grow cold. It was coming — what he had dreaded. Susanna ceased abruptly to fondle Pompon — which she had been nervously doing from the moment Miss Flynn took the stand — and fixed her eyes with a sort of resigned despair upon the coroner. Miriam flashed a significant glance at her, and Max's careless serenity of expression became slightly troubled.

The coroner's question appeared to increase Miss Flynn's indignation over the position into which she had been forced. She settled her eyeglasses with a belligerent air and viewed the coroner scathingly.

"I suppose you hope for an answer that can be twisted into incriminating evidence?"

The coroner bristled in defense of his official dignity. "I expect a frank answer, Miss Flynn."

Miss Flynn set her lips. "I think the question an unfair one and I will not answer it."

Susanna drew a little fluttering sigh of relief. Carrington felt profoundly grateful to Miss Flynn, but the coroner was angry and showed it.

"Perhaps you are not aware, madam, that your refusal to answer will incline the jury to believe either that you have something to conceal or somebody to shield."

The grim set to Miss Flynn's mouth became more pronounced. "The jury will believe what they choose, but I believe that there would be more progress made in this investigation if there were fewer deliberately incriminating questions asked and more attention devoted to solving certain palpable mysteries which apparently are beyond the comprehension of Scotland Yard. I am referring to the disappearance of a paper in cipher which was of paramount importance to the sister of Rajan Mohan and to Mrs. MacDonald, the housekeeper at Rose Gardens, and also to the disappearance of Nora Mohan herself. So far as I know, nothing has been accomplished in either direction. Act, not theorize, seems to me an excellent principle."

The coroner gasped. A wave of amused laughter swept through the room — an echo of that secret element of lawlessness in mankind which rejoices when those in authority are rebuked or derided. While the usher was peremptorily calling for order, Miss Flynn swept stiffly to her seat. The coroner, to hide his anger and confusion, hastily summoned the next witness.

This was Gupta Singh. As the aged East Indian, stalwart and upright in spite of his years, dignified, even majestic in his priestly garb of turban and flowing robe, which seemed to set him apart from, to raise him above commoner personalities, faced that eager gathering, alien to him and his, and consequently unsympathetic, if not actually hostile, Carrington was conscious of a sense of strength and power and resolution unconquerable emanating from the calm, stately figure of Brahma's priest. Empires would sooner totter than Gupta Singh abandon a set purpose. He could be inexorable, pitiless, too, if that purpose were thwarted — the harsh, grim lines of his countenance, the stern, farseeing, impersonal light in his eyes declared this. He looked beyond men and their petty deeds to great results, vast enterprises which had their root in the past, their growth in the present and their harvest in the future. Rajan Mohan had been a part of these enterprises, an aid to their achievement. It was not likely that Gupta Singh would show mercy to the one who had removed, or whom he suspected had removed, this integral link in the chain of his purpose. That Susanna was the object of his suspicion there seemed no doubt, for out of that whole roomful of men and women the East Indian's stern gaze sought out Susanna and rested upon her with concentrated hatred.

Carrington felt Susanna shiver. His resentment against Gupta Singh kindled to a flame. By what right did this man judge and condemn her without a hearing?

Miriam gave Carrington a little nudge. "Tom, don't scowl so, you're attracting attention."

Carrington made an effort to control his features as he listened to Gupta Singh's reserved testimony which the coroner drew from him with some difficulty and by dint of much questioning. The East Indian declined to state the nature of the business which had brought him and Rajan Mohan to England and had caused the latter to make such persistent efforts to obtain the lease of Rose Gardens, he intimated only that it was a purely private affair. When asked if they had been in England in June of the preceding year — June was the month in which Sir Robert Williamson had met his death — Gupta Singh answered that he had never set foot outside of India until six months ago.

"But was Prince Rajan Mohan in England in June of last year?" persisted the coroner.

"That I cannot say," was Gupta Singh's somewhat ambiguous reply.

As the coroner finally narrowed his questions to the period directly preceding the costume ball, the East Indian's replies became lengthier. It appeared that Rajan Mohan had gone to the ball against the advice of Gupta Singh. The old East Indian named no names, but it was plainly to be garnered from his words that he disapproved and had sought to prevent Rajan Mohan's growing intimacy with a certain member of the house party at Rose Gardens.

It seemed to Carrington, hypersensitive to any allusion, however covert, to Susanna, that everyone in the little courtroom must know to whom Gupta Singh was referring. Every chance look cast at her appeared to him deliberate and accusing. Perhaps Susanna felt the same, for she kept her head slightly lowered and her attention on Pompon, fawning against her. As Carrington stole a glance at her and saw the misery in her eyes and the nervous, agitated, persistently engrossed manner in which she fondled the Pomeranian, he understood better why she had brought the absurd little creature.

Gupta Singh concluded his testimony by solemnly exhorting English justice in the person of the coroner to leave no effort untried to discover the person who had stolen the Surya's Eye ruby and the whereabouts of Nora Mohan. Either he believed that the solution of these two minor mysteries would solve the greater mystery of Rajan Mohan's death or else he felt that Rajan Mohan, being dead and hence unable to further the undertaking which had brought the two East Indians to England, had become a nonentity, a thing without rating, and that in some way the reappearance of the ruby and of Nora — if the girl still were alive — would complete that chain of purpose broken by Rajan Mohan's death. Carrington guessed that the vengeance of a man who valued causes and effects above the lives of his fellow humans would be unremitting and pitiless, and he was obsessed by a primitive, protective impulse to snatch up Susanna and bear her away from even the shadow of the East Indian's suspicions. It was a relief to him when Gupta Singh resumed his seat.

As the name of the next witness was called Susanna sat up tensely. Edna MacDonald made her way to the witness-stand with nervous haste, obviously and wretchedly conscious of the battery of curious and appraising eyes bent upon her. This woman knew well what she must endure — only one year ago she had stood up under the fire of cross-examination and had struggled to evade insinuating and incriminating questions which later had caused her name and her reputation to be bandied about as common talk.

Carrington again felt sympathy for Mrs. MacDonald as she stood there so strikingly pale in her unrelieved black frock, steeling herself to composure, but unable to banish the fear in her eyes. Once she glanced furtively, almost pleadingly, at Susanna. Susanna responded by a slight, but encouraging smile which made her own face very gentle and sympathetic. It was just a flash, a brief message of womanly sympathy, but it brought a faint glow to Edna MacDonald's cheeks and lessened the fear in her eyes. With an increase of composure, she answered in her soft voice with its persistent undertone of sadness, the coroner's searching questions concerning her reasons for staying on at Rose Gardens after the violent death of its late owner.

She had fought against these insinuations before, but she did not lose her temper as she stated that she had remained out of deference to a clause in Sir Robert's will which had expressed his desire that she and Ahmed, the butler, remain indefinitely as caretakers in the event of his death.

"You had then no more urgent or more personal motive for remaining than deference to Sir Robert's wishes?"

"No." Mrs. MacDonald spoke calmly, but she looked a little anxious as though distrusting the intent of this question.

The coroner pressed his attack. "Do I understand rightly that Sir Robert in his will made no further provision for you than to establish you as permanent housekeeper — or caretaker?"

There came a bitterness into Edna MacDonald's eyes. "That was all the provision made for me.

The coroner leaned forward aggressively. "Had you reason to expect that Sir Robert would make further provision for you?"

At this Mrs. MacDonald became so agitated that her lips moved rapidly without framing an intelligible word. She clenched and unclenched her hands, patches of red came swiftly into her cheeks and disappeared as swiftly. Realizing what effect was registering on the faces of the jurors, she quickly regained her power of speech.

"Why — why, no. I always received my wages as housekeeper with due regularity, there was nothing more to expect."

"Then your willingness to follow out Sir Robert's wishes and remain as caretaker had nothing to do with any expectations you might have cherished — expectations which you thought might be realized through the discovery of that paper in cipher cunningly hidden in an East Indian idol and which you laid claim to as your 'right'?"

"No. Certainly not." But the question plainly had startled and dismayed her.

The coroner continued his aggressive methods. "But you knew of the existence of this paper, who had hidden it and why?"

"Yes!" There was passion in the single monosyllable.

"And you made a systematic search for this paper, did you not?"

Mrs. MacDonald hesitated and moistened her lips. In the pause Carrington glanced toward Gupta Singh. The East Indian was staring at Mrs. MacDonald with something of that concentration of hate with which he had stared at Susanna.

The coroner trenchantly added to his question. "Your search for this paper was so thorough that you mutilated several East Indian idols in your endeavors to locate it — is this not true?"

Mrs. MacDonald trembled with repressed passion. "It is true to a certain extent. I did mutilate some of the idols found broken, but not all. There were others interested in the discovery of that paper. For instance, it was not I who bored the hole found in the large statue of Brahma."

"Who was it then?"

Mrs. MacDonald clenched her hands again. "I only wish I knew!"

Her sincerity could not be doubted. The coroner slightly varied his attack.

"Who were the 'others' interested in the discovery of that paper?"

"Nora Mohan was one." Mrs. MacDonald's voice was hostile.

"And Prince Rajan Mohan?"

"Probably more so than his sister."

"You were acquainted with Prince Rajan Mohan?"

"Not in the least. A woman in my position does not have princes for acquaintances — but I knew of him."

"Did he ever visit Rose Gardens during the lifetime of Sir Robert?"

"Not to my knowledge."

"Would you have been likely to know if he had?"

"Not unless I had happened to see him. Sir Robert was not confidential with me." Mrs. MacDonald's tone was hard.

The coroner once more veered his questioning. "Will you state who concealed that paper in cipher?"

"Sir Robert Williamson concealed it."

"It was his then to dispose of in this way if he wished?"

"It was his, he could do as he wished with it — and did," a world of bitterness in the words.

"Then, Mrs. MacDonald," the coroner snapped back, "what did you mean by claiming this paper as your 'legal right'?"

Mrs. MacDonald started. An expression of consternation spread over her face. "I — I do not care to explain."

"I understand that you offered to do so on the night of the discovery and disappearance of this paper."

Mrs. MacDonald succeeded in recovering her poise. "For the sake of possessing that paper, I should have been willing to explain. Now that it has gone, I am not willing."

"Are you willing to state what you expected that paper to contain?"

"No." The single word was emphatic.

Carrington remembered Nora's similar uncommunicative nature in regard to the paper and his curiosity grew.

The coroner allowed the matter of the paper to rest. "Did you have conversation with Prince Rajan Mohan on the night of his death?"

"I have never spoken with Prince Rajan Mohan," sharply.

"Where were you during the course of the ball?"

"The early part of the evening I spent on the cliffs, by eleven o'clock I was in bed," she answered readily — almost too readily.

"Were you alone on the cliffs?"

Edna MacDonald flashed a peculiar glance at Susanna, hesitated an appreciable while, then answered hurriedly:

"I was alone."

Rathbone passed another card to the coroner. Carrington was commencing to dread these cards, and he was not surprised at the trend of the coroner's next question.

"Did you see any guest from the costume ball on the cliffs?"

Mrs. MacDonald studied this question before replying. "I saw no one from the costume ball," she said at length.

The coroner frowning, bent over his notes. Suddenly he sat upright and launched a shot that caused a tremor of excitement to pervade the room.

"Then if the man in the feathered hat and the courtier's dress who talked with you on the cliffs that night was not a guest from the costume ball — who was he?"

Mrs. MacDonald uttered a smothered cry; her face was like chalk. Her lips opened, but no words came. Susanna pressed against Carrington. He felt the trembling of her body, saw the horror in her eyes.

"Mrs. MacDonald, who was the man in the courtier's dress?" thundered the coroner.

There was no response. Edna MacDonald had fainted in her chair.

Susanna precipitated Pompon into Miss Flynn's lap and went hastily to Mrs. MacDonald's aid.

Max leaned across Miriam. His boyish, debonair look was gone.

"I say, Tom, if they get you on the stand, it will be just as well under the circumstances — as I told you before — not to proclaim the fact that I got myself up as the Crimson Knight. I was a silly ass to do it."

21

A QUESTION OF COSTUME

A dose of smelling salts restored Mrs. MacDonald to consciousness and she was assisted from the room by Susanna and Ahmed, the latter solicitous and deferential. The butler was immediately summoned to the witness-stand, but Susanna remained outside with Mrs. MacDonald. Carrington was rather glad that it happened so. Susanna would be spared the recital of much unpleasant testimony and would be free, for a while at least, from impertinent stares. Miss Flynn resigned herself to Pompon, Max resumed his usual careless serenity of expression, sand the courtroom generally quieted down and prepared itself to listen to Ahmed's reluctant and circumspect testimony.

That the East Indian, figuratively speaking, was on the rack there could be no doubt. Hitherto Ahmed's understanding and command of English had been perfect, but now it was necessary for the coroner to repeat his questions several times before they entered the East Indian's comprehension sufficiently to draw from him even the most monosyllabic response. Carrington fancied that the hard, searching gaze which Gupta Singh directed upon his unhappy compatriot as though he sought to probe the secret depths of his soul, was responsible in no small degree for the pitiful showing which the perfectly trained and efficient servant made on the witness-stand. Carrington dreaded the moment when Susanna must undergo the same scrutiny.

The coroner with admirable patience finally elicited from Ahmed a denial that he had had anything to do with the mutilation of the idols or the subsequent disappearance of the paper in cipher.

146

"I know nothing of anything, Sahib," the butler declared in his smooth, liquid voice.

"But you know," urged the coroner persuasively, "whether you ever admitted Prince Rajan Mohan to Rose Gardens during the lifetime of Sir Robert Williamson."

Ahmed's restless black eyes were suddenly lowered. "It is not so, Sahib, I have never admitted Prince Rajan Mohan to Williamson Sahib."

Carrington wondered if the fellow was lying, but the coroner was content to let the matter rest. He next forced the unwilling admission from Ahmed that it was he on the night of the costume ball who had called Miss Flynn's attention to the fact that the library door was locked. But he could not explain how it was that Miss Flynn had found the door unlocked, or how the key later had been discovered in the lock.

"What drew your attention to the library in the first place?" demanded the coroner.

Two repetitions of this question were necessary to elicit the reply that the door being closed had attracted his attention.

"Did you hear any sounds of moving about or disturbance within?"

"No sounds, Sahib." Ahmed seemed anxious to make this statement.

"Had you previously seen any person enter the library?"

"No, Sahib." Ahmed's answers came more quickly now.

"Did you see any person leave the library before you notified Miss Flynn?"

"No, Sahib," with greater haste, but so low as to be almost inaudible.

The coroner surveyed the East Indian thoughtfully. "Do you know if any person entered Rose Gardens that night which was not an invited guest?"

Ahmed was shaken by the question. Again the coroner was forced to repeat. The East Indian's response struck Carrington disagreeably.

"About ten o'clock, Sahib, a man came to the entrance door and asked that I would carry a note to Lady Susanna Helton."

It was the first specific mention of Susanna's name, and Carrington felt a weight settling on him. Rathbone, with eager haste and something of the hunter's look, commenced to scribble on another card.

"What was this man's appearance — how was he dressed?" asked the coroner.

"Like you, Sahib — dressed like any European."

"He did not then wear a hat with feathers and a queer fancy costume, red and tied up with ribbons?"

The audience leaned forward expectantly. They had all heard of the picturesque robber of the North Riding and they could guess what was in the coroner's mind. The question had startled Ahmed. He looked the embodiment of consternation.

"No, Sahib, no! The man was not in costume dress. He had the European clothes, but he was like what Williamson Sahib called a bloodsucking oaf."

The coroner frowned at the wave of laughter through the room. Rathbone finished his hasty scribbling and thrust the card at the coroner.

That official gave him an impatient glance, but proceeded to ask the question on the card.

"When you gave the note to Lady Susanna Helton what happened?"

The change in the trend of the examination seemed to afford Ahmed relief. He answered glibly that her ladyship had left the ballroom and gone outdoors to join the man.

The official pressed on, "Did you see her ladyship reenter the house?"

"Yes, Sahib, about half an hour later when I was passing through the hall, her ladyship came in alone."

Carrington started. Only half an hour later! But Susanna had been absent from the ballroom fully three hours.

"Did her ladyship return directly to the ballroom?" asked the coroner, still reading from the card.

Ahmed hesitated a moment. Then, "No, Sahib."

"Where did she go?"

Another pause. Ahmed was evidently the prey of some mental struggle. "Prince Rajan Mohan, Sahib," he said reluctantly, "spoke to her ladyship in the hall."

The coroner showed interest as intense as that of the spectators. The next question was put at his own initiative.

"Did Prince Rajan and her ladyship remain in the hall or where did they go?"

Ahmed looked genuinely distressed. "They walked down the hall, Sahib, toward — toward the library."

"Did they enter the library?"

"I did not see, Sahib. I carried refreshments into the ballroom."

"When did you see either of them again?"

Ahmed's tongue clove to the roof of his mouth. He cast furtive, helpless glances about the room. Pressed sternly by the coroner, he finally answered that he had not seen Prince Rajan until he had been discovered dead.

"And when did you next see her ladyship?"

"I saw her, Sahib, a few minutes before I went into the ballroom to tell the Mem Sahib that the library door was locked. I saw her ladyship come in from outdoors with the Mem Sahib's nephew."

"You are sure they did not come from the library?"

"They came from outdoors. Sahib."

"Was this outer door kept open during the ball?"

"Yes, Sahib, two footmen were watching it."

"Then no stranger — no unbidden guest — could have entered without being observed?"

"No, Sahib." Ahmed was beginning to look terrified again.

"And neither you, nor any of the servants, as far as you know, saw in the house or about the grounds, a man in a feathered hat and a red, ribbon festooned costume?"

Ahmed appeared quite desperate for a minute or two. Then suddenly he recovered his poise.

"The Mem Sahib's nephew wore a feathered hat and a red costume with ribbons."

"Confound that foreign chap!" muttered Max.

There was no humor now in the lines of his mouth. Hard, bitter, almost repellent his whole face seemed — but only for a moment. To those who bent curious stares upon him, he turned an indifferent countenance and now a smile, whimsical, yet with a suggestion of cynicism, played about his lips.

Miss Flynn was indignant with Ahmed for the innuendo in his answer, but she also was indignant with Max for having given ground to it by electing to copy the costume of a notorious character such as the Crimson Knight. She conveyed this displeasure to Max by a few whispered words, caustic and sharp.

Max looked comically repentant, also reproachful. "But, Aunt Ell, how the plague was I to know — "

His words were arrested by a sentence spoken by the witness who had succeeded Ahmed. Ivy Blake was on the stand and she was telling a startling tale.

The girl's cheeks were rosier than ever with embarrassment and excitement, but her round blue eyes were steady and convincing.

"Aboot an hour after t' ball began," she was saying, "Ah seed a man on t' terrace wi' a feddered hat an a ribboned suit. Ah wor in t' library trimmin' a candle and t' man wor lookin' in at t' door."

"Did you see his face?" demanded the coroner.

"Ah didn't wait ter see it Ah wor afeeard an Ah ran oot from t' library. Ah wor sure 'e wor t' — t' Crimson Knight." She lowered her voice impressively and glanced around the room with an air of pride in the sensation she was causing.

"Did you see this man again?" asked the coroner with official sternness.

Ivy looked more important than ever. "Ah seed 'im coomin' oot from t' library. Ah didn't see 'is face then either, on'y his back, but he went into t' ballroom."

"What time was this?"

"Varra late — aboot a half-hour afore t' murder."

"You mean before it was discovered that there had been a murder?"

"Ay, thot's what Ah mean."

"Did this man close and lock the library door?"

"He closed it, thot's aw he did."

"And what did you do? Did you attempt to look into the library?"

"Ah ran into t' servants' hall. Ah wor freetened."

"Then you don't know who locked the library door and later unlocked it in the short interval between Ahmed's discovery that it was locked and his informing Miss Flynn of this fact?"

"Noa, sur. Ah stayed in t' servants' hall until John — he's yan oh' t' footmen — cam cryin' theer wor murder done."

The next information elicited from Ivy was that which Carrington had long been dreading to hear — the repetition of her former statement that she had seen Susanna put the key in the lock.

"When was this done?" The coroner's tone was trenchant. He remembered Ivy's previous evasion as to the time.

Ivy again sought to elude the question, but the coroner pressed her so hard that she was finally forced to answer.

"It worn't varra long afore yo an th' doctor cam."

Carrington nervously adjusted his monocle and stared hard at Ivy. The girl was certainly telling the truth. But Susanna! She must then have had the key in her possession and have come downstairs, after all the others had gone up, to rid herself of this incriminating evidence. Undoubtedly she had been the one who had locked the door. But why and who had unlocked it in the interval of Ahmed's entering the ballroom? Not Susanna, for she had been standing near Miss Flynn when Ahmed approached. Carrington was coming to resent more and more the significant glances directed toward Susanna's vacant chair. Yet, in spite of himself, did not he too harbor the selfsame ugly doubts which excited this morbidly curious throng?

The coroner had not quite finished with Ivy. "What were you doing downstairs at that time?"

Ivy's eyes grew a little rounder and she seemed slightly dismayed. "Ah wor too freetened to go oopstaares to my room and Mrs. MacDonald axed me to coom in her room which is downstaares off t' servants' hall."

The girl hesitated as though unwilling to say any more, but the coroner forced her to continue.

"Theer cam a rap on t' door," she said somewhat sulkily. "It wor Lady Susanna, she wor nervous an oopset like. Mrs. MacDonald went out into t' corridor wi' her and closed t' door. She wor gone a long time an Ah got af eeard — aw alone in t' room — so Ah opened t' door and theer wor Mrs. MacDonald and Lady Susanna whusperin' afore t' library and Lady Susanna wor puttin' a key in t' lock." Ivy jerked her head defiantly. "Thot's aw Ah knaw aboot t' key."

Carrington thought it sufficient. Susanna then and that woman of mystery, Edna MacDonald, had been in collusion on the night of the murder. Now that this was manifest to every one, he wished that Susanna had not gone to Mrs. MacDonald's aid when she had fainted, he wished, too, that Susanna would no longer remain outside with the housekeeper. Suspicious minds would readily see more collusion in what he, who knew Susanna's generous and sympathetic nature, felt mire was only an act of kindness toward another suffering woman.

The coroner still had a last question to put to Ivy Blake. "Did you see anything further of this man in the knight's costume after, as you stated, he entered the ballroom?"

"Noa, sur." But there was a curious hesitancy in Ivy's voice.

"You seem to be doubtful on this point." The coroner spoke sharply. "Did you or did you not see him?"

"Noa, sur, Ah didn't— but Ah thought Ah did."

"Explain yourself, please."

Ivy twisted about worriedly. "Wann John cried to me theer wor murder done Ah ran into th' hall — th f entrance hall, sur — an Ah saw a man wi' a feddered hat an ribboned costume joost goin' oop t' staares. But warm 'e turned — Ah'd gi'en a cry oh' freet — Ah seed it worn't t' — t' Crimson Knight, sur."

"Well, who was it?" said the coroner impatiently.

Ivy drew a quick breath. "It wor Mr. Flynn, sur."

22

A QUESTION OF IDENTITY

Max, with a detached air of amusement, encountered the more than curious glances bent upon him. Miss Flynn bristled in defense of her nephew and stared out of countenance those who ventured to look at him too pointedly. To herself, she had lately been forced to admit that her favorite nephew was not all perfection, but she would not admit this to another nor allow any suggestion of it.

It seemed to be the general expectation that Max would be the next witness, but instead Carrington was called.

He took the stand with an unwillingness and apprehension which he tried his best to conceal and succeeded in doing. In fact, he presented an impassive countenance as he stood before the crowded roomful, dressed with immaculate correctness, an expression of amiable boredom filming his eyes, and answered with the elegant drawl peculiar to his kind, the coroner's searching questions. He was, however, careful to avoid Gupta Singh's gaze as the examination approached the danger zone, that is, events in which Susanna figured, preceding and following the death of Rajan Mohan. He felt somehow that if he were to meet the East Indian's hard scrutiny his self-control would be shaken.

As it was he came through the inquiry without making any damaging admissions in regard to Susanna and also spoke a word in Max's favor by substantiating Ivy's statement that the Crimson Knight had been in the vicinity of Rose Gardens on the night of the ball. He would no longer allow

154

himself to believe that it was Max whom he had seen from the terrace talking with Mrs. MacDonald.

The coroner, nevertheless, needed convincing. "You say, Lord Carrington, that you were on the terrace when you saw this man at the edge of the promontory. He must then have been at a considerable distance from you and it was dark in addition. How then did you know it was the Crimson Knight?"

"The moon was out, and I recognized him by his costume."

"But you could not see his face?"

"No, it was too dark for that."

"How could you be sure then that this man was not Mr. Flynn? He wore a costume resembling the Courtier's Knightly garb — according to the testimony of the two preceding witnesses."

Carrington found this question rather of a poser and he gave a lame answer. "I should suppose that Mr. Flynn would be in the ballroom instead of on the cliffs with — with a person who was not one of the guests," he finished hastily, not wishing to name Mrs. MacDonald.

But the coroner was determined to force him to it. Carrington, however, was equally determined and would admit nothing except that the Knight's companion had been a woman not in fancy dress. The coroner listened with interest to Carrington's account of having seen a man in Knight costume on the cliffs at dawn and of having met Max in the hall in conventional morning garb only a few minutes later.

"There seems then to be two Knights to account for," said the coroner with rather an unpleasant smile, as he dismissed Carrington.

This remark caused Carrington to wonder if he had really helped Max so very much after all. However, the knowledge that he had successfully diverted the questioning from Susanna was sufficient to content him. Since Max had foolishly chosen to impersonate the Knight, he must shield himself from the consequences.

Miriam was summoned next. There was something in her poise, her assured bearing — or was it the hard blue of her eyes — which gave Carrington a sense of uneasiness. She was jealous of Susanna, and he felt that she would not be likely to withhold evidence which might discredit her. Miriam was not generous-hearted, the only soft spot in her nature was her infatuation for Max, but this made her bitter against any one who caught his volatile fancy and it was particularly so in the case of Susanna. For over two years now Max had pursued her with untiring ardor — usually his passion cooled in half that time — but Susanna still remained its desired object. His trifling with poor little Nora was not to be taken seriously; she was just an amusing child, a pastime, and Miriam had not thought it worth while to be jealous of her. But Carrington knew that her jealousy of Susanna had reached fever heat and he listened in an agony of apprehension to Miriam's readily given testimony.

Yes, Miss Cramer admitted coolly, she had been absent from the ballroom about an hour and a half. She had gone outdoors because she had had a headache. She had joined Lord Carrington on the terrace and had remained there alone after he went inside. No, she saw nothing of a man in courtier dress nor of Mrs. MacDonald.

"Did you see Lady Susanna Helton go out from the house?" asked the coroner.

The audience, whose tension had somewhat relaxed, straightened up, metaphorically and literally, at mention of Susanna.

"Lady Susanna Helton had left the ballroom before I went outdoors," said Miriam quietly. "But about half-past ten o'clock, I saw her reenter the house. She was alone and came from the direction of the cliffs. She appeared to be in a hurry, and I thought that she was nervously upset."

Carrington felt an impulse to sweep Miriam's petite, assured figure from the stand. She might at least wait for direct questions instead of voluntarily offering testimony which she knew would discredit Susanna. Why verify until necessary Ahmed's statement that Susanna had reentered the house within a half hour after leaving it and so emphasize the fact that over two hours of her time from then until the discovery of Rajan Mohan's death was unaccounted for? Max apparently shared Carrington's indignation against Miriam, for his expression as he regarded her was almost contemptuous.

Miss Cramer, however, did not once glance his way, but looked persistently over the heads of the audience toward the outer door as though challenging Susanna to come back and defend herself. Rathbone was exceedingly interested in Miriam's testimony and proceeded to dash off another card.

The coroner's next question revealed its purport. "The terrace on which you stood extends, I believe, from the front entrance of Rose Gardens beyond the windows of the library?"

Miriam quickly assented. She seemed anxious for the next question. It came after a brief delay, during which the coroner studied again Rathbone's card.

"Did you happen to walk up and down the terrace — as far as the library windows for instance?"

"I walked several times from one end of the terrace to the other." There was in her voice a suggestion of information withheld which caused the coroner to lean toward her with eagerness.

"Did you look in at the library windows?"

"I looked in at the door." Miriam spoke as though regretfully, but Carrington, his sensibilities unusually keen, detected a false note.

"Miss Cramer," the coroner's tone though insistent was yet gentle — after all, Miriam was exceedingly pretty and chic and she had when she chose, as on the present occasion, a certain appealing way with her which most men found difficult to resist — "I must ask you to tell me frankly what you saw in the library."

Miriam's eyes became very regretful, her baby-like mouth quivered slightly. "I am afraid," she said with a little sigh, "that in telling you I may give an entirely wrong impression of — of what happened later."

A current of excitement ran through the room. Carrington was morbidly sure that Miriam's words were no less than an innuendo against Susanna. Max, leaning back nonchalantly in his chair, was studying Miriam with a sort of cynical, grudging admiration.

"Actress!" he muttered.

"Miss Cramer," urged the coroner, still gently, "it is your duty to tell all that you saw and leave the gentlemen of the jury to draw their own conclusions."

Miriam made a little depreciative gesture. "It really wasn't very much. Prince Rajan Mohan was in the library with Lady Susanna."

Miss Cramer's pause was significant and lent a dramatic touch to a statement in itself fraught with meaning.

"They were talking?" demanded the coroner.

"Talking?" Miriam elevated her carefully arched brows. "Well— yes."

"Amicably?"

Miriam appeared somewhat distressed. The coroner looked sympathetic and even Carrington was not quite sure but that her distress was genuine. Max gave a kind of twisted smile. Miss Flynn sat erect and frowning. She for one was not to be influenced by Miss Cramer's ingenuous ways.

The coroner repeated his question. Miriam firmly interlaced her little gloved hands as though to reassure herself of the integrity of her motive in answering frankly.

"It was not at all an ordinary conversation," she said in a low, deliberate voice. "Both were greatly excited, almost quarreling."

"How did this end, Miss Cramer?"

Miriam turned surprised eyes upon the coroner. "I cannot tell you. I walked away immediately."

Carrington felt a little bewildered. He did not believe that Miriam had walked away nor did he understand why she should conceal what else she had seen through the terrace door. Certainly it could not be from a desire to shield Susanna, and he had it from Susanna's own lips that her interview with the East Indian had been in the highest degree unpleasant There was no doubt that Miriam had seen more than she would tell. He remembered how white and agitated she had been upon her return to the ballroom. What had she seen and why should she conceal it? Had there been someone else in the library besides Susanna and the East Indian? Someone whom Miriam wished to shield? But whom would this self-seeking young woman be likely to shield except — Carrington stole an uneasy glance at Max.

At that moment the coroner dismissed Miriam and called:

"Mr. Maxwell Flynn!"

Max rose unconcernedly from his seat and walked leisurely to the center table. All cynicism and hardness was gone from his face, once more he looked carefree, irresponsible, boyish. There was a humorous gleam in his eyes, the faint beginnings of a smile on his lips as he faced the inquisitive glances leveled on him from every side. One might have said that he was amused, even a little bored, by the entire proceedings. His chestnut head high, his slim, elegant figure carelessly erect, he stood before the crowd, the coroner and the jury as he might have stood before friends and acquaintances in the grand stand at Ascot or in the stalls of a West End theater.

Miss Flynn bestowed on him a look of pride. "Flynn to the fingertips," she murmured.

Miriam nodded. Her sharp prettiness was softened and illumined as she gazed at Max. Hard-natured little adventuress as she was, Max had known how to touch some unsuspected chord of tenderness within her, how to rouse the hunger of love in a cramped and self-sufficient soul. Carrington found that he was beginning to envy Max his power to stir women's hearts.

The coroner now was putting certain preliminary questions which Max answered with an air of amiable condescension. Apparently he was unconscious of Gupta Singh's fierce scrutiny. It seemed to Carrington that the old East Indian viewed Max with hardly less hostility than he had Susanna. What the heck did the old chap know or suspect?

"At the fancy-dress ball," continued the coroner, "you wore the costume of the Crimson Knight?"

"I wore a representation of the Courtier's knightly costume." Max spoke with emphasis.

The coroner frowned. He did not like this nicety of distinction. "Was your costume a sufficiently accurate representation to allow of your being mistaken for the original courtier?"

Max's condescension grew. "Rather a difficult question that. I have never had the pleasure of seeing the Knight except indistinctly from my window the night the paper in cipher was stolen and I am sure I can't tell how my costume struck others."

Max's manner irritated the coroner. "If you have never seen the Knight except indistinctly," he flashed back, "how do you know that your costume was a representation of his?"

Max smiled tolerantly. "Partly from hearsay, partly because I had it copied from an old portrait in the dining-hall at Rose Gardens said to be the original Crimson Courtier rather the Crimson Knight, or else this present-day chap is said to be the reincarnated spirit of the other."

"You take a great interest in this old legend, Mr. Flynn. Why?" The coroner's tone was truculent.

Max looked at him lazily. "Why not? There's an epidemic of Knight legends throughout the North Riding. It's the one excitement here."

The coroner showed plainly that he did not like Max's nonchalance. "At any time during the course of the ball, were you out on the cliffs with Mrs. MacDonald?"

"I spent the evening in the company of my aunt's guests. At no time was I on the cliffs with Mrs. MacDonald." There was a certain arrogance in Max's voice and bearing which did not tend to propitiate the coroner.

"Were you out on the terrace?" he asked sharply.

"I was. The terrace was used as a promenade by many of the guests."

"Did you look in at the library door?"

"No, I did not go as far as the library door. I think that few of the guests did. The terrace forms a sharp angle just before reaching the first of the library windows. While I was on the terrace, I saw no one walk beyond that angle. To one not familiar with the house, it would seem in the darkness that the terrace ended there." Max's demeanor was once more amiable and indifferent.

"So then," pursued the coroner, "those on the terrace would not be likely to know what was happening in the library unless they made it a point to do so?"

"That is correct," Max assented affably.

Carrington glanced at Miriam, who was gazing with intensity at Max. Evidently she had made it a point to know.

"Did you enter the library at any time during the evening?" The coroner's voice was increasingly harsh.

"I did not enter or approach the library until the discovery of the death there."

Max answered with some sharpness. Apparently he saw, as others did, that the coroner was endeavoring to prove that there had been only one Knight in the vicinity of Rose Gardens on the night of the ball, and that Knight was Max himself.

The coroner stroked his chin thoughtfully, contemplating the witness before him. "Did you, Mr. Flynn," he asked at length, "see anything that night of another man dressed in Knight's costume?"

Max looked at him with a frankness which somehow seemed overdone. "I didn't happen to see the other — the original — Crimson Knight that night, but of course he must have been about since Ivy Blake and Lord Carrington too have vouched for his presence."

"But you personally saw nothing of him?"

"Nothing at all," said Max, lightly.

"If he had entered the ballroom, it would have caused some sensation, would it not?"

Max appeared a little puzzled. "Well, rather!"

"But you, wearing almost the identical costume could enter without sensation?"

The puzzlement in Max's eyes grew, but he responded readily enough. "Naturally, none of the guests wore masks; they would know my face and they had become accustomed to my costume."

"And yet," persisted the coroner, "if a person had seen the costume without seeing your face, that is, if you had been standing with your back to that person, he might have mistaken you for the real Knight?"

"Why," admitted Max with an uneasy smile, "I suppose so. My costume was a jolly good copy of the one in that old portrait."

The coroner straightened to the attack. "Did you not come out from the library, closing the door after you, about a half hour before the discovery of Prince Rajan Mohan's death?"

If Max felt the thrust, he successfully concealed it under an assumption of arrogance. "I have stated that I did not approach the library until after the discovery of the prince's death."

"A preceding witness has stated," resumed the coroner in harsh, judicial tones, "that she saw, a half hour before the discovery of the prince's death, a man whom, from his costume — she did not see his face, only his back — she took to be the real Knight, come out from the library and enter the ballroom. Apparently his entrance caused no sensation. Now, Mr. Flynn, since your costume, according to your own statement, was an exact reproduction of the real Knight's and yet you could enter the ballroom without causing sensation, why should we not think that it was you yourself whom this witness saw coming out from the library?"

Max's arrogant mouth hung slack. For a moment he stood gazing at the coroner in silent consternation. Then he pulled himself together and tried to carry off the situation lightly.

"I am afraid you'll have to take my word that it wasn't me."

The coroner's smile was not pleasant. "There seems to be no choice in the matter. That will do, Mr. Flynn." He turned to the usher. "Summon Lady Susanna Helton."

23

THRUST AND COUNTER THRUST

Susanna entered the inn parlor quietly and composedly, not with Max's air of half-contemptuous nonchalance, but with the calm bearing of a woman who has steeled herself for what she must undergo and has confidence in her ability to maintain self-control. The impression she made upon the coroner and jury was distinctly favorable, upon the spectators it varied according to their natures.

Miss Flynn's expression which had grown somber and even grim during Max's examination relaxed slightly and she bestowed a dutiful pat or two on the little Pomeranian who commenced to whimper at sight of his mistress. Into Max's face, now set in lines of cynical indifference, there came an ardent light as his eyes followed Susanna's graceful figure to the witness table, yet there was present too a suggestion of that appraising look with which Max invariably regarded women. In the case of Susanna Carrington had always more or less resented it — in the case of other women, it had not mattered to him — but now he found himself angry and the fact that Max's look was entirely probative did not lessen his resentment.

Miriam stared at Susanna through narrowed lids, and it seemed to Carrington that the ferocity of Gupta Singh's scrutiny was not more pitiless than Miss Cramer's cold gaze.

Out of the scores of faces turned toward her, Susanna's glance sought out Carrington's, he thought he read in her frank eyes the plea, "Stand by me, old friend!" He tried to convey to her by his answering glance the assurance that he intended to do so, and evidently she understood for she gave him a faint but warm smile of gratitude.

Max observed this smile and, taking advantage of Miriam's critical study of Susanna, whispered to Carrington, "Play fair, Tom!"

Carrington felt his color mount under Max's quizzing eyes. Somehow Max's knowledge of his sentiments toward Susanna made him uncomfortable. He had a notion that Max, confident in his own powers to attract women, was making mock of his poor pretensions. But perhaps — the consoling thought came to him — with one woman, the woman, his pretensions were not so poor after all. It was to him Susanna turned when in trouble — Max was for her lighter hours. But yet this did not content, Carrington wished to be something more to Susanna than a mental prop or solace, since that walk alone with her in the storm when his passion had forced utterance he realized that friendship could never satisfy, he must take as well as give. He would recall the foolish half-promise he had made to allow Max "free way" with Susanna. He could no longer hold to it; he must "play fair" with himself. It was as much his right to seek love as Max's — perhaps more.

A leading question put by the coroner arrested his reflections. That official had finished his preliminary questioning of Susanna and was now coming to the substance of the examination.

"Were you acquainted with Prince Rajan Mohan before you met him at Rose Gardens?"

Susanna's voice was quite steady as she gave reply. "I met Prince Rajan first at the Ascot Races in June of last year and later at the Russian Embassy ball in November, also at several other functions during the season."

The coroner looked slightly triumphant. Susanna had established what he had vainly endeavored to make Gupta Singh establish, namely, the fact that Rajan Mohan was in England the previous year in June, the month in which Sir Robert Williamson had come to his death. Gupta Singh squared his powerful shoulders, and his beetling gray brows drew together.

"What were your relations with Prince Rajan?" The coroner's tone was courteous and respectful rather than judicial. He was conscious of Susanna's charm and, moreover, was grateful for the information she had so freely given.

Susanna's frankness continued. "I saw a good deal of Prince Rajan. He called on me frequently, sent me flowers, and wrote to me when he was absent from London."

Carrington wondered why she had never mentioned the East Indian's attentions to him, but perhaps she had and the name had slipped his mind. Susanna had such a coterie of admirers.

"Was Prince Rajan — er — in love with your ladyship?" The question was put apologetically.

"I suppose so." Susanna spoke regretfully.

"And what were your feelings toward him?" The coroner looked as though he wanted to apologize for these personalities.

"I regarded him simply as an acquaintance," said Susanna briefly.

The coroner would have abandoned this line of questioning were it not for one of Rathbone's cards.

"Did Prince Rajan," he now asked, "ever make you a proposal of marriage?"

Carrington saw Gupta Singh straighten fiercely in his chair.

Susanna gave a queer little smile. "Yes, he offered me the honor of becoming his princess when I had made it plain to him that in England proposals of marriage were still the rule after declarations of love — even from a prince."

The spectators, in general, glad of any chance to relax, laughed at her words. But the ferocity of Gupta Singh's scrutiny of Susanna was intensified. Carrington became hot with indignation against all East Indians, but against Rajan Mohan in particular. If he had stayed in India where he belonged, Susanna would not have been mixed up in a murder trial.

"When and where did this proposal take place?" asked the coroner next.

A shade of annoyance came over Susanna's features. "Well really, I don't see — "

"It will be best to answer," interposed the coroner, still gently.

Susanna gave a little resigned shrug. "Prince Rajan made the proposal on the cliffs near Rose Gardens one afternoon a few days before the ball."

Carrington started. That must have been the day on which he had carried to Rajan Mohan Susanna's note asking for an interview.

"Did you accept the — er — offer of marriage?" asked the coroner.

Susanna slightly drooped her head. "I did."

This time Max as well as Carrington started.

The coroner, too, looked surprised. "Your feelings then toward Prince Rajan had changed?"

"Not in the least," said Susanna wearily.

"It was then to be a so-called 'marriage of convenience'?"

Susanna raised her head. "Not in the ordinary meaning of the phrase — no! His title, his wealth were nothing to me personally."

"But I understand that your finances have lately been in a straightened condition?"

Susanna flushed. "It is true, but that fact had nothing to do with my acceptance of Prince Rajan."

"Then what reasons did cause your acceptance?"

Susanna suddenly acquired hauteur. "Private reasons — and they must remain private."

"Your engagement to the prince was not made public?" The coroner's voice had grown harsh. In the effort to sound Susanna's soul, she had become to him witness, not woman.

"It was not made public. There were reasons on both sides why it should not be known for a while."

"Were you still engaged to Prince Rajan up to the time of his death?"

"No." The reply was sharp and distinct.

"When was the engagement broken?"

"The night of the ball."

"Where?"

She hesitated. Then, "In the library," she said half defiantly.

"At what hour?" persisted the coroner.

There was a tortured look in Susanna's eyes which made Carrington suffer with her.

"It was early in the evening," she said faintly, "not later than ten-thirty, I should think."

"Was it your ladyship or Prince Rajan who broke the engagement?"

"Does it matter?" she asked wearily. "Oh, I suppose it was me who actually broke it — but he forced me to do so."

"What do you mean by 'forced' you?"

"Well, he was unwilling to fulfill a certain promise private matter," she added with emphasis.

"This promise was the condition of your marriage to him?"

"It was," her tone infinitely bitter.

"You and Prince Rajan quarreled as the result of his unwillingness to fulfill this promise?"

"We broke the engagement," she answered evasively.

"Were there not mutual recriminations?"

"He made me loathe him!" The words burst from her passionately and as though against her will.

The coroner was quick to press his point. "Then there was a violent scene between you?"

Susanna attempted to retrieve herself. "I do not know what you mean by 'a violent scene'? We could not come to any agreement certainly."

"Did Prince Rajan threaten or attack you?"

The question startled her. "No!" she cried vehemently, but her eyes wavered.

"Think a moment," urged the coroner not unkindly, "did not Prince Rajan attack you and did not you in a struggle to escape him seize upon the only means of escape, one of the daggers on the wall above you?"

"No, no!" Susanna put out her hands in passionate protest. Her face was blanched and desperate, "He did not threaten or attack me," she reiterated with a feverish intonation.

"Then how," demanded the coroner sternly, "do you account for this torn piece of your gown being found clutched in Rajan Mohan's dead hand?" He drew from under the pile of papers before him the bit of spangled gauze which Carrington had dreaded to see.

The desperation in her face grew. "I cannot account for it. You must draw what conclusions you will."

"They will not be favorable," the coroner warned her gravely. Carrington's misery was intense. It seemed to him that Susanna was deliberately incriminating herself — and yet, perhaps not, for if she admitted that the East Indian had attacked her, as that damaging bit of spangled gauze intimated, the inference would naturally be that she had defended herself in the manner suggested by the coroner. Justifiable homicide this might be considered, but even under extenuating circumstances Carrington would not, could not bring himself to believe Susanna blood guilty. She was not a woman of unbridled passion, she would call for help, not stab a man.

"How long," resumed the coroner, "did you remain in the library?"

Susanna made a visible effort to calm herself. "Perhaps a quarter of an hour, perhaps longer, I cannot tell."

"Did anyone enter the library while you were there?"

"No," her reply quick and tense.

"Was the corridor door closed or open?"

"It was closed."

"And locked?"

"Yes, it was locked." Susanna's voice took on a reckless note. "I locked it to insure privacy. I did not want any person to come in casually and overhear what I was discussing with Prince Rajan."

"And the terrace door — was that locked too?"

"I suppose so. It was closed at any rate."

The coroner fixed his eyes steadily on Susanna. "Was Prince Rajan alive when you left the library?"

"He was."

But she shivered and the words seemed to drag from her. Carrington was morbidly certain they held a conviction for no one in the room except himself.

The coroner's expression was stern. "By which door did you go out?"

"The terrace door," hastily.

"Ah! Then you possessed a duplicate key? Miss Flynn has stated that, after locking the door, she retained the key."

Susanna made a quick effort to repair her slip. "I did not intend to say that the terrace door was locked — only closed. Certainly I did not possess a duplicate key."

The coroner favored her with an incredulous smile. "If you did not unlock the terrace door, who did?"

"I do not know."

Again her words failed to carry conviction. Carrington knew that well enough as his aching eyes wandered over the faces of the crowd, meeting hollow compassion, unwholesome curiosity, and even horror in the glances directed towards her.

"Where did you go upon leaving the library?" The coroner's manner was increasingly magisterial.

"I went down on the cliffs and stayed there for a long while. I wanted to be alone."

"Did you meet anyone there?"

"I met no one."

Why, Carrington wondered half angrily, could she not at least try to put some ring of truth into her tone? Did she deem the circumstantial evidence against her too strong even to make an attempt to extricate herself?

"You saw nothing," persisted the coroner, "of a man in a courtier's knightly costume?"

"No!" She spoke now with vehemence.

The coroner changed his line of attack. "Who was the man who sent a note in to you by the East Indian butler?"

"I do not care to give his name. He came on a matter of private business. He went away immediately after it was transacted — about ten-thirty — and did not return."

"Did you reenter the library after having left it?"

"I remained on the cliffs until very late. Then when I went up to the house, I met Mr. Flynn on the terrace near the front entrance and we went together — into the ballroom." Susanna's voice was even and deliberate, like one repeating a lesson learned by rote.

"Had you any reason to suppose that Mr. Flynn had recently come from the library?"

"Certainly not." The surprise in her tone was genuine. "He had come out from the ballroom to look for me."

"Did you unlock the library door leading into the corridor — the door which you had previously locked?"

"No, I did not go near the library. I went directly into the ballroom with Mr.

Flynn."

"But you still had the key in your possession?"

"Yes, I unconsciously took it with me when I left the library."

"My Lady, why were you so anxious on the morning after Prince Rajan's death to conceal the fact that the key had been in your possession throughout the evening, instead of being accidentally discovered by you on the hall floor as you then affirmed?"

Susanna moistened her lips. "Naturally I knew that some unpleasant inference would be drawn."

"You feared this inference so much then that you came downstairs after the other guests had gone to their rooms and slipped the key in the lock — or was your desire to consult with Mrs. MacDonald more impelling even than the desire to rid yourself of the key?"

Susanna for a moment looked startled. As she had not heard Ivy Blake's testimony, she was unaware of what the girl had divulged. "I went down to return the key," she said rapidly, "and I — I met Mrs. MacDonald in the hall."

The coroner showed his disbelief in words and manner as he asked, "What did you have to say to the housekeeper of Rose Gardens that could not wait until morning?"

"Something of a private nature." Susanna's voice was cool, steady, and determined. Her glance as it encountered his did not waver.

The coroner leaned back in his chair and surveyed her gravely. It seemed impossible to chip the armor of quiet and firm reserve which she had girded on. Her very frankness left no vulnerable spot to strike at, and she met his attempted thrusts with a calm refusal to answer which paralyzed a further attack in that quarter. As a last resort he tried intimidation.

"Do you realize that your repeated answers of 'private reasons' and matters of a 'private nature' cannot do otherwise than lead the jury to the very inference which you say you sought to avoid by surreptitiously returning the library key to its lock?"

But Susanna countered with the same disarming frankness. "I realize that fully." Her face was white, but her voice unmoved.

"And you still refuse to state the substance of your conversation with Mrs. MacDonald?"

"I do."

That ended her examination, and the case was given over to the jury.

24

THE HOUSE ON THE SEAWALL

The hours, passed in awaiting the verdict of the coroner's jury, were centuries of mental agony to the principal actors at the inquest. Susanna was the most composed of all but this very composure was disquieting to Carrington for it suggested the resignation of despair. It was plain that she expected to be held for trial and was prepared to go through with it. Mrs. MacDonald, still in a state of collapse, had sought her room immediately upon the return to Rose Gardens and still remained there with the door locked against well-meaning intrusion. Ahmed performed his duties as butler with, it seemed to Carrington's irritated nerves, more furtive glance and softer tread than ever. One could feel the brown fellow listening for the verdict they all dreaded.

Miss Flynn made no attempt at conversation herself and discouraged it in others. She even failed to respond to Max's affectionate raillery and sat apart from her guests, stiff and austere, in a corner of the great hall, working with grim diligence on some garments destined for the children of an Orphans' Home in the East End of London. But every now and then she would look up from her work and her gaze would fasten itself on Max with questioning anxiety. Carrington knew what a blow it would be to this authoritative, self-contained woman, with all her pride of race and family, if her idolized nephew, the only living being to whom her heart was really open, should be found or suspected to be, implicated in the death of Rajan Mohan, her guest and his.

Max, for his part, tried to keep up the others spirits and his own by going to the piano which had been moved into the hall and dashing off a cheerful little tune.

"I say, Susanna," he said lightly, "you know this. Come and sing it with me."

Susanna shook her head. "I can't now, Max, I simply can't."

Max swung round on his seat and looked at her with a face of whimsical tenderness. "Oh, come now, just a verse or two. It will brace you up. You know how well our voices blend, don't you, eh?"

Susanna smiled wanly and rose to humor his caprice, but a glance at Miss Flynn, frowning now over the orphans' garments, caused her to resume her chair. "It wouldn't do tonight, Max."

"I should think not," spoke up Miriam sharply.

Her eyes held a cold fire. "You seem to forget what the jury's verdict may mean to more than one here."

Max swung round again and brought his hands down upon the keys with a vicious crash. "By George! Miriam, you're the specter at the feast."

He got up abruptly and crossed the hall to the entrance door. His face had that haggard look which it had worn now and again during the inquest.

Miriam rose, too. "If you are going out on the terrace, I would like to walk with you. I promise to be very cheerful." The words were light, but her tone was still sharp.

Max turned quickly. A careless smile played now about his lips.

"Don't mind my grouchiness, Mimi. I dare say my nerves are a bit jumpy. Come along out. I think there'll be a moon later."

Miss Flynn frowned after them. "The way that the young woman pursues Max is disgraceful. You are responsible for her being here, Carrington. Why can't you take charge of her?"

"Oh, I'm going to look after her," he answered vaguely, hardly knowing what Miss Flynn said.

He was, in fact, absorbed in speculating upon Miriam's apparent hold over

Max. If it had any connection with Rajan Mohan's death, she should be made to speak for Susanna's sake. But how the heck was a man to make her speak? Mimi was uncommon tight-mouthed when she chose to be.

"It is a shame, Miss Flynn," remarked Susanna contritely, "that this house party should have brought you so much unpleasantness. I am heartily sorry for my share in it."

Miss Flynn sewed on with uncompromising zeal. "Your testimony was most unsatisfactory," she said irrelevantly and with severity.

"I know it," sighed Susanna, "but I couldn't help it."

She leaned her head back against the chair and closed her eyes. She looked utterly weary. Carrington felt indignant with Miss Flynn. A woman ought to be able to say consoling words to another woman.

Miss Flynn's needle flew in and out with greater rapidity. "If Helena Dormont," she observed tartly, "... if she had the common sense to engage herself to Max instead of to that young Army idiot, things might have been different. Max might not have needed a costume ball to amuse him."

"Damned inconsiderate of Helena Dormont," drawled Carrington.

Miss Flynn glanced up at him sharply, before she could administer a rebuke Rathbone appeared in the doorway. Carrington sprang to his feet with an exclamation of dismay. He knew instinctively that the detective had come to report the verdict of the coroner's jury.

Susanna opened her eyes suddenly and, recognizing Rathbone, put her hands to her throat as though she were choking. She, too, knew why he had come.

"Don't keep me in suspense," she said nervously. "I am to be held for trial? Please tell me quickly."

"You don't need to get worked up," said Rathbone with maddening slowness. "The verdict's a disappointment — it's murder by a person or persons unknown."

Susanna gave a little hysterical laugh. "The verdict might have been a good deal worse, Mr. Rathbone."

The detective eyed her significantly. "That's a fact; it might." He was plainly disgruntled.

"Now perhaps," remarked Miss Flynn, with a sigh of relief, "we will have an end to notoriety."

"Don't know about that, ma'am," answered Rathbone ominously. "Better read what the papers say, they're getting the extras out If you don't mind, I'd like a word with that girl, Ivy." Without waiting for Miss Flynn's permission, he went toward the servants' hall.

Miss Flynn's lips tightened. "So we are to continue to be harried and hounded by detectives and made the talk of every scandalmonger in the kingdom. If ever I get back to Cavendish Square among decent living, respectable people I hope I will have the sense to remain there and when I think of giving another house party I will invite the guests myself."

There came a stricken expression into Susanna's face. "I will take the morning train to London, Miss Flynn," she said quietly.

Carrington's features twitched, there was a peculiar light in his eyes. "Miss Flynn, no doubt your guests have caused you inconvenience, but you owe them a little courtesy since they are your guests."

Susanna raised her hand in protest. "Miss Flynn is justified in feeling annoyed, Tom. I did not exactly understand about the invitation — but I should not have come here. I am very sorry."

She turned to ascend the stairs. Miss Flynn checked her with one of her authoritative gestures.

"I am sorry too," she said jerkily, "sorry for what I said. I didn't mean you particularly. On the whole I should prefer that you stayed on a while."

A gentle smile lit Susanna's face. "You are very kind, Miss Flynn, but I think I ought to go back to London in the morning."

Miss Flynn frowned and cleared her throat. "I am not in the habit of repeating invitations, and it is not easy for me to apologize, but I say again I am sorry if I have been discourteous to you and I ask you once more to finish out your visit. I have grown accustomed to you and — well, I want you to stay."

Susanna hesitated a moment, then she impulsively leaned forward and kissed

Miss Flynn on the cheek. "You are awfully kind. Of course I'll stay if you want me to."

Miss Flynn snapped the moisture from her eyes as Susanna ran up the stairway.

"I'm no end grateful to you for your goodness to Susanna," said Carrington earnestly.

"You needn't be. I like her. I don't want to like her, but I do. Now where can I send for a paper? We may as well know the worst and have it over."

"I'll drive back to the Bay Town and see if the extras are out."

"That might be a good idea. Get back as soon as you can. I don't want to wait up all night."

A few minutes later Carrington stepped into the horse-drawn carriage and was driven rapidly away from the old turreted house on the promontory, now showing as a black irregular mass against the evening darkness. Miriam from the terrace threw him some sarcastic little remark about his impatience to secure a paper. Max had ungallantly left her to watch alone for the rising of the moon.

The coachman, a Yorkshire man, and consequently endowed with native superstition, did not enjoy this ride along the verge of the night-hidden moors with the solemn booming of the sea the only sound to break the silence. He was continually glancing about as though expecting some goblin shape to spring up before him and upon Carrington's asking what made him so "confoundedly jumpy," he launched forth into colorful tales of the Crimson Knight and his propensity for accosting belated travelers on the moors, appearing to them in all manner of fantastic shapes, but always contriving to wear the costume of the Merry Monarch's days.

Carrington stifled a yawn. The coachman was wearisomely prolix.

"I don't fancy you need to alarm yourself, Thomas. We are not actually on the moors and the Crimson Knight has lately kept himself under cover. He doesn't consort well with detectives."

"Do yo think, my lord, t' Knight be flesh an' blood?"

"What else, Thomas?"

"He wor hanged amaist tree hundred years ago."

The coachman's voice dropped to an awed whisper. "'Tis his picture hangs in t' dining-hall oop at t' hoos. Theer's nobbat one person in aw t' Riding — a wild slip of a laad — thinks t' Knight be flesh and blood. An' this poar laad's wits ha amaist fiigged away sence 'e took oop wi' t' Knight."

"Took up with the Knight?" encouraged Carrington. His speculations in regard to the Knight were beginning to formulate into definite suspicions, and he welcomed all information concerning him, were it no more than superstitious gossip.

"Ay, my lord," resumed Thomas, "t' laad took ter follerin' 'im aboot oh' neets, an' mebbe aidin' 'im in his devil's work. Mony a person ha seed t' laad follerin' t' Knight across t' moars. T' laad ha taaken too ter drink an' no one 'll ha speech wi' him."

"Who is this lad, Thomas?"

The coachman's volubility abruptly ceased. "Ah don't think Ah'd best naame 'im."

"Why not, Thomas?"

"Mebbe it wad get 'im an' soom yan else into trooble."

Carrington surveyed curiously the Yorkshireman's thick-set, obstinate shoulders. "How long have you been coachman at Rose Gardens, Thomas?"

"Aboot two year — mebbe," Thomas answered with true native caution.

Carrington tried again. "What did you think of Sir Robert Williamson? He was an eccentric, wasn't he?"

"It worn't my plaace ter think aboot t' Master," said Thomas bluntly. "Theer's alius foalk ter saay a maan's queer in 'is head like if he do different from they. Yo'll ha ter ax others aboot 'im."

The horse-drawn carriage was winding now among the narrow streets of the Bay Town, and Carrington had no further opportunity for trying to break through Thomas's stubborn cautiousness. Fisher-boys crying "extras" were keeping the little old-world town of smuggling fame awake and Carrington had no difficulty in possessing himself of a half dozen papers.

A hasty reading of the front page stung him into a belligerent humor which made him want to fight the world — particularly the newspaper world — In order to force the retraction of these insinuations against Susanna. Of what use was the jury's verdict of "persons unknown" in the face of calumny like this? The worst interpretation was put on every phase of her testimony. She was not spared in any instance, it was even practically stated that the jury had been flagrantly negligent of their duty in failing to indict her. But what angered Carrington perhaps more than all was the unnecessary dragging in of the details of her unhappy married life and the putting of the blame for the divorce on her shoulders instead of where it belonged — on the shoulders of her cad of a husband. Everything possible was done to blacken her character and prejudice the public mind against her.

Carrington's burning sense of the injustice of it all drove him to a step which he had been contemplating for some days but had hesitated to undertake through dislike of interfering in concerns which were not his affair. Now, however, he felt that matters had come to a crisis where the suspicion that had been troubling him must be verified and Susanna's name cleared before the world. That she would make no effort to vindicate herself, he knew. But he would attempt it, come what might. Things could not be worse than they were.

Heedless of Miss Flynn's injunction to return as quickly as possible he bade Thomas wait for him by the mailbox in the center of the town and proceeded, on foot, to the queer, tall, furtive-looking houses near the water's edge from a window of one of which a man had peered down upon them as they were driving to the inquest. The memory of Susanna's bitter expression as she had stared up at that window quickened Carrington's pace. He had no difficulty in finding the house he sought. He had made careful mental note of it, the last except for one other set upon the seawall and built fairly on top of its neighbors.

The house, as he mounted the stone doorsteps, was dark save for a single light in an upper window obliquely facing the sea. An elderly woman of unprepossessing appearance answered his summons at the door. She carried a candle in one hand and held it in such a fashion that its light illuminated his features, but left hers in shadow. She seemed in fact like an anachronistic survival of those days when the inhabitants of this very house perhaps were roused from sleep by excise officers, armed with warrants authorizing them to search for smugglers.

"I wish to speak with Captain Bartholomew Helton," said Carrington in a confident tone.

"He doan't live here, sur." The woman tried to close the door.

Carrington put out his foot and prevented. "That won't do, my good woman. I have seen the man here."

The woman kept her face persistently shaded. "Then 'tis anoother naame he calls 'imself. Ah doan't knaw ony such person as yo speak of. This is a respectable lodging-hoos an' he might ha coom here ter see yan oh' th' lodgers."

"No, I am sure that he is staying here." And Carrington set to work to describe the man whom Susanna had met at the ruined tower on the cliffs, the same man, he was convinced, though he had merely caught a transient glimpse of him, who had peered down from the window of this house. Captain Helton in his proper person he had seen only once in his lifetime — at Susanna's wedding. She had met the young officer while traveling abroad, and immediately after the wedding they went back to the continent for the honeymoon from which Susanna returned alone some months later. Scandalous tales of Captain Helton began to be spread in army circles and finally he resigned his commission to avoid being forced to do so. Susanna, out of pity for the ruin he had made of himself, joined him in Vienna and attempted a second time to live with him. It ended two or three years later in her instituting divorce proceedings against her husband.

In the midst of his description of the supposed Helton, Carrington heard someone coming down stairs.

"What's all the fuss about, Mrs. Barker?" demanded a boyish, excited voice from the hall.

Mrs. Barker, startled by the interruption, let the door swing open and Carrington, quietly pushing by her, stepped into a stuffy, box-like hall. He found a slim youth in a rakishly tilted cap confronting him. The light from Mrs. Barker's candle showed the lad to be possessed of a shock of copper colored hair, shifty eyes of an uncertain brownish hue, and a pasty, unwholesome complexion. He was singularly like, and yet unlike, someone whom Carrington could not at that moment name to himself. In age the boy might have been seventeen or eighteen.

Carrington repeated his query and the description of the man he sought.

"He doesn't lodge here," said the boy. "Does he, Mrs. Barker?"

The landlady shook her head. "Noa, thot's what Ah told t' gentleman, Master Leon." Her tone was conciliatory.

She had forgotten to shade her face, and Carrington saw that it was thin and shrewd and furtive — not at all pleasing.

The boy slouched toward the door. "Well, I'm off, Mrs. Barker." He stared curiously at Carrington. "Want any guiding through the town? I take it you're a stranger."

"Thanks," said Carrington briefly, "I can find my way without a guide." He had taken an instinctive dislike to the youth.

"Master Leon" bestowed on him another curious prolonged stare, at once insolent and suspicious, then swung on his heel and went out, giving the door a vicious bang.

Carrington, more than ever settled in the conviction which had sent him to this house, addressed Mrs. Barker with sternness, saying he had reason to know that the man he sought was amongst her lodgers and that if she wished to avoid trouble with the police, she would see that he had opportunity to speak with him.

The mention of the police served to quicken Mrs. Barker's wits and make her complaisant. She admitted that one of her lodgers resembled the person Carrington had described to her, but his name was Mr. Lucius. She thought that Mr. Lucius was out now, but she would go up to his room and make certain. She left the candle on a corner table and mounted a steep flight of stairs to a dimly lit upper hall.

Carrington had just decided that it would be best to follow her up to Mr. Lucius' room in case she should lie about his presence there when he heard someone come up the doorsteps and insert a key in the lock. He felt a thrill of expectation. This might be Helton himself. It certainly was a lodger since he was provided with a key. Carrington, not wishing the sight of him to alarm Helton into flight as had happened at the tower on the cliffs, drew back into a dark corner of the hall. He kept his eyes fastened on the door which, with a single turn of the key, swung open as though the newcomer was accustomed to unlocking it.

The door closed softly and a man in a silk hat and evening clothes stood in the hall. The candlelight shone full on his face. Carrington with difficulty repressed an exclamation of astonishment.

The "lodger" was Max!

25

"MISS MERTON"

Max, not observing Carrington in the dark corner of the hall, immediately ascended the stairs. He did not, however, run up with his usual light, boyish step, but went up slowly and deliberately. His expression, too, unlike its wont, was neither careless nor carefree, on the contrary it was resolute and a little grim. For the first time Carrington noted a resemblance between Max and Miss Flynn.

Max mounted the first flight of stairs, and Carrington heard him ascending a second with quickened step. Some instinct stronger than idle curiosity impelled Carrington to follow the moment those footsteps were no longer audible. It was not without purpose that Max was provided with a key to the lodging-house where Bartholomew Helton was presumably staying, and Carrington intended to find out if this had to do with the murder in which public opinion implicated Susanna. He was just mounting the second flight of stairs when he heard a woman's steps coming along the hall below. Supposing this to be Mrs. Barker returning from "Mr. Lucius" room and not wishing to be discovered prowling through her house he leaped up the remaining stairs and found himself in a dimly lit hall, the four doors leading from which were tightly closed. Which door had Max entered?

There was no means of telling, no sliver of light under any threshold, no sound of voices. Carrington had practically no detective instincts and so was at a loss what to do. Finally a straightforward, but unsleuthlike idea occurred to him. He approached the nearest door and knocked on it authoritatively. A startled movement within warned him that someone was there.

He grasped the handle of the door; it turned, and he stepped into a room shadowy with the first rays of the moon.

At his sudden entrance an indistinct figure blotted against the side wall, rose hastily to its feet and resolved itself into a slim woman's form.

"I beg your pardon," began Carrington in some embarrassment, "but I was looking for — "

"Hush! Please lower your voice," entreated the young woman — he judged from her slenderness that she was young — in an eager whisper and down she went on her knees again, apparently listening at the wall.

Carrington stood in the silence of amazement, looking down at her and perplexedly twirling his monocle. Suddenly a light flashed along, or rather through the wall, illuminating the delicate features of the young woman crouched against it and showing above her a curtain of heavy, dark plush which she was holding back with one slim hand. Carrington moved closer. He saw then that the light came from the next room through a small hole cut in the wall.

"I say," he began again.

The young woman with an impatient gesture checked him and letting the curtain fall into place, and in this way shutting out the light, rose once more to her feet.

"Don't you understand," she demanded in an angry whisper, "that if you talk you can be heard in the next room?"

Carrington understood that something was going on in that next room which it might behoove him to know about so, rather unceremoniously drawing the young woman aside, he pulled the curtain back and crouched down by the wall in his turn. At first he could make out nothing save a round hole of light, partially obscured by the legs of some piece of furniture, but finally by twisting his head about and closing one eye, he contrived to see a section of the interior of a typical lodging-house room. By the mantel, stood Max reading a note, an exasperated smile on his lips. As far as Carrington could see he was alone in the room.

Max crumpled up the note impatiently, thrust it into the flame of a lamp, then stamped it under foot until only black wisps remained. Then he blew out the lamp and crossed to the door.

Carrington got up and he, too, crossed to the door, resolved to accost Max in the hall, though he had no idea what he was to say to him.

The young woman laid a restraining hand on Carrington's arm. "Please wait a moment. Let him at least get by the door. Since you forced yourself into my room — I'm sure I don't know why — you might show me a little consideration and not walk out of it in the very face of another gentleman."

Carrington stopped short. "I beg your pardon," he muttered awkwardly.

Then it seemed to him that the young woman stifled a little mocking laugh. She struck a match and lit a candle, and he gazed into a pair of large brown eyes, in which mirth struggled with a proper demureness.

His mouth hardened, and he put up his monocle. "I should like to know the reason for your extraordinary interest in the gentleman who has gone out from the next room."

"Most women find Mr. Maxwell Flynn extraordinarily interesting, do they not?" she parried.

Her amused expression irritated Carrington and her ingenuousness he set down as mockery. "You know Mr. Flynn?"

She shrugged lightly. "As well as most people do, I fancy." She picked up a little flower-trimmed hat from a chair and began to pin it on hastily. "I don't think I need detain you any longer. Mr. Flynn must have reached the ground floor by now."

"You mean to follow him?" Carrington demanded with directness.

She smiled. "Perhaps. Do you?"

Carrington flushed. "Mr. Flynn is a friend of mine."

"And to me," she said coolly, locking the door as they stepped into the hall, "he is an interesting study. I think we are justified in following him, Lord Carrington. Oh yes, I know your name," observing his start of surprise. "I believe everybody in the Bay Town knows by sight the guests at Rose Gardens."

Mrs. Barker confronted them in the lower hall. She seemed rather apprehensive. "Ah thought yo mun ha gone, sur. Ah've been oop to Mr. Lucius' room, he's not in. Ah'd noa notion yo knew Miss Merton, sur," glancing suspiciously from him to the young woman by his side.

"We're old acquaintances, Mrs. Barker," Miss Merton spoke up readily.

She opened the outer door and preceded Carrington down the steps. Mrs. Barker closed the door sharply after them. As Carrington had feared, Max had lost himself from their sight in the labyrinth of passages and little alleys intersecting the narrow street. Miss Merton, however, wasted no time in indecision but turned at once into a little court which looked like a cul-de-sac, but instead terminated in a hidden flight of steps leading down to another passage, similarly provided with a series of steps. This second flight descended directly upon a narrow stone pathway running alongside the seawall. Here the waters were beating angrily against the bastion. The moon, stretching a band of silver across the sea, disclosed a flat-bottomed rowboat tossing at anchor near the wall. At the further end of the miniature embankment Carrington made out the figures of a man and girl walking slowly in the opposite direction.

"Your friend, Mr. Flynn," said Miss Merton softly. "Whenever he visits the Bay Town of an evening, he walks on this little esplanade. He must be a lover of the sea, is he not, Lord Carrington?"

Carrington ignored the question, put in a quizzical, half mocking tone, and advanced with rapid and determined pace toward those two distant figures. The sight of that girlish form in fluttering white aroused a suspicion that grew into certainty as he came nearer. Miss Merton made no effort this time to restrain him, instead she tripped along by his side, a curious smile on her lips and a tense, eager look in her eyes which made them very dark and brilliant. Most men would have pronounced her an exceedingly attractive young woman and would have felt a thrill of adventure in their unconventional meeting and her cool appropriation of him as an "old acquaintance" but Carrington, singularly insusceptible to all women save one and, in this instance, moreover, intent on fathoming the reason for Max's mysterious actions, failed to be impressed in any way by Miss Merton.

Max, at the sound of their approach, whirled about with a rapidity which proved the state of his nerves.

"Thomas!" he cried in angry dismay.

Max shrugged indifferently. "My dear child, do as you think best. I don't know that I'm qualified to advise you. Mrs. Barker's doesn't appear to be a particularly secure hiding-place — if you want to hide."

Nora seemed both perplexed and hurt by his offhand answer and cool manner. Then after a moment she threw up her head with a defiant little gesture.

"I'm tired of hiding. I will go back to Rose Gardens, Lord Carrington, and Gupta Singh can ask me questions if he chooses."

"Now it's a brave little Lotus-Flower," said Max in a caressing voice. "You have been foolish, haven't you, child, to run away and hide just for a caprice, a fancy?" There was a smile of tender amusement on his lips.

Nora's defiance suddenly melted. Her eyes filled with tears. "Have I been so — so very foolish?"

Max laughed softly and pinched her cheek. "You wouldn't like me to say so, now would you?"

Nora gave him a smile of tremulous content, her brief resentment gone. Max's power to change her mood at will had never been more obvious. The adoration in the dark eyes of the young East Indian girl angered Carrington. He felt that Max merited no woman's worship.

"We had better be getting back to Rose Gardens," he remarked curtly.

To his surprise Nora hung back. "I do not want to go tonight after all — perhaps tomorrow — "

"Now, little girl," said Carrington in a gentler tone, "the thing for you to do — the right thing — is to come along. Nobody is going to scold you. Miss Flynn will be relieved to see you and — and if you need a friend — there's Lady Susanna. She would be a jolly good friend too."

Nora, however, was not to be persuaded. Max said nothing at all, but stood watching her with his smile of tender mockery, which Carrington somehow felt had more influence over her than any words of his.

"Look here, Nora," Carrington exclaimed at length, "I have half a mind to take you back by force. You shouldn't stay at that lodging-house, you know."

Nora seemed to be waiting for advice from Max. Receiving none, she drew herself straighter.

"Perhaps I will go back to Rose Gardens tomorrow, Lord Carrington, if you will come for me and — and I think I should like Lady Susanna to come, too."

"Why not make it a family gathering," laughed Max, "and let me come, too?"

Nora turned to him eagerly. "Would you come, Mr. Flynn?"

He pinched her cheek again. "Of course, if my respected aunt allows me to after she hears of my share in your running away, you foolish child. She will have more questions to ask me than Gupta Singh could find to put to you."

At mention of the East Indian, Nora shivered. "If I do come back, Lord Carrington will he have to know?"

Carrington patted her arm reassuringly. "Now don't you worry about that old chap. He won't be allowed to bother you."

Carrington and Max accompanied Nora to the door of Mrs. Barker's lodging-house. Carrington did not ask again for 'Mr. Lucius.' He preferred to do so when Max wasn't there.

Nora promised that she would be ready to return to Rose Gardens the next morning. "And you will come for me, too, Mr. Flynn?" her eyes searching his wistfully.

"Oh, I shouldn't wonder," he answered with a laugh. "Goodnight, little Lotus-Flower."

For some reason Carrington felt vaguely uneasy as the door closed behind Nora. He did not like the idea of her spending another night in Mrs. Barker's lodging-house. But what could he do? He could hardly take her away by force. In silence he and Max made their way up the queer old streets darkened by the weird shadows of the tall, narrow houses guiltily crouched one against the other. Still in silence they went on to the mailbox and climbed into the waiting horse-drawn carriage. Carrington could not bring himself to speak, and Max was strangely disinclined for conversation.

Finally, however, Max could stand the strain no longer. "I say, old man," he began persuasively, "I know you think me an awful rotter but — I give you my word — I haven't harmed the little Lotus-Flower. I promised Susanna I'd play the deaf adder and — well; I have my virtuous moments."

Carrington surveyed him gravely. "If I thought you had harmed that little girl I should not be riding with you now. But all the same you have treated her caddishly. You have stolen her love to suit some purpose of your own, and I don't think it is wholly to gratify your pride of conquest. Max, you know more than you should about Rajan Mohan's death. Is Nora shielding you?"

Max's face showed a whiteness not due altogether to the paling light of the moon. "Thanks for your opinion of me, Tom," his voice hard, "but you are wrong. I did not kill Rajan Mohan."

"You know more about his death than you have told. Max, it is your duty to speak — for Susanna's sake. Do you know what the papers are saying of her? They practically call her guilty."

"It is an infernal shame!" declared Max with genuine indignation. "But honestly, Tom, if I were to say any more than I did at the inquest it would put Susanna in a worse mess than she is in now."

"What do you mean?" Carrington scarcely knew his own voice.

"Hang it all! Old man, don't you know I'd give my eyes for Susanna? But I tell you there is nothing to be said nothing to be done. She hasn't been indicted, and the thing will gradually blow over. You'll have to let it go at that."

"No," said Carrington determinately, "it will not go at that. I am going to put the best private detective in London on the case."

Max drew a prolonged whistle. "The heck you are!"

26

DOUBTS AND SUSPICIONS

Upon their arrival at Rose Gardens, Carrington handed the newspapers to Miss Flynn and warded off her rebuke for his delay in returning by giving a brief and rather incoherent account of his meeting with Nora. He left to Max all explanations of the latter's share in her disappearance and went off by himself for a quiet smoke and reflection. Susanna, he learned, had gone to bed with a headache.

He, too, felt anything but fit. Max's statement that, were he to add to his testimony at the inquest, Susanna would be further implicated, made him sick at heart. For all his increasing distrust of Max, he felt that in this instance he had spoken the truth. Yet Carrington did not for a moment believe in Susanna's guilt, he was convinced that she was the victim of circumstantial evidence from which she could not or would not extricate herself. But how was he to prove this to the world? He determined that he would make another attempt tomorrow, perhaps when he went for Nora, to speak with Mrs. Barker's lodger, 'Mr. Lucius.' Failing this, he would communicate his suspicions to Rathbone the detective.

But just what were his suspicions? Why simply that 'Mr. Lucius' was Bartholomew Helton, Susanna's divorced husband and possibly the Crimson Knight also. Still, granting that these hypotheses were true, it would not go far toward clearing Susanna. It had been brought out fairly conclusively at the inquest that the only costumed Knight who had been in the house on the night of the masked ball was Max. Although it had been suggested — and Carrington himself believed it was so — that the real Knight had been hanging about the grounds, it had by no means been proved. However, it seemed to him, since he refused to credit Susanna's guilt in spite of the cumulative evidence against her, that one of these two men in Knight dress was the murderer. The question was which one?

He doubted Rathbone's ability to handle the case alone, and he intended to send a telegram early in the morning to a private detective in London, a young woman professionally known as Pamela Wainwright. This young woman had established a reputation as a solver of apparently unsolvable mysteries and had distinguished herself especially in that recent affair involving a prominent aristocratic family and a priceless necklace. Carrington turned toward the library to see if there were any telegram blanks there. The door was closed and, upon opening it he was surprised to see Miriam, usually the most illiterate of people, seated near the bookshelves, intensely absorbed and bent over a ponderous tome and making pencil notes as she read. She started somewhat guiltily as he entered and hastily closed the book.

"I am trying hard to amuse myself, Tom," she said, affecting a little yawn. "Everybody has run away and left me."

He looked curiously at the morocco-bound volume over the title of which her tiny, ringed hands were clasped. "What were you reading, Mimi?"

"Oh, some stupid old thing not worth the printing."

He went up to her and before she could realize what he was doing, he had taken the volume from her lap.

"Cryptography — Ancient and Modern," he read in a queer voice. "I didn't know you were interested in cipher-writing, Mimi."

She tucked the paper of pencil notes in the bosom of her dress. "But I'm not in the least interested," with another little yawn. "I took that book down at random. The cover rather attracted me — but it is hopelessly stupid. Put it back for me, Tom, there's a dear boy."

He pushed the volume into the only empty space in the mahogany bookcase — between two equally heavy tomes on the upper shelf and was obliged to stretch his tall body to reach it.

He glanced down oddly at Miss Cramer's petite form. "You go to no end of trouble to take down a book at random, Mimi. How the heck did you ever reach it?"

"What does it matter?" petulantly. "You seem to be immensely interested in that book."

He screwed in his eye-glass and studied the other titles on that shelf. "Funny thing," he commented dryly, "all the books on this shelf are about cryptography. Have you taken down any others 'at random,' Mimi?"

Miriam paled — she always did when angry — and her eyes took on that hard light which they had held at the inquest. "I do not understand your questions. Is it a crime for one to touch a book in this library? What makes you so disagreeable to me all the time?"

Carrington surveyed her reflectively. "I don't mean to be disagreeable to you, Mimi, but frankly, I think you're behaving cattily to Susanna. What made you tell all that rot at the inquest about her quarreling with Rajan Mohan?"

"Because I was asked — and because it was the truth."

Carrington lost his temper. "By Jove! You took precious good care to put as black an interpretation on it as possible."

Miriam rose deliberately. "Oh, I don't know about that. I might have told more — a great deal more. As it happened, I didn't walk away immediately from the window."

"I never supposed you did." Carrington spoke with unwonted roughness. "But whatever else you saw couldn't have been prejudicial to Susanna or you would have told it."

"I wouldn't be too sure of that, Tom," Miriam's tone cut like a lash. "Why don't you ask her all that happened?"

Carrington felt suddenly helpless before Miriam's innuendos. "She wouldn't tell me," he muttered.

"Exactly, she wouldn't tell you. Then I think that is all that need be said." Miriam moved to the door, carrying her small figure with an aggressive dignity. "Goodnight, Tom. I trust you will feel better natured in the morning."

For an instant Carrington stood rigid, then he strode to the door. "Miriam! I say, Miriam!" he called sharply.

On the threshold he almost collided with a young male person who showed a desire to run at sight of him. But Carrington held his arm in a grip that could not be shaken off.

"By George!" he said slowly, "what the heck are you doing here?"

His captive's pasty white face wore a sullen look. "Lemme go! You hurt. I'm doing no harm."

"Whom did you come here to see, eh?" Carrington did not relax his grasp on the youth's arm.

"Master Leon's" shifty, brownish eyes for a moment looked impudently into his. "Not to see you, guv'nor, that's sure."

"What seems to be the trouble, Tom?" a rather excited voice from the great hall suddenly demanded.

Carrington glanced surprised at Susanna who was coming toward them. He had supposed her to be in bed long since, nursing a headache. She still however, wore her dinner frock.

"I say," burst out Leon, "you tell him to let go of me."

"Tom, let him go." There was an anxious little pucker on Susanna's forehead. "He isn't here to do any harm."

Carrington reluctantly loosed the boy's arm. "You know this — this chap?"

"He has been here before," she evaded, "with messages."

"To you?" Carrington asked with his usual directness.

"Oh, cut the questions!" said Leon airily. "I've got a right to be in this house if I choose."

He slipped past Carrington into the library and went out through the open terrace door.

"Susanna," said Carrington gravely, "I wish you would be frank with me — perhaps I could help you. I could try anyway. What kind of a mess have you gotten yourself into?"

Susanna smiled drearily. "It's a shocking mess, Tom, and the worst of it is there is no way out."

"But old girl, there must be — There will be. If you will only tell all that happened in the library that night — "

"I will never do that, Tom. I couldn't." Susanna spoke in a tone of finality.

"But it is your duty to yourself. Have you seen the papers? — what they are saying?"

She shook her head. "I don't want to see them. I can guess what they are saying."

"Now look here, Susanna, I've figured this all out. You're shielding somebody, that's what you are doing. And Bartholomew Helton is mixed up in this, now isn't he?"

The suddenness of this thrust left her speechless for a moment. Then she said with a little laugh, "What an absurd idea, Tom! Don't you know that Bartholomew Helton is in Australia?"

Carrington's jaw set obstinately. "I know he is supposed to be in Australia, but I have seen him here in Yorkshire at least twice. He was the man you went to meet in that tower, Susanna, and I've a jolly strong suspicion, too, that he is that very Knightly chap Inspector Rathbone would give a good deal to lay his hands on."

Susanna paled slightly. "What you say is too absurd, Tom. But please don't say it to any one else. It — it might be believed."

"It would be," he declared with conviction.

"Then please, please don't suggest such things," she laid an appealing hand on his arm.

"You are shielding Helton then?" His voice was hard.

"I cannot have Bartholomew accused!" she fenced. There was agony in her eyes.

Carrington shook off her hand. "Susanna, you don't still — you can't — love that — that cad?"

"Love Bartholomew Helton?" The bitterness in her tone was extreme. She looked at Carrington almost with exasperation, then the sight of his troubled face caused hers to break into a smile of tender humor. "You dear, foolish — foolish boy!"

With a little choking laugh that sounded like a sob she hurried down the corridor toward the servants' hall. Carrington stared after her in a kind of hopeful bewilderment. Could she mean — Then his heart suddenly sank.

Susanna had entered Mrs. MacDonald's room. Why was she mixed up with this woman of mystery whom many believed to be implicated in Sir Robert Williamson's death, and whose position before and after' that event was, to say the least, anomalous? It was all right to be kind to Mrs. MacDonald, of course she was to be pitied, but Susanna was something more than kind, she clearly had some understanding with the housekeeper. And the housekeeper clearly had an understanding with the East Indian butler. Now Carrington was certain that no good could come of anything in which an East Indian was concerned — it did not occur to him that he might be prejudiced — and the fact that Susanna had gone into Edna MacDonald's room where she might be drawn into even a worse mess than she already was involved in made him resolve to send off a telegram immediately to Pamela Wainwright.

Susanna might consider herself under obligation, through some mistaken sense of duty, to shield Bartholomew Helton, but he did not feel himself obliged to support her in this ridiculous notion. It was like Helton to skulk behind a woman's skirts and it was equally like Susanna to permit him to do so. She had said at the time when his misconducts had at last driven her to seek relief in divorce that she felt herself a deserter. Well, however she felt about it, she should not be permitted to sacrifice herself further for the worthless fellow who had taken the first bloom off her life.

Miss Flynn, to whom Carrington applied for a telegram blank, expressed approval of his resolve to send for Pamela Wainwright.

"I have no personal experience of women as detectives," she said, "and it seems to me a very unusual pursuit for them to engage in. However, it's a fad for women to do very unusual things nowadays, and I hear that this particular one is highly successful in her profession. Of course she is quick and intuitive. You men for the most part are slow-witted."

"Shouldn't wonder but we are," Carrington admitted good-naturedly, "still we are useful at times — as escorts to country houses — if nothing more, eh,

Miss Flynn?"

His hostess did not smile. "I may as well confess that I have not passed one enjoyable hour here."

"It's a jolly shame," declared Carrington sympathetically, "that East Indian chap's being killed here, the notoriety and all."

"It isn't that. It is Max. Carrington, I am beginning to — to distrust Max."

"Oh, but that's — that's silly of you, Miss Flynn."

"No, it is not. You distrust him yourself Carrington, if I really believed that Max was concerned, even indirectly, in Rajan Mohan's death I — " Her firm voice broke. "He is my brother's child, my heir," she finished unsteadily.

Carrington of a sudden became tremendously busy with his cigarette-case. "Perhaps — ah — perhaps it will not be necessary to send for Miss Wainwright. Rathbone may be slow but I dare say he will plod along very well by himself."

"No, I wish you to send for Pamela Wainwright." Miss Flynn straightened and settled her glasses decisively. "Whatever comes of her investigations, I want an end to doubt — I want the truth. Let me know as soon as you receive an answer to that telegram. And, Carrington," she turned as she was about to ascend the stairs, "I want you to drive over to the Bay Town tomorrow and bring back that East Indian child. Tell her I will not scold her — I have scolded Max instead. He had no business to look up lodgings for her even if she did ask him to. He knows what I think of his conduct."

"Oh, I dare say Max meant it for a kindness," said Carrington, trying to be consoling.

Miss Flynn came a step nearer. Her face looked older and sharper. Her tightly combed red hair, graying at the temples, seemed to him to show more silver threads.

"Carrington," her tone was almost imploring, "has it ever occurred to you that Max might have persuaded Nora to run away so that she could not be called on to testify at the inquest?"

It had occurred to him, but he hastened to assure Miss Flynn that it had not.

"Why, she was afraid of that old graybeard, that's why she ran away. It is my belief he was the one who sent her those bullets of salt. They had some meaning, you know."

"Max," said Miss Flynn harshly, "also received a bullet of salt."

Carrington's jaw dropped. "That's — that's a fact," he admitted helplessly.

$$27$$

IN SIR ROBERT'S CHAMBER

It was well past midnight when Carrington, after sending a telegram to Pamela Wainwright, went up to his room. On the way he was obliged to pass the door of the chamber which he understood had been Sir Robert Williamson's. This door had always, so far as he had noticed, been closed and presumably locked. The reason why had never interested him. If the housekeeper chose to have the chamber of her late master remain closed against intrusion, it surely was no concern of his and he was about to pass by with his usual indifference when a vague sound from within — Or was it imagination? — caught his ear.

He stopped and listened, even his phlegmatic temperament a little stirred as he waited there in the dark corridor, whose lights had long since been extinguished, for the repetition of an indistinct sound which suggested more than anything else the furtive scraping of wood on wood. But the noise was not repeated, on the contrary, the silence was so intense as to seem unnatural, strained, as though someone else were listening, and listening breathlessly, until his footsteps should continue down the hall. As Carrington stared in doubt at the door, he fancied he could detect under the threshold a pale, very pale sliver of light as from a shaded lamp. At all events the outline of this particular doorway was certainly less obscure than that of its neighbors. And now he did hear another sound from within — a cautious step, someone was in the room — someone who did not want his presence known.

Carrington laid his hand on the yielding knob. At the same instant the outlines of the door faded, became blurred into the dark walls of the corridor.

The light had been put out! Carrington stopped only long enough to ascertain that he was well provided with matches, then he made a rather melodramatic plunge into an absolutely dark chamber whose musty odor proclaimed the fact that it was a place of disuse and avoidance. He could make out nothing in the darkness, but he knew that person of the cautious step was hiding somewhere in the shadows engulfing the room and might even elude him if he were not careful. Consequently, with little regard for quiet, he closed the door and stood with his back against it. Then he struck a match.

In its flickering glare there loomed up heavy old furniture and a high, canopied bed behind which, half-concealed by its curtains, lurked an odd-looking figure at sight of whom a Yorkshire peasant would, no doubt, have fallen to muttering prayers.

Carrington merely struck another match. It illuminated the plumed hat, and the ribbon festooned suit of the person behind the bed and revealed the domino across his features.

"It's about time, Captain Helton, to unmask, isn't it, eh?" asked Carrington sternly.

Just then his second match blackened and crumpled to the floor. Before he could strike a third, the Knight had sprung upon him and was trying to throw him back from the door. Carrington, though taken by surprise, held his ground and, with a well-directed blow, reminiscent of his Oxford days, drove his assailant half across the room, where he stumbled against a chest of drawers and sprawled his length. Before he could pick himself up, Carrington was upon him, holding him down by the weight of his own body and warding off his counter-swings with one hand while with the other he tore off the Knight's mask.

"The game is up, Helton, time to show your face."

In spite of the Knight's struggles, Carrington succeeds in striking another match.

"By — by Jove!" He rose slowly to his feet, not heeding the match that stung his Angers.

The Knight got up painfully. "Confound you! Tom. You hit out like a prize-fighter."

"I should be glad of some explanation," said Carrington severely.

He went over to the fireplace and lit one of the tall candles which he had glimpsed on the mantel. The darkness was intolerable.

Max met his accusing eyes with an easy smile. "Fooled again, old man! You never could tell me from the real Knight."

Carrington's face held a hard contempt. "I think that very few people have been able to distinguish you from the other."

Max's answering laugh was not entirely pleasant. "Never blessed with any saving sense of humor, were you, Tom? By George! Old chap, if you could have seen the way you pounced into this room and then set about pommeling me — "

"I asked you," interrupted Carrington sternly, "for an explanation of your being in this room in such a costume."

"Perfectly proper costume, Tom," Max's tone was mocking. "Can't you see, old child, I was trying to have a little fun? — was going to walk into Aunt Ell's room and give Aeronwen a few thrills. Instead, I thrilled you, eh?"

"What were you doing in this room?" repeated Carrington uncompromisingly.

Max suddenly lost his air of good-humored raillery. His whole countenance hardened.

"Who the devil gave you the right to cross-examine me? I came into this room because I chose, and that's all you'll get for your confounded curiosity."

"I shouldn't advise you," returned Carrington in a cold, steady voice, "to wear that costume again either in this room or anywhere else. I don't fancy that Inspector Rathbone's sense of humor is much stronger than mine and he might mistake you for that Knight who came out of the library shortly before Rajan Mohan's murder was discovered."

It seemed to Carrington that a grayish color came over Max's features. "You mean the real Knight?" he asked somewhat thickly.

"I have been wondering," Carrington answered with deliberation, "if that man was 'the real Knight.'"

Max again lost his habitual self-control. "Why — Why, confound you! Are you daring to accuse me? — "

"It is not my place to accuse you." Carrington turned on his heel.

Max caught him by the arm. He had forced a persuasive smile to his lips. "Hang it all! Old top, we mustn't quarrel. We have been friends too long."

"I don't want to quarrel with you, Max." Carrington's voice was gentler. He could not forget that he had once given to Max the love that he would have given a younger brother had he possessed one. "But honestly, I don't like a host of things you have been doing lately."

"Oh, I say, I'm not as bad as you think me. You might at least give me the benefit of the doubt; you do — Susanna."

Max spoke with a whimsical boyishness which Carrington had never been proof against. He began to be half ashamed of his suspicions.

"I dare say I'm — I'm rather of an ass."

Max gave him an affectionate clap on the shoulder. "That's what you are — a regular old idiot! But I'm uncommon fond of you even if you did try to batter me into jelly. Oh, by the way, Tom, what did you mean by hailing me as 'Capt. Helton'?"

Carrington felt that it was impossible to explain this to Max. "Oh, I — I don't — know," he said lamely.

"You think Bartholomew Helton is mixed up in all this, Tom?"

"I don't know anything about Bartholomew Helton. He is supposed to be in Australia."

Max gave a short laugh. "Oh, all right," he said carelessly, "be mysterious if you like. I'm off to bed. Think I'll get out of this costume. Your pommeling has rather taken away my enthusiasm for thrilling poor Aeronwen. Whiff out the candle, old man."

Max strolled toward the door. Carrington, still full of misgivings as to Max's garb and his presence in this disused room, was about to blow out the candle when the door was opened suddenly from the hall. Max started to dodge back behind the curtains of the bed, but it was too late.

There was a little cry, quickly suppressed, in a woman's voice, and Edna MacDonald, dressed as for motoring, stepped swiftly into the chamber and closed the door.

"So it was partly a trick to get me away," she began angrily. "It wasn't enough for you to share — "

Then for the first time, she saw Carrington standing by the mantel. She checked herself in consternation and the slight flush which anger had brought to her face faded, leaving it more colorless than ever. Max was standing with his back persistently turned toward her. His attitude seemed to make her distrustful. She glanced suspiciously from him to Carrington. Then she went rapidly up to Max and forced him to look at her.

"Mr. Flynn!"

"Whom did you expect it was, Mrs. MacDonald?" demanded Carrington sternly.

She cringed under his gaze. Her bronze-colored eyes were imploring. Her lips moved, but she said nothing.

Max smiled mockingly. "Took me for the real Knight, did you, Mrs. MacDonald?"

His insinuating words, the hard raillery in his eyes seemed to infuriate her. Carrington saw again something of the tigress in her.

"I took you, Mr. Flynn, for a thief. I still take you for one."

Max said something under his breath. There was a shade of fear on his face, though his smile remained. "I suppose the charitable conclusion would be that you have allowed your nerves to run away with you."

He turned toward the door, but Mrs. MacDonald stepped in front of him and barred his way. "I wish to know why you came into this room."

Her agitation had the effect of restoring his usual assurance. "Suppose I ask you the same question?"

Again his words stung her beyond control. "I will take this matter to the police, Mr. Flynn."

Max surveyed her with an expression of quizzical amusement "I don't think you'll go to the police, Mrs. MacDonald."

Mrs. MacDonald could not sustain his gaze. She shivered and drew back.

Max's smile broadened. With a shrug he swung on his heel and sauntered to the door.

"I'll not keep you talking longer, Mrs. MacDonald. You must be tired after your drive."

Edna MacDonald looked after him fearfully. Carrington felt awkward and out of place.

"Hadn't you better turn in?" he suggested finally. "Of course you are tired."

"Lord Carrington," she said with emphasis, "I have not been motoring tonight. I could not sleep — thinking of the inquest and all — so I went out on the cliffs to walk. The wind was so strong that I wore a hat and veil. Mr. Flynn was mistaken."

Carrington had little faith in her explanation, but he had not the heart to call it into question. She seemed to be almost dropping from nerve exhaustion, so he simply suggested again that she go to her chamber and try to sleep.

"Lord Carrington," she asked with searching intentness, "why did you come into this room?"

Because it appeared the best thing to do, he told her the truth, that he had heard sounds which had made him suspect someone was in this disused chamber.

"What sort of sounds?" she urged, nervously.

"Why— er — footsteps."

"No other sounds? You are quite sure?"

"It is difficult to distinguish sounds at night," he evaded. "It was the footsteps that made me come in.

She gave a sigh of despair. "Of course you will not tell me — Mr. Flynn is your friend.”

She stepped into the corridor and Carrington followed. She then closed and locked the door with one of a bunch of keys which she took from a small handbag.

Carrington watched her curiously. “Does Miss Flynn desire this room to be locked?”

“I do not know what Miss Flynn desires.” There was hostility in Mrs. MacDonald’s voice. “But this was Sir Robert Williamson’s room, he would not wish people poking about in it, he did not allow even the servants to enter.”

She turned abruptly as though to avoid further discussion and hurried down the corridor.

Carrington went on to his own chamber. A subdued purring sound outside drew him to the window. There he saw a long, low automobile gliding almost noiselessly away from the house. Apparently Mrs. MacDonald had returned from a drive, after all. It was now sufficiently near dawn for him to make out the figure of the chauffeur, and there was something in the youthfulness of his appearance and the rakish tilt of his cap which suggested “Master Leon.”

28

THE CRIMSON KNIGHT UNMASKED

The next morning Carrington and Susanna drove over to the Bay Town to bring Nora home. Max, despite his half promise to the young East Indian girl, did not accompany them. Instead, he went for a ramble over the moors with Miriam.

Carrington had purposely refrained from telling Susanna to which house they were going and when he would have led her up the doorsteps, she drew back, startled.

"Tom," with direct reproach, "I did not suppose you would try to lay a trap for me. Of course I do not need to tell you that I should not have come here had I not supposed it was to see Nora."

Carrington flushed uncomfortably under her pained look, but the consciousness of the integrity of his motives gave firmness to his voice as he answered:

"I won't deny that I am trying to pry into your affairs, but I think you know why I am doing this, and it is the truth that Nora is in this house and wanted you to come with me."

"Tom," Susanna's voice was low and decided, "If Bartholomew Helton is accused of Rajan Mohan's murder, I will stand with him. He is not more guilty than I am."

"Susanna!"

"I mean it, Tom, Now let us go in to Nora."

It seemed to Carrington that Mrs. Barker's appearance was more unprepossessing than ever. He fancied, too, that she looked at Susanna with a glint of recognition in her furtive eyes. This time she was not inhospitable and her manner was unctuously propitiating.

The young lady he asked for was to be found in her room, she never went out in the daytime.

Would he and the lady like to go upstairs at once?

Carrington signified that they would. On the first landing he intercepted a glance of understanding between Mrs. Barker and Susanna. A feeling of deadness weighed upon him. He could not understand Susanna nor her quixotic devotion — if it were no more — to Bartholomew Helton. As they passed Miss Merton's door, he saw that it was tightly closed and he wondered if when she heard voices in Nora's room, she would gratify her curiosity by peering through the peep-hole in the wall.

Several knocks, increasingly vigorous, on Nora's door eliciting no response, Mrs. Barker shook the handle which turned readily. The room presented an appearance of disorder and confusion which Carrington had not observed the evening before when he had looked into it through Miss Merton's point of vantage. A couple of chairs were overturned, a small glass jar lay broken on the floor, its shattered bits of crystal sending forth a peculiar, heavy fragrance as of exotic flowers, a little white slipper stood nearby, its mate not visible, and the coverlets of the bed were tossed back as though its occupant had sprung from it in haste. Of Nora herself there was no sign.

"T' yoong laady mun ha' gone out, aafter arl," suggested Mrs. Baker, her eyes meeting no one's.

"Without dressing herself, with nothing over her night clothes?" Susanna pointed to a neat little pile of lingerie on a chair in the corner and to a thin white frock, limp and rain-soiled, hanging from a peg on the wall.

"She mun ha' had other clothes," volunteered Mrs. Barker.

Susanna dismissed the suggestion with impatience. "I believe the poor child has been forcibly taken off in the night. What do you know about this, Mrs.

Barker?"

The landlady cringed under Susanna's accusing gaze and broke out into protestations of her ignorance of the entire matter. The house had been quiet all night, there had been absolutely no sound of disturbance and no one had entered it — of that she was sure, for she slept in a front room on the ground floor — since "t' yoong laady herself had come baack."

At this juncture a violent ringing of the door-bell below afforded Mrs. Barker an excuse for going downstairs and so avoiding further questioning — an excuse of which she immediately availed herself.

"I think," remarked Susanna, "that here is another proof that Nora was forcibly taken off. She would not have left this."

Susanna indicated a photograph of Max, encased in a satin frame and standing erect in solitary state, on the top of the battered old bureau.

"Poor little girl," she said softly, "I am afraid she has been very foolish. Max ought to be ashamed of himself."

The bare little lodging-house room revealed no further clues as to the manner of Nora's disappearance nor her present whereabouts. Once again the young girl had utterly disappeared. Carrington felt that Max this time could not be held responsible, but this fact only increased his apprehensions. Nora, seemingly, had been carried off by force and he could not forget those bullets of salt which appeared to presage some evil threatening her. He had no doubt that she possessed knowledge of her brother's death and it was not unlikely that she had been carried off either to insure her silence or to make her divulge this knowledge. Either supposition seemed equally tenable since Nora admitted that she feared to be questioned by Gupta Singh. If that implacable old chap suspected that she had knowledge which might solve the mystery of the death of his compatriot, the man on whom he had built all his hopes for the glorification of India, he would stop at nothing to make her speak. Carrington had heard of the tortures resorted to by the East Indians in crimes like this. What would one poor little life count for when weighed in the balance against the epoch-making enterprises which stirred the soul of Brahma's servitor?

Before going downstairs Carrington knocked at Miss Merton's door. She ought to know something of Nora's disappearance. But Miss Merton either was not in her room or was unwilling to be questioned. Carrington, after several vain attempts to elicit a response, turned away from the locked door which piqued his interest to the point of irritation. It was then he discovered that Susanna had quietly slipped away without a word of explanation. He hurried down both flights of stairs, hoping to catch a glimpse of her in one of the halls, but he was unsuccessful She had evidently entered one of the closed rooms which must, of course, have been known to her. At that moment he would have given much to be able to hand Bartholomew Helton over to the police.

Mrs. Barker was cowering against the newel-post in the entry-hall answering in frightened monosyllables the questions put to her by a stockily built man in a tweed suit. This individual bore the unmistakable stamp of the police official. Since the commencement of Miss Flynn's house party, Carrington had become unpleasantly familiar with the type. He had no desire to stay longer in this house — if Susanna chose to conceal herself, he would not attempt to find her — so he went toward the outer door.

Mrs. Barker's inquisitor, after a comprehensive glance which included the minutest details of Carrington's appearance, tipped his hat politely and addressed him by name. The notoriety which Carrington had gained as one of the guests at Rose Gardens was highly offensive to him and he returned the official's salutation with scant cordiality.

The detective chose not to take offense. "I saw your lordship come in here. I have a telegram for you. It came in just as I was sending off one myself."

Carrington took the pink envelope held out to him, he turned it over with a frown. "This has been opened."

The detective smiled blandly. "A little official liberty, my lord."

"A piece of confounded impertinence, I call it."

"That's just as you look at it, my lord. To me it's all in the day's work."

Carrington gave a short laugh. "I didn't find much incriminating evidence in it, did you?"

The detective laughed, too. "I wasn't exactly looking for it, my lord — just professional curiosity. But, I say, if you are going to meet the lady — your lordship'll excuse my mentioning it — you'd better be stepping. She's always on time, and she doesn't like to be kept waiting. Rathbone," he added confidentially, "will be hot when he finds out she is going on the case. Jealousy, I call it. Now I," with expansive magnanimity, "don't feel that way about her. She doesn't do bad for a woman. No, by George! She's devilishly smart."

Carrington lost no time in entering the inn opposite, where the telegram from Pamela Wainwright had stated that he would find her at ten o'clock, the hour which was just striking. The inn brought back unpleasant memories of the inquest, and he made his way as quickly as possible to the back parlor, designated by Pamela Wainwright as their meeting place.

In answer to his knock, the door was opened by a young woman, at sight of whom he stood for a moment speechless.

"Miss Merton!" he exclaimed at length.

Her brown eyes were mirthful. "You didn't expect to meet me so soon again, did you, Lord Carrington?"

"I beg your pardon," — he turned to withdraw — "I must have made a mistake in the room. I expected to meet a — another lady — "

"Pamela Wainwright, perhaps?" smiled Miss Walton.

He stared. "My telegram must have become public property."

Miss Merton's look of amusement grew. "Not necessarily — I am Pamela Wainwright."

"You will pardon me, Miss Merton," he said stiffly, "but I am not in the mood, nor have I the time, for joking."

Miss Merton laughed. "You don't believe me, eh? Will this convince you?" She drew from a silver mesh bag the telegram which he had sent the evening before.

In the face of this, he could no longer disbelieve and yet this slim, girlishly pretty young woman with mirthful brown eyes, skin fair as a child's and soft brown hair simply coiled in her neck was not at all his idea of the detective who had already won an enviable name in her chosen profession.

The pseudo "Miss Merton" appeared to find his puzzlement highly diverting. "Am I so very very different from what you expected? Is the disappointment too great to be borne? I am afraid the prying 'Miss Merton' made an unfavorable impression upon you."

"Why, no, not at all — now that I understand. I — I am delighted to — to have met you before."

She laughed again — a low, amused laugh. "Really, you almost make me believe you mean that." She stood a second surveying him.

He remained grave and silent, slowly drawing off his gloves.

"Lord Carrington," the mirth died from her eyes, her tone became crisp and business-like, "you wish to employ me to unravel the mystery at Rose Gardens, and particularly, I understood from your telegram, to clear the name of Lady Susanna Helton in spite of herself."

"That is so," he assented. "I believe that you alone can do this."

"Perhaps," she agreed with a calm confidence that was by no means vanity or arrogance, "but I cannot at present undertake to do this. As a matter of fact, I am already at work on the case; my employer is the East Indian priest, Gupta Singh, and the clearing of Lady Susanna's name is of little importance to him. When a prince of India has been murdered, the Surya's Eye ruby stolen, and a princess abducted, what does the tarnishing of a mere Englishwoman's name matter to him?"

"But," Carrington urged, "have you not discovered anything in your investigations so far which might clear her?"

Pamela Wainwright shook her head. "Ah! No, Lord Carrington, I cannot give away professional secrets. The results of my investigations belong to Gupta Singh and to the proper officials, and that, too, only when I think it wise to make them known."

"But you don't think her guilty as that — that ass of a Rathbone does?"

The detective's brown eyes danced. "You have precisely expressed my opinion of Mr. Rathbone. No! Lord Carrington, I will not say one word more."

She had no opportunity to do so. The door was torn open and a slender, wiry man, his hair windblown, and with the look of a hunted creature plunged into the room. At sight of Pamela Wainwright, he uttered an oath of consternation and made a movement to dart out again.

The detective, however, was too quick for him. She sprang to the door, closed it, and leveled at him the barrel of a tiny revolver, not more than four inches long and mounted with mother-of-pearl.

"Surely you cannot wish to leave us so soon, Capt. Helton?"

The excited voices of men in the room beyond maddened Helton. He looked with desperation at the slim young woman, coolly holding him prisoner, Carrington placed himself by Miss Wainwright's side, her girlish figure accentuating his height and the broadness of his shoulders.

Helton hesitated a second, calculating. Then, ducking his head, he leaped toward the window. The toy revolver flashed fire. Helton, with a scream of pain, threw himself through the closed window, the glass splintering and cutting.

Pamela Wainwright calmly replaced the little revolver in the silver-mesh bag from where she had snatched it. "Capt. Helton will not row very far. His right arm is useless. Ah! Mr. Rathbone" — as that official and two subordinates precipitated themselves into the room — "you are a trifle late, our friend has just gone out through the window."

Rathbone and his two satellites, with a fine disregard for splintered glass, vaulted over the windowsill upon the bastion on which the inn was built.

Pamela Wainwright went swiftly into the hall and thence out onto the bastion. Carrington followed. Some yards beyond the seawall a flat-bottomed, red row-boat was tossing at anchor. Toward it a man was swimming, struggling on with one-two strokes. At that moment Rathbone, throwing off his coat and vest, dove into the water and with long, reaching strokes, began to pursue the one-armed swimmer. His subordinates, shouting encouragement, laid bets on him as the winner.

Carrington felt his arm seized in a convulsive grasp. Turning, he looked into the despairing face of Susanna.

"Tom! That is Bartholomew — Out there in the water. I did my best, but I couldn't save him. Rathbone knew too much. Oh, he — he is going under! He will drown before our eyes!"

Carrington tried to draw her toward the inn. "Come away, Susanna. You can do no good."

She shook her head. "I must see it through. Tom!" — her voice suddenly rising to a scream — "he has capsized the boat — he has gone down — under it!"

Carrington forcibly drew her away now and she submitted like one whose endurance was utterly broken down.

When Rathbone, dripping and panting — as a swimmer he was not in practice — was pulled out of the water by his two subordinates, the red row-boat was drifting out to sea, bottom side up. Of Helton there was no trace.

A half-hour or so later his body was recovered. Efforts at resuscitation proved fruitless, but were maintained, at Susanna's urgency, long after every hope of reviving life had been abandoned. It pained Carrington to observe that she seemed to consider herself in some way responsible for Helton's death.

Rathbone, on the other hand, accepted his responsibility with an exultant air which was decidedly unpleasant.

"I'll confess," he remarked confidentially, "that when I started out some weeks ago to trail the Crimson Knight, I didn't expect to bag so big a game."

Pamela Wainwright regarded him with interest "What do you mean by so big a game, Mr. Rathbone?"

Rathbone expanded under the stimulant of success. He even condescended to become facetious. "Oh, come now, Miss Wainwright, you ain't so blind as you're trying to make out. Didn't I tell you I was working on a double trail?"

"Why yes," she assented, "but I understood you to say that there was a petticoat at one end of this double trail."

Carrington listened apprehensively. He was glad that Susanna had gone from the room.

Rathbone's manner became increasingly pompous and assured. "Now I don't give away the inner workings of a case any more than you do, Miss Wainwright. When I said there was a petticoat at one end of the trail, I meant a little more than that. The petticoat was shielding someone. Begin to see a little glimmer of light, eh?"

Pamela Wainwright regarded him with a curious smile. "No, Mr. Rathbone, I am still hopelessly in the dark."

The look Rathbone gave her was almost pitying. "Well, I'm hanged! Miss Wainwright, I gave you credit for at least being able to put two and two together."

"Yes?" her voice was dangerously sweet, "and what do yon make of two plus two, Mr. Rathbone?"

Rathbone scowled. He had learned to distrust that tone of voice. "What's the use of beating about the bush? Scotland Yard has come out on top — as it always will in the long run. While you've been eliminating suspects, I've run down my suspect and bagged two birds in one."

"What two birds, Mr. Rathbone?"

His scowl deepened under her mocking eyes. "Why, confound it all! The Crimson Knight and the murderer of Rajan Mohan. They are one and the same — Helton!"

It was Pamela Wainwright's turn now to look pitying. "My dear Mr. Rathbone, isn't it possible that you have mistaken your vocation? Your conclusions are as far from being correct — "

Rathbone lost his temper. "Anyone must be a silly idiot who can't see that Helton was the Crimson Knight and — "

"Of course, he was the Crimson Knight. Any amateur would have discovered that immediately, but he was no more the murderer of Rajan Mohan than I am."

Rathbone looked positively savage. "If you know so much more than Scotland Yard, perhaps you will be good enough to tell — "

Pamela Wainwright smiled gently. "Like you, Mr. Rathbone, I do not give away the inner workings of a case, but, I assure you, you have still to discover the person or persons who killed Rajan Mohan, stole the Surya's Eye ruby, and the paper in cipher, and abducted the little East Indian Princess."

29

ON THE TRAIL

It was sundown before Carrington and Susanna returned to Rose Gardens. The latter had been harried with questions by the detectives who, under Rathbone's lead, had tried, but vainly, to make her incriminate herself as the confederate of the Knight and the sharer of his spoils. Pamela Wainwright finally rescued her from these inquisitors — they, like Rathbone, were still inclined to believe Helton guilty also of Prince Rajan's death — and requested a seat in the horse-drawn carriage as she wished to make some investigations at Rose Gardens.

During this drive, a sympathetic understanding began to establish itself between Susanna and the detective. Pamela Wainwright did not hector Susanna with questions, but tried to divert her mind by talking entertainingly on general topics. Carrington learned from their conversation that Susanna had met the detective previously in the character of 'Miss Merton'.

As they came within sight of the Rose Gardens, Pamela Wainwright's face became grave.

"I am sorry, very sorry for Miss Flynn," she said musingly, more to herself than to her two companions.

Susanna flashed a peculiar glance at the detective, "Why are you sorry for Miss Flynn?"

Pamela Wainwright bit her lip as though regretting her words. Her voice was emotionless and wholly professional as she answered:

"Because of the notoriety this affair has brought upon her. It is, of course, very distressing."

Miss Flynn received the detective with correct courtesy which, however, was not cordiality. Her manner made it clear that she disliked Miss Wainwright's profession and considered it reprehensible for a woman to follow it. On the other hand, Miss Flynn was unwontedly gracious in her reception of Susanna. The news of the identity of the Crimson Knight and of his death had reached Rose Gardens and Miss Flynn found it impossible not to feel pity for Susanna as being more or less his victim. Susanna showed herself touched by this sympathy.

Carrington wished that the ability to express his emotions had been vouchsafed to him. There was so much his heart prompted him to say, and yet he sat now by Susanna's side, as he had sat during the drive back to Rose Gardens, in awkward silence, finding no word to say.

Miss Flynn handed to Pamela Wainwright a note enclosed in an envelope of thick, foreign paper.

"This was brought here for you."

The detective broke the seal and read the note, a little frown gathering between her brows.

"It is from Gupta Singh. He fears that I am cooling in the chase. He intends to pay his respects to you this evening, Miss Flynn, and, incidentally, to give me my walking papers unless I have some information to impart to him. Oh, I do not blame him for feeling as he does. My progress, in this case, has been slow. But, you see, there were so many threads to pick up and I wanted to be sure. By the way, Miss Flynn, I should like a few words with your interesting housekeeper."

"Mrs. MacDonald has been confined in her room all day with a headache," observed Miss Flynn.

"I will go to her then," said Pamela Wainwright gravely. "She must be told of Capt. Helton's death — if she does not already know."

Susanna unexpectedly intervened. "Couldn't you let the poor woman rest until morning? She may know already — through Leon. But if she does not know, it will be a terrible shock. I think she really loved him."

The detective's expression softened. "I think she did. I suppose it is her justification. But I must speak with her tonight, a little later will do just as well, however. Miss Flynn, will you ask your nephew to come here, please?"

"My nephew!"

"Yes, there are questions he must answer."

Carrington and Susanna exchanged swift glances. The same suspicion had come to both.

Miss Flynn bristled with indignation, but her cheeks were a little grayish.

"Surely, you are not accusing my nephew — "

"At present I am accusing no one," said the detective gently. "I want simply to ask your nephew certain questions. Please send for him, Miss Flynn."

Max entered the detective's presence with his confident air, his mocking smile. Miriam, on the contrary, who accompanied him, showed perturbation. Max's surprise at beholding 'Miss Merton' metamorphosed into a detective was by no means as great as Carrington's had been and he carried off the situation lightly.

"I knew that you were something more than an ordinary woman, Miss Wainwright. You interested me from the first."

"The interest was mutual then," she smiled. "You have been in my thoughts very frequently the last few days, Mr. Flynn."

"You flatter me, Miss Wainwright." His eyes laughed into hers.

"Not at all, I am speaking seriously." Her tone hardened. "My interest in you has been so intense that on the day before the inquest I went up to London on the same train which you took."

Max's audacious glance fell, the lines of his mouth stiffened. His voice, however, was still bantering as he said:

"By George! If I had only known it, we would have had a jolly entertaining ride together. I say, Miss Wainwright, why didn't you make yourself known?"

The detective looked him straight in the eye. "Because I feared that if I did, it might cause you to postpone your business interview with Mr. Jermayne of Tottenham Court Road."

Max smothered a snicker. His face was ashen.

Miriam suddenly stepped before him. Her eyes, of a harder blue than ever, flashed hate at the detective.

"I do not know what you mean by all this, Miss Wainwright. Mr. Flynn went to see Mr. Jermayne at my request. He was kind enough to try to raise money for me on some old jewelry which had belonged to my mother."

Pamela Wainwright turned her searching gaze on Miriam. "How did your mother happen to have in her possession the Surya's Eye ruby, Miss Cramer?"

The silence in the room was intense. Miss Flynn, alone, was not looking at Miriam, white and defiant, but at Max who had forced to his lips a trace of his old careless smile. A bitter conviction was struggling into being on Miss Flynn's face.

Miriam collected herself. "Your question is absurd, Miss Wainwright. Of course the Surya's Eye ruby was never in my mother's possession."

"In that case then," shot back the detective, "Mr. Flynn was trying to dispose of stolen property."

At this Miriam completely lost control of herself. She burst into a storm of denial and vituperation.

Carrington laid a kindly hand on her arm. "Better not say any more, Mimi."

Miss Flynn addressed herself to Max who had preserved silence. "If you have any explanation to offer, you will oblige me by stating it."

Max fought hard to regain his nonchalance of bearing. "My blessed Aunt, I could give you a dozen, only, you see, I prefer to have Mimi — "

Miss Flynn cut him short. "That is sufficient. Do not put the responsibility of your crimes on a woman. It is bad enough to be a thief — and a murderer!" Her voice shook in spite of herself.

"I am no murderer!" Max cried sharply.

Susanna rose in agitation. "No! You are not that, Max."

"We cannot be too sure of that," said the detective coldly. "It is impossible for Mr. Flynn to prove his innocence. Circumstantial evidence declares him the murderer of Prince Rajan Mohan. He had incentive and opportunity. Oh, let me finish, Miss Cramer. You will not help the case against Mr. Flynn. His appalling debts were his incentive and his opportunity — you all know he had that. He was absent from the ballroom a considerable part of the evening and he was twice seen, in his Knightly costume, to come out from the library where Rajan Mohan was murdered."

"See here," burst out Max, "you seem to forget that this chap who came out from the library could just as likely have been the real Knight."

"That is impossible, Mr. Flynn. If he had been the real Knight, he could not have gone into the balls room unmasked and mingled with the guests as this man — as you did, Mr. Flynn. You cannot prove an alibi and the fact that you were detected trying to sell the ruby stolen from the murdered man would be sufficient for any jury to convict you."

Max's lips still wore their persistent smile — though now a wholly cynical and sneering one. He had always prided himself on being a philosophical loser. He meant to keep up his reputation.

"By Jove! Miss Wainwright, you present the paradox of a pretty woman and a logician combined. But — your conclusions are wrong. I did not kill Rajan Mohan."

Pamela Wainwright smiled satirically. "Didn't you, Mr. Flynn? I don't believe that you would care to stand trial — Against my logic. I think what you want is not justice — but mercy. What will you trade for mercy, Mr. Flynn?"

Max fell in with her humor. "Have I anything left to trade?" his tone bantering.

"You have that bone of contention, the paper in cipher which, by the way, was not stolen from you at all."

"You're jolly clever, aren't you, Miss Wainwright?" Max was careful not to glance in his aunt's direction.

"It is my business to be 'jolly clever,' Mr. Flynn. Well, what do you say? Should we trade?"

"She is trying to trap you," warned Miriam in a low, tense voice.

Pamela Wainwright caught the words. "I am not trying to trap him. I do not need to. I offer him in exchange for that paper in cipher — which he has found useless — an opportunity to make his escape from the country. Otherwise, he will be charged with the murder of Prince Rajan. I think he realizes the impossibility of proving his innocence. It is for him to choose."

Max's sangfroid was unshaken. "You've got me fair and square, Miss Wainwright. If I do give up this bone of contention, can you assure me safe conduct from the country?"

"I can. I have considered and planned everything. There is a train leaving for London within an hour which you can catch. At London you should be able to make the early morning clipper for — well, I should advise, Australia."

Max's eyelids stretched wide in dismay. "Australia!"

The detective nodded. "I should say that Australia was the safest refuge for you. Your debts, I understand, have made you rather too familiar a figure on the Continent. Australia will be new ground for you."

Max made a wry face. "Damned dull ground — but oh, well! I'll try it for a few years until this affair blows over."

"I think you are wise, Mr. Flynn. The paper in cipher, please, and really you haven't many minutes to lose. I have taken the liberty of ordering a carriage. It should be waiting for you now."

Still with imperturbable nonchalance, Max drew from an inner pocket the paper in cipher and, with a mock bow, tendered it to Pamela Wainwright.

During this time Miss Flynn had spoken no word. Only the gray rigidity of her features showed that she was suffering.

Max turned to her now, his smile growing whimsical. "Aren't you going to wish me 'bon voyage', Aunt Ell?"

Miss Flynn raised her eyes. The scorn in her gaze withered the smile on his lips. "I am going to wish that I may forget I ever had a nephew."

Max turned away sharply, with a hard laugh. "And what are you going to wish me, Susanna? A short road to perdition?"

Susanna took his hand impulsively in both her own. There was a great pity in her face.

"I am going to wish that you will pull yourself together and live a different life. You can do it if you will."

"It is too late for that," his voice a little unsteady, his smile more regretful than bitter. "If I had loved you years ago — and you could have given me your love — " He broke off abruptly, a mask of cynicism hardening his face. "Miss Wainwright will be reminding me that I haven't the time for sentimental rot. So long, Susanna, old girl!" He wrung her hand convulsively, released it and, with an indifferent nod at Carrington and Miriam, sauntered leisurely toward the door.

At last Carrington found his voice. It was his friend of long-standing, his boyhood's playmate, who was being banished for this in disgrace.

"Max," he said huskily, "I wish you the best of luck! I'd like awfully to hear from you."

Max turned, his eyes bitter, his mouth hard. "I'll not need to wish you luck. As for writing, I don't fancy there'll be much news to chronicle from the wilds of Australia. So long, everybody!"

Miriam suddenly ran forward and caught his arm beseechingly. Her eyes now were softly lustrous.

"Max, let me go with you!"

Max turned around, surprised. "Don't you understand I'm ruined — a Pariah?"

"What does that matter to me? Max, take me with you!"

"Miriam," interposed Carrington, "I don't think you quite realize — "

Miriam stamped her foot. "Be still, Tom! I realize that Max is being driven into a strange land — disgraced you call it — Well, what does disgrace matter to me? I want to be with him — anywhere — I don't care where — so that I am with him. Max, you will take me?"

Miriam trembled with the intensity of her emotion as, with flushed cheeks and beseeching eyes, she begged to be allowed to share disgrace and exile with the man who had long ago tired of her and had been at no pains to conceal the fact. Carrington was touched by the devotion and self-sacrifice of one whom he had always known as a Becky Sharp. Great indeed, must be her love for Max that it has transformed her.

Max surveyed her coolly, appraisingly. Carrington grew hot with indignation.

"Mimi," he pleaded, "think twice, don't ruin your life."

Miriam utterly ignored him. She was fighting for a few hours of happiness, she would not think of what must inevitably follow — knowing Max as she did. The clasp of her hand on his arm tightened, her eyes were full of passionate appeal, she swayed against him. "Take me with you!"

Max continued to survey her appraisingly. In the stress of her emotion, she looked uncommonly pretty. His own eyes lit up — but not with tenderness, his mocking smile deepened.

"Of course, I'll take you, Mimi, if you are so set on going. I'm bound to be damned lonely out in the wilds."

Miriam did not shrink at the brutality of his words. She had gained what she sought. She knew it was dross, but it was what she wanted.

Carrington, however, gave Max a glance of hopeless contempt. He forgot their long years of friendship and remembered only the pitiful little East Indian girl whose love Max had stolen for his own selfish gains and now here was another woman on whose misplaced devotion he meant to batten and divert himself until, once more satiated, he cast her off again.

"Max," he said with conviction, "you're no end of a bounder."

Max shrugged indifferently. "You are frank, to say the least. Mimi, should we say goodbye?"

Miss Flynn stood up. "Wait a moment. I hope I know my duty by my brother's son. If you communicate with my bankers, they will see that you are supplied with money, sufficient for necessities."

"Thanks, Aunt Ell," responded Max coolly. "I will probably be forced to avail myself of your bounty. My assets at present are nil. Come along, Mimi."

As the door closed behind them, Miss Flynn sank into her chair. She looked old and worn.

"Thomas," she said unsteadily — she had not called Carrington by his first name since he was a boy — "I am going back to Cavendish Square tomorrow or the next day. I hope you will come to see me often. I will be lonely — at first — until I get used to having no nephew."

Carrington pressed her hand. He could not seem to find anything to say.

Susanna went over to Miss Flynn and said, a little timidly, "I wish that sometime I might come with Tom."

Miss Flynn hastily passed her handkerchief across her eyes. "Please do, I should like to have you."

Pamela Wainwright stepped forward. Her face like Susanna's was gentle and sympathetic.

"Miss Flynn, perhaps you are thinking a little more hardly of your nephew than you need to. With your permission I am going to ask Mrs. MacDonald and Ahmed, the butler to come here. This case is by no means closed."

30

THE EYES OF BRAHMA

The detective had scarcely finished speaking when Ahmed shakily ushered in Gupta Singh. The old East Indian was in a state of agitation bordering on frenzy. He altogether forgot the courtesy due Miss Flynn and addressed himself solely to Pamela Wainwright.

"I come to give you dismissal. You neglect my interests. You let a thief escape — The man who has stolen the Surya's Eye ruby. As I enter the house, I see him; the thief, riding away like — 'like mad,' as you English say, in a motor cab. I demand the explanation!"

Pamela Wainwright sustained the East Indian's furious eyes with provoking calm. "Perhaps I have misunderstood your object in engaging my services. Was it the apprehension of the murderer of Rajan Mohan or simply the recovery of the Surya's Eye ruby — and its mate?"

"And its mate?" Miss Flynn, Carrington and Susanna stared at the detective in amazement.

Ahmed's dark face paled. Gupta Singh scrutinized the detective in a curious, reflective fashion. "You have found then the stolen paper and you have the knowledge of cipher writing?"

"Yes. Naturally so, since I am a detective."

The East Indian continued to study her quiet face. "And the mate of the

Surya's Eye, it is safe?"

"I presume so. The person into whose possession this paper came was unable to decipher the location of its hiding-place."

"But the Surya's Eye itself, where is that?" The light of fanaticism shone now in the old priest's eyes.

Pamela Wainwright smiled reassuringly. "The Surya's Eye is under the protection of representatives of Scotland Yard. It did not seem safe in the shop of the London jeweler where it was offered for sale. The person offering the ruby did not think it prudent to carry so costly a jewel about on his person and preferred to leave it in Mr. Jermayne's care in exchange for a rather substantial sum on credit until that gentleman could beg, borrow — or possibly steal — the entire amount demanded. To make the ruby doubly safe, I decided to take it out of Mr. Jermayne's hands and put it in those of Scotland Yard. You need not be apprehensive, Gupta Singh, the ruby will not be stolen again."

The old East Indian shook with emotion. "You are aware, of course, that both rubies belong to me as the priest of Brahma. They must be restored at once."

Pamela Wainwright gave a little shrug. "That is not my province, but I rather fancy that you will have to apply to the Government for permission to remove them from the country."

The East Indian's features were convulsed with a righteous wrath. "There was no permission asked when the mate of the Surya's Eye was stolen fourteen years ago by Sir Robert Williamson from the image of supreme Brahma in the temple at Delhi."

The mention of Brahma caused Ahmed to cower as Carrington had once seen Nora do.

Pamela Wainwright made a little deprecatory gesture. "However that may be, the ruby has been so long in this country and is of such inestimable value that you will find complications in attempting to remove it."

Gupta Singh towered above her in his wrath. "You English cannot understand. The Surya's Eye and its mate formed the eyes of the image of Brahma. Sir Robert Williamson's crime was more than theft, it was desecration — sacrilege! Outraged Brahma can be appeased only by the restoration of both rubies."

Carrington put up his monocle. "Sir Robert Williamson, as I understand, stole only one eye. Then why the heck did you or Rajan Mohan blind the old chap entirely by taking out his other eye and parading up and down England with it? Wasn't that sacrilege, eh?"

Carrington was not familiar with Hindustani, but, from the force of Gupta Singh's delivery, he was able to comprehend vaguely the old East Indian's opinion of himself and other scoffers at the true religion.

After a moment Brahma's priest controlled himself and said in his slow, stilted, but none the less impressive, English, "You will be made to understand. The royal House of Mohan for generations have had under their special protection the temple of supreme Brahma at Delhi. To guard this temple has been esteemed their highest prerogative. But when the English descended upon India and subjugated her proudest princes, Ananya Mohan, the grandfather of Prince Rajan, forgot the past glory of his race, consorted with the English usurpers and made no effort to shake off the foreign yoke. Arjun, his son, forgot still more his high duties. He welcomed, he cherished, the insidious poison of the West" — Gupta Singh's burning gaze, bitter to the point of accusation, was fixed now upon Susanna, as though in her he saw the epitome of that "insidious Western poison."

"This poison so entered Arjun's veins," the old priest went on, in a voice of suppressed fury, "that for his English myrmidons and English gold he was willing to betray his great trust, the prerogative of his House, the guarding of Brahma's shrine. He would have money and more money to fling at the feet of English houris. He would not himself violate Brahma, for he was a coward as all traitors are, but he would give to another the opportunity to do so. This other was Sir Robert Williamson. For years this man had been robbing the men of India and outraging their gods. It was agreed between the traitor Arjun and this perfidious foreigner that a certain door of Brahma's temple which could be entered only by the head of the House of Mohan should be left unguarded one night. Through this door Sir Robert Williamson was to enter the temple and steal the two sacred rubies which formed the eyes of Brahma. The proceeds from the sale of these holy jewels was to be divided between Arjun and the Englishman. At the eleventh hour Arjun came to realize the atrocity of the crime that was about to occur. He dared not confide in the priests of Brahma and call them to the aid of the god who was about to be desecrated, so he went alone to prevent the crime. Well, he was unsuccessful. The consciousness of his baseness robbed him of strength, and he was stabbed to the heart by his English friend on the threshold of Brahma's shrine.

"Sir Robert Williamson, fearing discovery, stayed only long enough to remove one sacred eye. Some hours later I found Arjun dying. At the feet of the violated Brahma, he poured out his confession. From that day a curse has rested on the House of Mohan. The restoration of the stolen ruby alone can remove it. From the hour of Arjun's death, I took his young son, Prince Rajan, under my charge and forced him to vow his life to the appeasing of Brahma and the restoration of the past glory of his race. In order that he might never forget his high mission, I removed the remaining eye of Brahma and placed it on his breast where its red fire did not cease to burn him until the night it was stolen in the midst of that Western poison which had been his father's undoing."

Again the East Indian's gaze, bitterly contemptuous, settled on Susanna, who shivered a little.

Carrington was stirred to anger. "I shouldn't say, Miss Wainwright, that we had far to look for the murderer of Sir Robert Williamson."

"You are wrong," said Gupta Singh authoritatively. "It is true that Rajan Mohan at my tutelage was destined to be the instrument of Sir Robert Williamson's death, but he was cheated of his vengeance and his hope of recovering at the same time the sacred ruby."

Carrington grew nettled and even apprehensive at observing how Gupta Singh continued to glower at Susanna.

Miss Flynn was strangely silent, she had sat in a sort of apathy since Max's departure.

Pamela Wainwright broke the general silence which had fallen when Gupta Singh ceased speaking.

"I am going to question Mrs. MacDonald now. No, Ahmed," as the butler made a swift movement toward the door — "I wish you to remain here. Lord Carrington, may I ask you to tell Mrs. MacDonald that I must speak to her here?"

Ahmed flashed a furtive, miserable look at Gupta Singh, but the old priest did not deign to glance in his direction.

Carrington was obliged to knock several times on Mrs. MacDonald's door before he received any response. Then there was the sound of some inner door opening and closing, and dragging steps crossing the room. Carrington was moved to pity at sight of Mrs. MacDonald. Her face had been colorless before, it was now ghastly, but it was the hopeless misery in her eyes which affected Carrington most deeply. She was like a woman who, at one stroke, had seen swept away the cherished hopes of years of hardship and repression. Even the capacity to suffer seemed to have been taken from her. She presented an appearance of passivity and total apathy, evinced no emotion whatever at the detective's summons and followed Carrington in silence.

As they came into the hall, Susanna went forward in her impulsive manner and, taking the housekeeper's hand, drew her into a chair by her side, screening her as much as possible from Gupta Singh's scrutiny. Edna MacDonald let her hand lie listlessly in Susanna's, but there was the flicker of emotion on her features and a sudden moisture in her eyes.

"I hope," said Susanna, addressing Pamela Wainwright, "that you will ask Mrs. MacDonald as few questions as possible. She is ill and ought to be in bed."

"I will not need to ask her many questions," responded the detective gently, "but she must tell us the story of Sir Robert Williamson's death. It is time that the world knew it."

At mention of Sir Robert Williamson, Mrs. MacDonald shook off her apathy. A flush dyed her cheeks; her eyes glittered.

"Why should I add infamy to anyone's name because of him? He deserved to die! He was a monster of cruelty to every one — Except to the girl he called his ward. He was good to her only because she was like a conscience to him. She reminded him of the crimes he had committed in India, and he hoped that by being good to the daughter of the man he had ruined and then murdered, he could beg off from punishment in the other world. He was obsessed with the fear of death — and no wonder! The only happy moment I knew from the time I entered his service as housekeeper was when I saw him lying dead in the library."

"You should have left his death to the agents of Brahma," spoke up Gupta Singh in his heavy, sonorous voice. "You took it upon yourself because you hoped to get possession of the sacred ruby he had stolen. You dared to plan another violation of Brahma. You corrupted to your service that base creature" — his eyes now on the cringing Ahmed — "who forswore the gods of India and followed a foreign master over the seas."

"Williamson Sahib he — he saved my life in the jungle," whimpered Ahmed.

"And destroyed your soul," admonished the old priest harshly. "You dared to protect him against the vengeance of Brahma. You would warn him when the servitors of Brahma came to punish. But — when the Englishwoman with the pale face commanded you to kill — so that she might have the ruby — you killed!"

Ahmed slid to his knees. "No, no! It is not I to kill Williamson Sahib! Prince Rajan will not believe that!"

"Prince Rajan," said Gupta Singh severely, "would believe all an Englishwoman told him — he was the son of Arjun. You, by cheating vengeance, will later know Brahma's wrath."

On his knees Ahmed dragged himself to Mrs. MacDonald.

"Sahiba! You tell Gupta Singh it, not I who kill Williamson Sahib."

Edna MacDonald raised her white face to the old priest's.

"Ahmed is telling the truth. He did not kill Sir Robert Williamson."

"Then who killed him?" demanded the old priest fiercely.

Edna MacDonald dropped her face in her hands.

Susanna placed a kindly arm about her shoulders.

"Capt. Bartholomew Helton killed Sir Robert Williamson," she said quietly.

Gupta Singh turned upon her. "If you knew, why wouldn't you tell?"

Susanna met his eyes calmly. "Because I had no interest in Sir Robert Williamson, dead or alive. It was not my business to tell."

Pamela Wainwright, with a little gesture of command, checked the harsh speech on Gupta Singh's lips. "Mrs. MacDonald, I am going to ask you now to tell the story of Sir Robert's death. In return I will tell the story of Rajan Mohan's death."

The detective's words caused a stir through the little gathering. Miss Flynn sat stiffly erect, a strained look about her features. Carrington knew that she was dreading to hear Max's name spoken. A glance of understanding passed between Susanna and Edna MacDonald. The latter's face now showed a hopeless acquiescence. Ahmed, still crouched by her chair, presented a pitiful appearance of abject terror. He was acutely conscious of every movement on the part of the old priest; he seemed to be in a kind of paroxysm of guilty fear, and Carrington for the first time felt sorry for the poor wretch.

Inspector Rathbone, his jaw set more aggressively than ever, had quietly entered the hall and now stood, note-book and pencil in hand, waiting for the housekeeper to speak.

"I think it will be best," said Pamela Wainwright in a crisp, business-like tone, "for you to state clearly the relation in which you stood to Sir Robert Williamson."

Mrs. MacDonald raised her eyes. They held a world of bitterness. "I was legally his wife — Morally his slave. Why he married me I don't know, unless to make sure that I should not escape his persecutions. I was his lawful prey, and he used his right to heap upon me every sort of humiliation and insult. He knew why I married him — to make a permanent home for myself and Leon, my poor boy. Oh, I paid for it!"

Leon! Carrington knew now why "Master Leon's" face had seemed so familiar.

Mrs. MacDonald went on with her story in a dreary monotone; her features without expression save for the bitterness smoldering in her eyes. "I was a widow without friends, without money and newly come from Australia when I secured through an advertisement in The Times the position of the housekeeper here. Sir Robert had just returned from India and had with him Nora Mohan, then a child of three or four, and Ahmed who was butler and valet too. Sir Robert soon made it plain that he desired more than a housekeeper. At least I can say to his credit — or that is, I thought then it was to his credit — that he suggested no mere temporary relation, only stipulated that the marriage should remain secret until it pleased him to announce the fact. Well, what could I do but accept? Leon was only five years old, I thought this marriage would secure him a home." Mrs. MacDonald gave a short, hard laugh. "Instead, it secured for him harsh treatment and even blows and made him what you have seen, a drunken loafer.

"I endured all this for years — what else could I do — Sir Robert had bound me to him — And of course I was counting on his death. Who wouldn't have? Well, the inevitable happened finally, another man came into my life. He had made friends with Sir Robert for the purpose of robbing him later. I knew that, but he gave me compliments in place of abuse and I — I came to love him."

She looked around the hall with a little defiant gesture. Susanna gently pressed her hand. Gupta Singh was visibly chafing with impatience, but he preserved silence. Ahmed was regarding Mrs. MacDonald with the mournful eyes of a whipped dog.

After a moment she resumed the thread of her story. "This man — Capt. Helton," — her voice shook over the name — "was a distant relative of Sir Robert's and he knew of his theft of the ruby and other crimes he had committed. He intended to make him give up the ruby by threatening disclosure. Then we were going away together. I had learned by that time that I had little to expect at Sir Robert's death. He intended everything to go to Nora Mohan and I could not prove the legality of our marriage. The clergyman who had married us, and the witness were both dead, there had been some confusion over the license and Sir Robert had taken the certificate from me and destroyed it. I had nothing to hope for except discovering the hiding-place of the ruby, and this was only indicated by a paper in cipher which also was hidden. He intended to give the key of this cipher to Nora and also a clue to the hiding-place of the paper. He could not resist torturing even her by making the discovery of the ruby doubtful. For me he made it impossible."

"Capt. Helton, of course, knew of all this, and he planned an interview with Sir Robert in which he intended to force him to give up the ruby. He had no thought of killing him, but he knew Sir Robert's violent nature and that he always carried with him a poisoned dagger as a protection against his East Indian enemies. Capt. Helton persuaded me to steal this dagger so that Sir Robert would be unarmed in case, as was very likely, he should lose control of himself at this interview. I had no idea that Capt. Helton intended to carry the dagger with him. But he did, and both men lost control of themselves. The rest you know." Her voice was still emotionless.

"I shielded Capt. Helton. He and I together made the murder appear as much as possible the work of those East Indian enemies Sir Robert was always in fear of. I gained nothing by Sir Robert's death; Capt. Helton was financially and socially ruined so he stayed on here secretly and we searched for the ruby and the paper which would give a clue to its hiding-place. Capt. Helton needed money and he wanted excitement, so he revived the legend of the Crimson robber, his ancestor as well as Sir Robert's. His likeness to this man whose picture hangs in the dining-hall was rather striking, and by impersonating him, he got both money and excitement. Then Prince Rajan Mohan began to make attempts to get into the house, and for some reason he came to suspect that Capt. Helton had killed Sir Robert. From then until the day of his own death, we both went in fear of our lives. I cannot say who killed Prince Rajan. I have told you all that I know."

Her words carried conviction and Pamela Wainwright seemed content to accept them.

Gupta Singh, however, was still unsatisfied. "Prince Rajan's death remains a mystery — the English detectives have so bungled the matter; things are done differently in India — but the rubies, the eyes of Brahma — "

Pamela Wainwright interrupted him. "Brahma perhaps must remain blind indefinitely, but Prince Rajan' s death is not to remain a mystery. English detectives are not so bungling after all. Lord Carrington, may I ask you to go once more to Mrs. MacDonald's room and this time request Princess Nora Mohan to come here? Mrs. MacDonald, you will kindly give his lordship the key to the priest's closet leading off your chamber. You will find the door to this closet, Lord Carrington, concealed behind the long mirror on the wall."

31

GATHERING UP THE THREADS

It was a terrified little princess indeed whom Carrington discovered in the enclosure leading off Mrs. MacDonald's chamber. He had no little difficulty in persuading her to accompany him to the hall when he had told her, in response to her tremulous question, that Gupta Singh was there. Like Ahmed she seemed to stand in a kind of guilty fear of the old East Indian. At last, however, Carrington succeeded in convincing her that he was capable of protecting her against even Gupta Singh.

But on the threshold of the hall, at sight of the old priest's stern face, her courage forsook her again, and she clung terrified to Carrington's arm.

"Buck up, little girl," he whispered consolingly, "there isn't anybody going to hurt you while I am here."

"You don't know — you don't understand," she shivered.

As a matter of fact, Gupta Singh's gaze as it fastened upon Nora might have withered the courage of a more considerable person than this little East Indian girl.

"There are many things you must tell Miss Flynn and her guests," said Pamela Wainwright, addressing Nora in a purposely gentle tone. "First you must tell how you happened to be here in Mrs. MacDonald's chamber."

Nora looked at her pitifully. "But you know — you know everything."

"The others do not," the detective answered, still very gently, "and I prefer that you tell your own story."

As Nora, after a glance of appeal at Mrs. MacDonald, remained silent, the housekeeper suddenly spoke for her.

"I brought her here. I went at night to Mrs. Barker's lodging-house at the Bay Town and forced her to return with me. I hoped through her in some way to get possession of the two rubies."

"You did this at Capt. Helton's suggestion?" Pamela Wainwright's voice became once more crisp and professional.

The flush that suffused Mrs. MacDonald's face was her only answer, but it was sufficient.

Pamela Wainwright turned again to Nora. "You must tell us now what you saw in the library here on the night your brother was killed."

Nora drew in her breath. "I will not tell!" Her hands were clenched. She looked like a frightened but very obstinate child.

"You will not harm Mr. Flynn by telling the truth," said the detective incisively. "He is already on his way to London where he will take the earliest train, then boat for Australia. We" — she nodded toward Inspector Rathbone, waiting grimly, pencil in hand, to take down whatever testimony might be wrung from Nora — "we have promised him safe conduct until he leaves the country."

"He — he is not to come back — ever?"

Carrington turned away that he might not see the misery in Nora's eyes.

"No, he will never come back." Pamela Wainwright seemed to be forcing herself to treat this tragic-faced child with professional coldness. "I think that Miss Cramer, too, will never come back."

"Miss Cramer! He — he took her with him?"

Pamela Wainwright nodded. "They went together." In spite of herself the detective's expression was compassionate.

A lightning-like change came over Nora's face. All its childlike appeal was gone, her mouth was hard, her eyes dry. She looked as her brother had looked when the hot blood of his East Indian forefathers had burst through the constraints of Western refinement. For the first time she forgot her fear of Gupta Singh, forgot even his presence. She stepped nearer the detective, her slim, as yet unformed, figure trembling with the intensity of her passion.

"I will tell you what I saw in the library. My brother lay on the floor — he was dead — And Mr. Flynn was tearing the Surya's Eye from his breast. There was a dagger at Rajan's side and — and blood on Mr. Flynn's hands."

Miss Ellery tried to smother a groan.

Susanna suddenly pressed forward. "For Miss Flynn's sake, if not for her nephew's, the whole truth should be told. Prince Rajan was dead before Max came into the library."

Rathbone's pencil dug eagerly into the pages of his notebook. Carrington, at that moment, was conscious only of a mad desire to snatch that pencil and break it and its owner into bits.

"How do you know that Prince Rajan was dead before Mr. Flynn came into the library?" Pamela Wainwright asked quickly.

"I saw him lying dead on the floor before Mr. Flynn came in."

"You are sure of this?"

"Perfectly."

"And what makes you so sure of this?" demanded Rathbone in his most truculent tone.

Susanna met his bullying gaze with composure. "Because I looked in at the terrace door after I had seen that Prince Rajan was dead. Mr. Flynn was bending over his body. I thought he was discovering that he was dead, so I went away immediately — out on the cliffs."

"You didn't then," heckled Rathbone, "first lock the library inner door so the murder shouldn't be discovered by others?"

Susanna's composure was not to be shaken. "As I stated at the inquest, I locked the inner door when I first entered the room in order that no one should interrupt my conversation with Prince Rajan. So far as I know, the door remained locked."

"It was locked when I came in from the terrace," spoke up Nora sharply. "I thought I would leave it so to — to help Mr. Flynn, but — but he," her voice broke — "he is a bad heart; he forgets what I do for him, what he promises me — "

Miss Flynn went forward resolutely and, drawing the girl back, forced her to sit down. "My nephew is not worthy of your thoughts. I am going to look after you from now on."

With a tenderness that Carrington for one had never observed in her before, Miss Flynn drew Nora's head down upon her breast, consoling her as one might have consoled a broken-hearted child. Nora clung gratefully to Max's aunt, sobbing out her griefs in the arms of the woman of whom hitherto she had always stood in awe.

Rathbone turned to Susanna. "Perhaps now, my Lady," his tone still truculent, "you will be good enough to explain how a piece of your gown came to be found in Rajan Mohan's hand."

"And perhaps, Mr. Rathbone," spoke up Pamela Wainwright crisply, "you will be good enough to remember that I am conducting this inquiry."

Rathbone scowled. "Fire ahead with it then."

"I will tell you exactly what happened in the library between Rajan Mohan and myself," said Susanna quickly, before Pamela Wainwright could address her. "The truth cannot harm the guilty person now. As I testified at the inquest, I broke my engagement to Rajan Mohan in the library because he refused to fulfill a promise he had made to me. This promise concerned Capt. Helton. Prince Rajan had discovered that Bartholomew had killed Sir Robert Williamson and also that he was the Crimson Knight. Prince Rajan considered that Bartholomew by killing Sir Robert had not only prevented him from recovering the Surya's Eye ruby, but had also cheated him of his vendetta and his hope of appeasing Brahma's wrath against this whole family. For this Prince Rajan had determined to have Bartholomew's life. I wanted to save Bartholomew. I felt more or less responsible for the wreck he had made of everything — if I hadn't divorced him, I might have been able to put him on his feet again. Well, he appealed to me for help; I was sorry for him, awfully sorry, and Prince Rajan kept urging his love upon me. I knew I should always blame myself for anything worse that might happen to Bartholomew, so finally I told Prince Rajan that I would marry him if he would give me his promise to let Bartholomew alone. He gave me his promise, and then later, in the library that night, told me he could not keep it. When I refused to marry him as a consequence, he lost control of himself and showed me then the little respect which men of the East have for women. I repulsed him and that is how, Mr. Rathbone, a piece of my frock came to be found in his hand."

"I was about to call for help, when Bartholomew, dressed as the Knight, stepped in through the terrace door. Prince Rajan was so astounded at seeing Bartholomew that he loosed his hold on me, and I ran out of the terrace door, out onto the cliffs. I felt that I could not endure Rajan Mohan's presence another instant. Then, after a few minutes on the cliffs, I thought of what might happen between him and Bartholomew and I went back to the library. Bartholomew was gone, but Rajan Mohan lay on the floor — dead! I think I was half-crazed by the horror of it all, my head seemed to be bursting, and I ran back to the cliffs again. Bartholomew came to me there a few minutes later. He was in a pitiful state of terror. At first he denied that he had killed Rajan Mohan, but he finally saw how useless denial was and said something which has been haunting me ever since, 'I did it for your sake — because of the insult he offered you. Now it's up to you to get me out of this mess.'"

Carrington's indignation against Helton swelled. Of course he was just cad enough to hold this over Susanna in order to impose the more effectually on her generous nature.

Gupta Singh, while Susanna was speaking, had not removed his stern eyes from her face. Ahmed, too, was watching her with fixity. It seemed to Borrow dean that there was a sort of incredulous relief on his features.

Edna MacDonald broke the brief silence that had fallen, "I do not believe, as I have told you repeatedly, that Capt. Helton killed Rajan Mohan. Capt. Helton is dead and why blacken his memory more than is necessary?"

Susanna turned to her with a quick glance of sympathy. "It is true there is only circumstantial evidence against Bartholomew. If it makes you happier to believe him innocent of this crime, I hope you will continue to believe it."

"It is more than belief," cried Mrs. MacDonald passionately, "to me it is certainty. I have not only Bartholomew's word — he never thought it worth while to lie to me — But I have the testimony of my own eyes. I was outdoors near the library the greater part of that evening. When Bartholomew entered through the terrace door, he had just left me. He did not intend that either you or Rajan Mohan should see him. You were quarreling, and he hoped to slip in without being observed. His purpose was — well, I suppose you can guess what it was — He needed money. You know as well as I do that he stood in deadly fear of Rajan Mohan, he would never have had the courage to kill him, and he did not have the time. I saw you run out from the library, and less than half a minute later Bartholomew ran out too. He was running from Rajan Mohan, for I saw the East Indian spring to the door as though to pursue him, and then some person — I couldn't make out whether it was a man or a woman — Moved away from the shadow of the house and entered through the terrace door. I did not stop to see what happened then — Capt. Helton called to me."

"A no end remarkable tale, Mrs. MacDonald," remarked Rathbone with the exasperating drawl which he assumed at times.

Mrs. MacDonald flushed. "I didn't expect anyone to believe me" — a world of bitterness in her tone.

"I believe you, Mrs. MacDonald."

Pamela Wainwright met with a slight and baffling smile the amazed glances bent at her.

"It was you, Mrs. MacDonald, was it not, who unlocked the library door in the interval between Ahmed's discovering that it was locked and his announcing of the fact to Miss Flynn?"

"Yes, it was me. Lady Susanna had already told me that she believed Capt. Helton had killed Rajan Mohan. I wished to make sure that the East Indian was really dead. I turned the lock with a duplicate key, but before I could open the door I heard people coming from the ballroom, and so I hurried away."

Carrington took occasion here — he could not have told just why — to glance at Ahmed. Once more he was struck by the abject terror in the brown man's face.

Nora still sat with her head on Miss Flynn's breast, catching her breath now and then with a heartrending sob. The means and the author of her brother's death were of far less import to the little East Indian than the desertion of the man who had once seemed the handsome ideal of her girlish dreams. Miss Flynn, still with that grayness to her features, was stroking Nora's dark hair, but abstractedly, and Carrington knew that her thoughts too were with Max.

"You were saying," pursued Pamela Wainwright, still addressing Mrs.

MacDonald, "that you saw some person move away from the shadow of the house and enter through the terrace door and that you could not make out whether this was a man or a woman. But you must have gained some impression of the person's sex from the dress."

Mrs. MacDonald shook her head. "From the very brief glimpse I had, I judged that the person was one of the guests in masquerade costume, and it appeared to be a costume that could be worn by either a man or a woman."

Pamela Wainwright turned quickly to Ahmed. "What happened when you entered the library through the terrace door?"

Ahmed stared at her with mingled amazement and terror. "It, not I, Sahiba, who enter through the terrace door."

"Be careful what you say," the detective warned him.

"It, not the terrace door, Sahiba," he protested earnestly. "I do not go outside the house all that evening — I will swear it — so it cannot be the terrace door I enter through."

"Ah! But you did enter the library before calling Miss Flynn."

The East Indian turned a sickly yellow-white. "I have not said so, Sahiba!"

"You do not need to." Pamela Wainwright's voice became more severe. "It is known that you entered the library directly after Lady Susanna and Capt. Helton left it When you left it, Rajan Mohan was dead."

"I did not kill him, Sahiba!" The East Indian's voice rose almost to a shriek.

Pamela Wainwright gave a peculiar smile. "Can you prove that you did not?"

Ahmed started to burst forth into a torrent of avowals of innocence, then suddenly checked himself. "I cannot prove!"

With the admission, he lost all control of himself, and dropped again to his knees, groveling in terror at the detective's feet.

Gupta Singh strode over to his compatriot and stood looking down at him with a sort of majestic contempt.

"Miserable deserter of Brahma, it is not for you to gain glory by falsely confessing to be the avenger of Brahma."

The old priest turned to Pamela Wainwright and drew himself up proudly. "It is I who killed Rajan Mohan. Like Arjun, his father, he would have deserted and betrayed Brahma for the English — for an English woman."

Again Susanna shivered under his glance. Carrington quietly interposed himself between them.

Ahmed had raised his head and was staring up at Gupta Singh with that expression of fascinated terror with which he ordinarily regarded him.

"You will know the truth now," the old priest went on in his sonorous voice, "It was me who caused Rajan Mohan to break the impious promise he had made to Lady Susanna Helton. Also, I commanded him to see her no more. The son of Arjun was not to be trusted with an English woman. But he disobeyed me, he would go to this masquerade ball. I knew the influence this woman would have upon him, and I went there to see that he gave her no more promises. I made Ahmed play for me the spy. He told me that Rajan Mohan was in the library with this woman. I went to the terrace door to put an end to this interview, but before I could go in, Lady Susanna ran out. She was followed a minute later by the man, Helton."

"I stepped into the library. One would say Arjun was alive again in his son. Rajan Mohan was mad with passion for the English woman. He openly defied me, flaunted in my face a spangled piece torn from her gown and swore that for the sake of holding her in his arms again he would denounce the gods of India, and Brahma might forever go unavenged. I killed the blasphemer as he stood there. And this was execution, not murder, as you English call it."

There fell a tense silence. The gaze of all was fixed upon the old East Indian with a kind of awe, approaching admiration. He, on his part, presented an aspect of lofty calm, mixed with contempt for those who failed to comprehend his motives.

Rathbone, that ever zealous bloodhound of the law, was the first to shake off the atmosphere of Eastern gods and their vendettas which the sight of this majestic old priest, assured of the righteousness of his act, conjured up, and to return to the realities of twentieth century England.

"You can give any fancy name you like to the killing of Rajan Mohan," he said gruffly, "but here in this country, you'll answer to the charge of murder."

As he spoke, he advanced toward Gupta Singh with the obvious intention of clapping handcuffs upon his wrists, but before he could carry out his purpose, the old East Indian had snatched a small phial from the folds of his robe and swallowed the contents.

The poison had an almost instant effect A grayness spread over the East Indian's features, he staggered back.

"It is not for unbelievers to pass judgment on a servant of Brahma."

These were his last words.

32

AFTER THE STORM

Two or three days later, after the excitement caused by Gupta Singh's rather spectacular death had partly subsided, Pamela Wainwright found time to give Miss Flynn and Carrington an insight of the inner workings of the case and the line of reasoning which she herself had pursued.

"I always follow to a certain extent the process of elimination," the detective explained. "Take, for instance, Rathbone's first suspect, Lady Susanna. The most superficial reader of character would know that a person of so frank and open a nature could never successfully conceal her guilt and would very probably scorn to do so. You remember the frankness with which she refused to answer certain incriminating questions, although she knew the interpretation that would be put upon her silence. But, although I mentally acquitted her of actual guilt, I had no doubt from my observations of her that she either knew the murderer or thought she did and was trying to shield him. You see, I had been studying this case before Gupta Singh engaged me to hunt up his rubies. Rose Gardens has been of interest to me ever since the murder of Sir Robert Williamson, and if it had not been for other more urgent cases, I should have tried on my own account to solve this murder."

"Lady Susanna's unhappy married life was a matter of common knowledge and I soon found out by inquiring of certain money-lenders the cause of her recent desperate betting at the races. She was staggering under not only her own debts — and you'll have to admit, Lord Carrington, that she is not a particularly frugal person — but also under the debts of that precious husband of hers, and was trying to buy up the money-lenders. These gentlemen had discovered that Helton had ventured to return to England at the risk of arrest for various crimes. The payment of his debts was the price of their silence. For a short while I allowed myself to be misled as Rathbone was, in thinking Helton the murderer of Rajan Mohan as well as of Sir Robert Williamson. It was simple enough to prove that he had killed Williamson — that is, as soon as I discovered that he was the Crimson Knight and the lover of Edna MacDonald. These two facts I discovered during the day I spent at Rose Gardens in the capacity of a housemaid — in fact, as Ivy Blake's predecessor."

The detective gave a little laugh. "I will have to confess that I was dismissed without a 'character.' Mrs. MacDonald came upon me at night, prowling about the house, and dismissed me on the spot. But I had found out more even than I had hoped to. I was morally convinced also that Mrs. MacDonald had been Williamson's wife, in spite of the aspersions cast upon her at the inquest. She was too clever a woman to allow herself simply to be entangled with a testy old reprobate. She wished to better herself in the world, and in addition she had a son to provide for — I discovered that, too. Of course, she was Williamson's wife, and of course he ill-treated her — he ill-treated every one except the little East Indian girl as I learned by inquiry. Then — enter the lover — and the result was easily to be guessed at. But, to prove Helton the murderer of Rajan Mohan was another matter. As Mrs. MacDonald said, he had not the opportunity to kill the East Indian. I happened to be trailing Helton that night, and I can account for all of his movements from the time he left Mrs. Barker's house in the Bay Town to go to a cave along the shore where his Knightly costume was hidden, and from there approached Rose Gardens. With my own eyes I can vouch for the truth of every one of Mrs. MacDonald's statements regarding his actions on that night. He was not in the library long enough to kill Rajan Mohan."

"I, too, saw the person whom we know now to have been Gupta Singh, come out from the shadow of the house and enter the library. But I took him to be one of the guests in fancy costume and so I continued to follow Capt. Helton, for I hoped to discover him in some act which would make it possible for me to have him arrested as the Knight. You understand that both Rathbone and I had known for some days that he was the Knight, but we had not been able to find sufficiently definite evidence to make his conviction certain. When I learned that a murder had been committed while T. had been trailing a person who did nothing more criminal that night than bully Lady Susanna on the cliffs — I could not, of course, get near enough to hear their conversation — and then return to his cave on the beach, I called myself some rather hard names. Still, from these observations of mine I was able at once to eliminate two other suspects in addition to Lady Susanna, Helton, and

Mrs. MacDonald, who had been in his company from the time he reached the vicinity of Rose Gardens until he entered the terrace door."

"This left then in my mind as possible suspects, Ahmed, Maxwell Flynn, Nora, Miriam Cramer, and Gupta Singh. The first four apparently had the opportunity as I found out by making careful inquiries among the guests in regard to the different periods when they were absent from the ballroom. As to incentive, Ahmed and Nora both seemed to be in Rajan Mohan's power and presumably would welcome his death as a relief from the bondage he held them in. The Surya's Eye ruby was incentive enough for the other two, but — I had seen an unknown person enter the library from the outside, at or near the time when Rajan Mohan must have been killed. Now I, like Mrs. MacDonald, could not swear to the sex of this person, but I had the impression that it was a man and a man too powerfully built to be Maxwell Flynn."

"Later I tried to identify this person with someone of the guests from the neighboring houses, but I did not succeed. I even asked Rathbone's aid, but he stamped the whole story as 'silly rot' and persisted in believing that Helton had had sufficient time in which to kill Rajan Mohan in spite of all I could say. This attitude of Rathbone's threw me entirely upon my own resources and for a while I seemed to be facing a blind wall. Then, unexpectedly, Gupta Singh engaged me to search for his rubies. The moment I saw him in his East Indian garb, I thought of the mysterious person I had seen to enter the library. I questioned him as narrowly as I could without arousing his suspicions. When I discovered that he not only cared nothing about apprehending Prince Rajan's murderer, but was even unwilling to discuss the matter, I became mortally convinced of his guilt. Finally, by continued questioning. I led him on to betray some bitterness against Rajan Mohan. That was what I wanted. He had then incentive. I could learn nothing of his movements on the night of the ball from his servants, but I found out a good deal by putting Ahmed through a sort of 'third degree.' He knew more than he should about the murder and be regarded Gupta Singh with a superstitions fear that made him day in the old priest's hands. I saw that no ordinary measures would make him betray Gupta, and so, as a last resort, I tried to terrorize him into speaking. I was more successful than I had dared to hope. As far as I am concerned, the case is closed. It is for the government to decide what will finally become of the rubies. I wonder if I have made every point clear to you both?"

Carrington reflectively swung the black ribbon of his monocle. "I suppose it was Gupta Singh, eh, who put those bullets of salt on the little girl's plate and also on Max's?"

The detective shook her head. "No, it was Ahmed. Gupta Singh by threats based on the superstitious fear in which he, as a priest of Brahma, held Ahmed, forced him to do this. He suspected, as he told me, that Mr. Flynn had stolen the Surya's Eye and that Nora knew it and was shielding him. He hoped to terrorize Nora into betraying Mr. Flynn."

"That point is clear," said Carrington slowly. "The old chap, of course, knew that Ahmed would never say a word about his being around the house the night of the murder, and he wasn't mistaken in his man. But I don't exactly understand why Ahmed should report the murder — that is, why he should tell Miss Flynn that the library door was locked and so call attention to the room. He must have known there had been some sort of a scene between Prince Rajan and Gupta."

"It was Mrs. MacDonald who ordered him to do this," answered the detective. "Lady Susanna had told her that Capt. Helton had killed Rajan Mohan. Mrs. MacDonald knew that this was impossible as Helton had not had the time, but the poor woman was so upset that she could wait no longer for the murder to be discovered and some solution attempted. For the first time she had difficulty in persuading Ahmed to obey her — He always had obeyed her with a dog-like devotion. This devotion explains the hatred which he always felt toward Helton — he must have known that this man was using her love for his own purposes. As I was saying, Mrs. MacDonald finally persuaded Ahmed to inform Miss Flynn of the locked door, but when she saw that he was actually going she became desperately afraid that Helton would somehow be accused of the murder, so she unlocked the library door with the intention of satisfying herself that he had left no traces of his having been in that room. The sound of your footsteps, Miss Flynn, drove her in terror to the servants' hall. That explains, I think, the mystery of the locked and suddenly unlocked door."

"And now" — with a hurried glance at a tiny gold watch — "it is time for me to be driving to the station if I am to catch the next train to London. If you think, Miss Flynn, that I have left any point unexplained, please remember that my head now is full of the murder at Notting Hill House. I have scarcely thought of anything else since I received the telegram asking me to take the case."

Carrington assisted the detective into the waiting horse-drawn carriage and then joined Susanna on the terrace. She was watching the setting sun gild the waves of the North Sea with ruddy gold.

At Carrington's step, she turned with a welcoming, tinged with sadness, smile.

"Our last chance, Tom, to watch the sun set over the North Sea. In spite of everything that has happened here, I believe I have grown fond of this wild spot. I will be almost sorry to leave for London in the morning."

"I will not," Carrington spoke with decision. "This has been a silly unpleasant house party for the hostess and every one concerned. Miss Flynn is no end sensible to plan a trip on the Continent and try to forget it all."

"I am glad she is going to take Nora with her," said Susanna. "Traveling will make the poor child think of something besides Max. Oh, by the way, Tom, have you heard how kind Miss Flynn has been to Mrs. MacDonald? She has engaged Malcolm French of Lincoln's Inn Fields to put forward Mrs. MacDonald's claim to Sir Robert Williamson's estate."

Carrington gloomily dangled his monocle. "Mark my word, Susanna, everybody but me seems to have people to look after them. I hear that some old maid cousin of yours has asked you to finish out the summer at her place in Kent."

Susanna made a little moue. "Yes, but I would rather stifle in London than listen to Cousin Serena's dissertations on the wickedness of my ways. I'm not going to Kent, Tom. Perhaps you will look in on me once in a while. It will be dull in London."

The sun brought out the auburn glints in Susanna's hair, the dusky violet hue of her eyes seemed more pronounced, her lips more red.

Carrington caught both her hands in his. "Susanna! you don't need to stifle and be dull in London. Don't you think we could 'hit it off,' eh? That is, I mean, couldn't you? — couldn't you — ah — contrive to many me?"

A wonderfully tender expression came into Susanna's face. "Dear old boy, I'm awfully fond of you. I think we might try to 'hit it off.'"

THE END

ABOUT THE AUTHOR

Carsten Ford has made his career in the written word milieu since graduating from university in Literature. For the last 2 decades he has been both an editor and a content writer for various in-print publications, a variety of on-line informational websites, as well as several academic institutions. He performs research and supplementary commentary as an archivist for a non-profit organization.

Gladys Locke was an author and librarian. She had a deep fascination for mysteries and the solving of said crimes.